A vision of the massacre she had seen flitted through Anne's mind.

Though she had dreamed of Sam touching her, she couldn't completely forget the blood that ran in his veins. "No, I . . ." Slowly, she became aware of the cool wet cloth that covered her right leg from ankle to hip. She blinked. "You bandaged my leg?"

"Washed the grit off, mostly," he said, one eyebrow raised now.

Anne could feel the hot flush of color on her cheeks. "Then you . . . My leg, I mean . . . You saw . . ."

Sam could barely suppress his grin. "Your leg? The whole blessed limb, from ankle to hip."

Her blush deepened. "Oh, my goodness," she breathed. "Well?"

"Well what?"

"I don't know," Anne stammered. Even Daniel had never seen that much of her. "Just well."

His dark eyes bore into her. "What is it you want, Mrs. McIntire? An appraisal or an apology?"

Dear Reader,

This month we are pleased to bring you a quartet of historical romances, all set in the Wild West.

In *Blessing* by Debbi Bedford, Uley Kirkland is caught in a lie when her relationship with an accused man forces her to come to terms with the woman she has become.

Years ago, Lucas Chandler refused Rachel Hawthorne's marriage proposal with a laugh. Now, in *Winter Fire* by Pat Tracy, he must woo the young woman he rejected in order to reclaim his family ranch.

Mary McBride's first book, *Riverbend*, was one of our 1993 March Madness titles. We are delighted to bring you her second book, *Fly Away Home*, about a sheltered Eastern girl and a half-breed Indian who find unexpected love.

Blinded during a roundup, cowboy Winn Sutton woke up to darkness. But widow Cynthie Franklin teaches him that love can find the way in *Wait for the Sunrise* by newcomer Cassandra Austin.

We hope you enjoy all four titles. And join us next month when we will be presenting Veronica Sattler's lavish historical reissue set in Regency England, *The Bargain*—as well as three other exciting books—only from Harlequin Historicals.

Sincerely,

Tracy Farrell
Senior Editor

Fly Away Home

MARY McBRIDE

Harlequin Books

TORONTO • NEW YORK • LONDON
AMSTERDAM • PARIS • SYDNEY • HAMBURG
STOCKHOLM • ATHENS • TOKYO • MILAN
MADRID • WARSAW • BUDAPEST • AUCKLAND

Harlequin Historicals first edition September 1993

ISBN 0-373-28789-5

FLY AWAY HOME

Books by Mary McBride

Harlequin Historicals

Riverbend #164
Fly Away Home #189

MARY McBRIDE

comes by her romantic streak naturally—what else from the daughter of two people who met on a blind date on Valentine's Day? Mary lives in St. Louis, Missouri, with her husband and two young sons.

This one's for you, Loren

Prologue

Syracuse, New York, 1870

Anne McIntire descended the great oak staircase slowly. Her knees trembled beneath her velvet dressing gown. Her knuckles were white as pearls on the polished banister. Out of habit, she paused on the landing and lifted her hand to straighten the gilt frame of her husband's portrait. Strickland's brush had captured Daniel's military expression perfectly—the arrogant angle of his chin, the firm line of his mouth, the blue eyes as dark as his uniform.

Her hand hung in the air a moment, then drew back. What was the use? The portrait would be out of kilter again tomorrow. Who would adjust it then?

She continued down the staircase, her pale hair streaming over her fragile shoulders, her light blue eyes downcast. Each step on the rich pattern of the Persian carpet was slow and precise, like a last deliberate caress. She would never mount these stairs again.

The Meissen clock in the parlor struck two just as the butler appeared at the foot of the stairs. As always, he stood in profile to conceal his black eye patch. His good eye met hers for a moment.

"I've laid a fire for you, Mrs. McIntire," he said.

"Thank you, Corporal Rumsey." Her own voice startled her. It was clear and calm, unlike her heart. Unlike her very soul.

The butler shifted his lean body as Anne passed, keeping himself in profile. "The colonel's having another bad night," he commented.

The walnut-panelled parlor echoed with the final chime of the clock. "Yes. Another bad night," Anne said. His last, she thought as she settled in the platform rocker by the fireplace.

"Will you be needing anything else this evening?" the butler asked.

She shook her head, then folded her hands in her lap and stared into the blue depths of the flames.

He cleared his throat. "Shall I take the colonel's sleeping draught up to him now?"

"No," she said sharply. Then, with a softer edge to her voice, she added, "Not tonight."

Rumsey lingered in the doorway a moment. "Very well. Good night then, madam."

At the sound of her husband's footsteps, Pauline Rumsey turned from her saucepan of milk on the stove. "How is she?" she asked.

Peter Rumsey faced his wife straight on. The black patch did not completely cover the scar tissue around his eye. Its jagged edges reddened now, as did the butler's entire face. "She doesn't want me to give him his sleeping draught tonight."

Pauline shrugged as she raised her eyebrows in the general direction of upstairs. "He's quiet now. Does she want anything?"

When her husband shook his head, Pauline poured the warm milk into two cups and carried them to the cloth-covered table where he now sat. She was a thin woman, and she slid into a chair without pulling it out from the table. She sprinkled a generous teaspoon of sugar into her cup, stirred it thoughtfully and frowned at the white liquid as it swirled around the spoon.

"I wonder if she ever regrets marrying him," she mused.

Peter Rumsey sipped from his cup.

When he failed to respond, his wife continued, "I'd regret it. No, that's not true. There'd be nothing to regret, because I wouldn't have gone through with the wedding."

His good eye widened as he looked at her over the rim of his cup. "Are you telling me that if we were betrothed and I became that severely wounded, you would have walked out on me?"

"Yes," she said. "And you would have encouraged me to go, Peter. You wouldn't have done to me what Colonel McIntire has done to her. She was only eighteen years old. Still a girl, with her whole life ahead of her." Pauline clucked her tongue. "She's had no life at all for the last five years. Such a dreadful waste."

"Colonel McIntire is an officer and a gentleman," he snapped.

She shook her head sadly. "Corporal Rumsey, you may still have one good eye, but you're blind as a bat. You can't see past your own loyalty to him. He's not what he used to be. And he's making her life hell on earth."

"It's not for us to say, Pauline."

She drummed her thin fingers on the table. "Well, I'd have plenty to say if she ever asked me," she grumbled. "I'd tell her to get out of here while she's still young enough to find a man who can—"

Her husband's dark scowl cut her off. Pauline scowled back briefly, then reached across the table to touch his cheek beneath the eye patch.

"I wouldn't make a very good martyr, Peter." She poked her thumb toward the parlor. "Or a saint."

The thin woman frowned into her cup, then idly spooned in more sugar, wondering if Anne McIntire ever wished the colonel were dead.

In the nighttime quiet of the huge house, Anne imagined she could hear the nib of Daniel's pen as it clinked against the lip of the crystal inkwell and scratched over a sheaf of cream-colored vellum. Or was it only the sound of mice skittering behind the walls? Or the clicking of june bugs against the windows? And why—why was it taking him so long?

Then the pistol shot rang out upstairs. Anne jerked slightly, like a limp puppet whose strings had been twitched. Tears welled in her eyes, then streamed down her pale cheeks and splashed onto her folded hands.

For a moment there was only the ticking of the clock, the crackling of the fire and the creak in the chair as she kept rocking. Then she heard Rumsey's quick footsteps ascending the stairs.

Anne stood up. She tore away the velvet dressing gown that covered her black silk travelling suit. Her hands trembled fiercely as she slipped off her wedding ring and placed it beside the Meissen clock on the mantle.

As she walked out of the house, the clock began to chime. She closed the door before the third and final knell.

Chapter One

Anne was the sole passenger now, and she planted herself firmly in the center of the seat, trying to sway with the rhythm of the big Concord coach. The canvas side curtains were closed in an effort to keep out the dust, but as far as she could tell it only succeeded in keeping the heat in, for the dust still seeped up through the floorboards and sifted down from the coach's roof. Her black travelling suit was covered with it, and she had long since given up shaking the folds of her skirt to rid herself of the infernal grit.

Right now she didn't mind that she couldn't see outside. All day the wide, rough landscape had overpowered her senses and made her feel small, delicate, even breakable. Like a porcelain figurine. A dusty one, at that.

The farther away from Syracuse she travelled, the more her apprehensions grew. Now, in New Mexico Territory, she was frankly afraid. What had possessed her? she wondered. She must have been demented to have even considered such a journey. But she had done much more than merely consider it. She had planned it methodically, as secretly as a lover plans an elopement, as stealthily as a murderess plots a crime. In her letters to her Aunt Emma in New Mexico, Anne had played the role of widow long before the fact. Her mourning clothes had been fitted and stitched by a crosstown dressmaker while her husband still drew breath. Her bags had been packed and stowed at the railroad station weeks before she had had the courage to leave.

For what? she wondered now. She didn't even know her mother's eldest sister, who had journeyed west forty years before and was her only surviving relative. Who else could she have turned to? Emma Hook seemed friendly enough in her letters, glad to have the opportunity to meet a niece she hadn't known existed. She had described her ranch, her own two-year widowhood, and had mentioned the fact that she lived with her two grown sons, Jay and Sam. In Syracuse, Anne had thought it seemed the perfect place to go. An aging aunt and her two fussy bachelor sons... Seeing this strange land, however, made her more than apprehensive about the strangers whose lives would soon be linked to hers. She wasn't looking for links or bonds of any kind. She was done with all that.

In the dim interior of the rocking coach, Anne gazed down at the ring finger of her left hand, surprised once more that there was no mark from the wedding band she had left behind. At the very least, she thought, there should have been a thin, worn impression on her skin; at worst, a deep, dark scar. But her pale skin was unblemished, as if she had never worn Daniel's ring—as if she had never been married at all.

She had to clutch the edge of the seat then as the stage coach ground to a halt. It was too soon, she was sure, to have arrived in San Miguel. When she raised the side curtain, all she could see were the sun-darkened folds of flesh at the back of the driver's neck and a few damp locks of russet hair. All she could hear was the man's low, indrawn whistle.

"Is something wrong?" Anne asked, craning her neck to see around him. "Why have we stopped?" She began to open the door to get out.

"You best stay inside, ma'am," the driver said over his shoulder. "This ain't a pretty sight." He scraped his hat from his head, then moved away from the coach.

"Let's get out of here," the man riding shotgun called down in a tight, tense voice. "There's nothing we can do now."

"Hold on a damn minute," the driver said. "Lemme just see if I can figure out who they are, so's we can tell the sheriff in San Miguel."

"It's still smoldering, Rusty," the guard whined. "Them damn Apaches are probably close by. Hell, those savages might even be watching us right now, for all we know."

Smoldering? Savages? Anne's curiosity overrode her fear. She opened the door and leaned out.

The beefy, red-haired driver stood with his bandanna over his mouth and nose, poking through the charred ruins of a wagon. Wisps of smoke straggled up, only to be blown away by a hot, dry wind. Anne saw a burnt log lying beside a broken wheel, but when the wind twitched a remnant of red plaid shirt, she realized that it wasn't a log at all. It was a man. Her eyes widened with horror and her stomach turned over just as the driver shouted back from the other side of the wreckage.

"Looks like Ed Haney's wife. Hard tellin', though. They gutted her." His eyes shifted to Anne, who was clinging now to the door, half in, half out of the coach. "Sorry, ma'am," he said.

The driver plodded back up the slight incline and helped Anne back into her seat as the guard called frantically, "You'll be a hell of a lot sorrier if we don't get going right now, Rusty."

"Are they...are the Indians still nearby?" Anne asked weakly.

"Naw," Rusty said. "Those devils got what they wanted. They're long gone now. Don't you worry, ma'am. We'll get you to San Miguel in one piece."

Anne rolled her eyes, knowing he meant to comfort her, but finding little reassurance in his choice of words. When the coach jerked forward, she sagged back against the seat. Her stomach was roiling. Her hands were shaking and her heart was as heavy as lead. What in the world was she doing here? Whatever had made her think she could be free out here in this wide, wild land? It was too wide, too wild—a land where women were slit open like sawdust dolls and men were left to smolder like logs on a grate.

She had dreamed of freedom, of spreading her wings and flying. But this was a land where buzzards ruled, and birds of prey. New Mexico made her feel small and helpless and afraid, like a pale canary that had inadvertently escaped its cage. For a bleak and desperate moment, she longed for the life she had left behind in New York.

No. She bolted upright, stiffened her spine and shook out her skirt furiously, filling the coach with dust. She might be small, but she wasn't helpless, and she absolutely refused to be afraid. Pale canary or not, this bird was going to fly.

Emma Hook was a sturdy woman. Thick waisted now at the age of sixty, with more salt than pepper in her hair, she seemed the perfect mistress for the parlor in which she stood, her coloring a match for the thick stucco walls, her figure not unlike the heavily carved Spanish furniture. Her hazel eyes were trained out the window at the distant Sangre de Cristo mountains whose peaks were still lightly capped with snow even though it was early June. Emma was waiting. She felt sometimes that was all she did. So much of her life had been spent standing at this very window, watching, waiting.

Judging from her niece's last letter, this should be the week of her arrival. The stage might be coming through one of those mountain passes right now, hurtling down and driving hell-bent for San Miguel. If she had it to do all over again, Emma thought, she would have told Anne not to come. But the Apaches had all gone to the reservation when she had posted her invitation, and it had seemed a safe-enough trip for a young woman to make.

Not now. Emma castigated herself for not anticipating the present dangers of travelling in the territory. But how could anyone have predicted that Raging Owl would refuse to stay on the government land, or have imagined the havoc and destruction he and his band of followers would wreak in their effort to remain free? If anything happened to her sister's child, she'd never forgive herself.

A rising cloud of dust in the distance caught her eye. She remained at the window, silently watching, until she discerned a single figure on horseback—Jay. Emma's heart clenched. If Jay was returning from San Miguel alone, it could only mean one thing—something had happened to Anne.

Emma was on the front porch tapping her foot restlessly when her son rode up to the door. "What happened?" she asked, her hand over her heart.

Her son ignored her as he dismounted, and shouted, "Natividad!" in the direction of the bunkhouse. Then his harsh glare fell on his mother. "Where is that lazy Mexican? I want him out here to tend my horse the minute I ride in. Is that too much to ask?" Jay yelled again, "Natividad!"

Emma crossed her arms over her bosom, staring at the man who so resembled her. He had the same green glint in his hazel eyes, the same slightly sallow cast to his skin. His nose was long and narrow like hers, and his lips were not generous, but thin and pale with a tendency to pull down at the corners. Age had softened Emma's features, but on her twenty-nine-year-old son, they were still axe sharp. Like her, he tended to put on weight around the middle while his legs and arms remained thin. He was not particularly strong, nor was he agile. He was, in fact, a singularly graceless man. All of which, she thought now, he could have overcome with a pleasant disposition and a generous heart. But Jay was surly and cruel. Why did she forever expect him to be different? What magic, after all this time, did she think was going to change him?

"What happened to Anne McIntire?" she asked as he glared in the direction of the bunkhouse.

"How the hell should I know?" he snapped. "She wasn't on the stage that came in Tuesday. I'm not going to piss away my life waiting for a damn stagecoach and some widowed cousin who's probably destitute and damn ugly to boot." His thin lips whitened as he watched the Mexican cowhand scurry from the bunkhouse. Jay Hook's fist tightened as if he meant to strike the young man.

"I did not hear you ride in, Señor Jay," Natividad said, reaching out a hand to take the horse's reins.

Jay slapped them across his palm. "See that it doesn't happen again," he said, turning his back on the horse, the cowhand and his mother as he stormed into the house.

Emma stalked after him. "Jay, I want a word with you."

In the clay-tiled vestibule, he whirled on her. "What, Mother?"

"There was another stage today," Emma said, trying to control her temper. "I want you to ride back into San Miguel tomorrow and—"

Jay cut her off with a shrill laugh. "Not on your life. Anyway, the half-breed's in town. I told him to meet today's stage just in case our cousin is on it. He said he would, but you know him." He burned his mother with an acid gaze. "I expect he'll do it if it doesn't interfere with his drinking or whoring or brawling."

Emma's eyes flared. "Your brother's name is Sam," she spat. "I've had enough of your vile tongue, Jay."

A cruel smile edged his mouth. "The lioness defends her half-breed cub again. Aren't you tired of it, Mother?"

He left her standing in the vestibule, her eyes stinging with tears that would not fall. A lioness. Yes, perhaps. But then, she had to be.

In her mind Emma wandered back forty years. So long ago, and yet it seemed like only yesterday she had married the strapping, young John Hook in Rochester on a fine spring morning. The very next day she'd packed her wedding dress away and the newlyweds had headed southwest. Months later, when their wagon broke down a few miles from the little mission of San Miguel, John had taken it as a sign that their long journey was meant to come to an end.

He'd bought a tract of land, rolled up his big sleeves and set to work. Ten years later The Hook was a prosperous ranch. They had healthy cattle and flourishing crops, but the children they so dearly wanted didn't come.

Emma had been keeping watch at the window that afternoon as John rode into the dusty yard bare-chested, his shirt bundled in his arms. He was grinning when she greeted him at the door. Without being told, she knew. Her arms had gone out instinctively to take the plaid bundle from him, and while she carefully unwrapped it, John narrated the story of finding the babe still bloody, curled in his dead mother's arms.

"God only knows what she was doing up in those mountains, Em," he'd said. "Near as I can figure, she was trying to get away from the Apaches. Pretty little thing. Real delicate. She had herself a strong son, that's for sure."

As he spoke, Emma was smiling down on the baby's tawny face and full head of black hair. She touched his hand and the baby grasped her finger firmly. John covered their joined hands with his.

His voice was thick. "I meant to take him straight to the mission, but . . ."

"You did right, John."

"He's a half-breed, honey. This won't be easy."

Emma nodded. She knew this baby was destined for a hard life no matter how much love and warmth she gave him. Her heart ached for him already.

Then, as if little Sam hadn't been miracle enough, nine months later Emma gave birth to Jay. How she had loved her sons. How she'd cherished them.

Emma's shoulders sagged now as she walked to the window once more. The sun was just dipping down, warm and honey gold, into a mountain pass. She loved her sons. Both of them. Only...

Chapter Two

When the stagecoach rattled into San Miguel, the town's adobe buildings reflected the turquoise of the sky and the fierce pinks and oranges of the sunset. As soon as the coach stopped, Anne climbed out, intending to shake herself like a dust cloth. But when she did, her skirt only raised more dust from the dry street. She stood in a little gray cloud, coughing, as the guard tossed her bags down from the luggage rack.

"Just those two, right, ma'am?"

She looked at her leather valises. The grime on them was so thick she could have carved her initials in it. "Yes, just those two." She sighed.

Rusty, the driver, shifted around in his high seat. "Pardon my askin', but is somebody meetin' you, Miz McIntire?"

Did she look as forlorn as his gaze implied? Anne wondered. The courage she had coaxed back to life after seeing the burned wagon suddenly failed her. This was a terrible mistake. She wasn't ready to be on her own. After five years in a cage, her wings were stiff and useless. She had wanted so to fly, but she simply didn't know how. Maybe, she thought, she should just go back the way she'd come. Maybe in another year or two...

"Would you put my bags back on top, please? I've changed my mind," she said as she hiked up her skirt and prepared to climb back into the coach.

"Did I hear you right, ma'am?" the guard called down.

Anne had one foot inside the coach now, the other still on the narrow metal step. "You heard me," she said. "Put them back."

"Anne McIntire?"

The deep voice startled her. Her hand jerked to her throat, and when she twisted in the direction of the sound, her foot slipped from the step. Arms flailing, she pitched backward in a flurry of black silk, then hit what felt like a rock...with arms. Anne looked up and opened her mouth to speak, but nothing came out.

The boulder that had broken her fall was an Indian. Long black hair framed a face that was bronzed in the light of the setting sun. His dark eyes glittered. And a slow gleam of a grin twitched across his full, sensuous lips.

"My mother said you were a widow, Mrs. McIntire. She failed to mention that you were also a mute."

Anne blinked, trying to dismiss the image of the charred wagon, the burned body, the echo of the driver's voice calling "they gutted her." She forced a dry croak. "I . . . but you're—you're . . ."

His grin vanished. "I'm Sam Hook," he said bluntly as he set her down. He jerked a thumb at the leather valises. "These yours?"

She could only nod dumbly, then stare as he shifted his heavily muscled body and bent his long, buckskin-clad legs to pick up the bags as if they were empty.

"Hold on there, half-breed," the guard called from atop the coach. "Just what do you think you're doing?"

Sam Hook raised his dark eyes slowly. The fiery sunset played over his high cheekbones and chiselled nose. Standing just a foot away, Anne could have sworn she felt a rush of heat from his big body and saw a whiplash of tension cross his features. But they were belied by his even tone.

"I'm walking my cousin over to Mrs. Thiel's, if that's all right with you," he replied.

The guard deferred to the red-haired driver, who chewed his lower lip a minute as if considering his responsibility to his female passenger. "I 'spect that'd be all right. We're gonna sit here and watch you though, 'breed, just to make sure the lady gets there."

"You do that," Sam Hook grunted. He swung his gaze to Anne then, rage still suffusing his dark eyes. "The woman who runs the mercantile has a spare room she rents out. You'll be spending the night there. Tomorrow I'll take you to The Hook." He didn't wait for a reply, but, with one of her bags in each hand, strode across the street.

Anne cast a quick, bewildered glance at the men on the coach, then picked up her dusty skirts and followed the big Indian, three of her steps equalling one of his lengthy strides. She was trailing after him like a lost puppy, she thought. Like a scared little pup. Well, she was scared, dammit. She'd never been more than fifty miles from Syracuse in her life. For the past five years she'd barely been out of her own house. Now here she was, traipsing after some enormous Apache who claimed to be her cousin. Anne figured she had every right to be frightened out of her wits.

But she had made it this far, hadn't she? All the way from New York to New Mexico. This trip was supposed to be the start of a brand-new life. A new life where she expressed her wants and needs. A life in which she said, "I want," instead of always asking what she could do for somebody else. Acting like a scared puppy wasn't the way she had envisioned that new life commencing.

She halted dead in her tracks. "Just one minute, Mr. Hook."

The tall, dark man turned slowly, regarding her through narrowed eyes.

Oh, Lord! Her heart began to thump in her chest and the palms of her hands were wringing wet. Did she really want a confrontation now, here, with this savage-looking man? But she had to do it. If she didn't try to use her wings, she'd never fly. Never. And she wasn't going to let anyone—not even this scowling dark Indian—deny her the freedom she had earned.

She met his flinty gaze. "I'd like some dinner, before going to my room, if you don't mind." There, she thought. That was a reasonable demand. And she *was* hungry.

Sam Hook closed the distance between them in two long strides. "I'm sure Mrs. Thiel will—"

"I'd like to take my meal there," Anne cut in, angling her head toward a sign that proclaimed Good Food just down the street. "Won't you join me if you haven't already eaten dinner?" She had a strong urge to chew on a fingernail, but kept her clammy, trembling hands at her sides.

He simply stood there, staring down at her, his face expressionless.

"People do eat dinner in New Mexico, don't they?" Anne asked, rattled by his dark, penetrating gaze.

He nodded silently, his black hair shifting slightly over his wide shoulders.

"Well, why are you staring at me that way? Really, Mr. Hook!" Anne was flustered now. She had at last taken a firm stand, had made what she considered a very reasonable demand, only to be answered with silence and an obsidian stare that was making color flood her cheeks.

Almost lazily, he shifted one of her bags under his arm. "I'm trying to figure out if you're deaf or just plain stupid, Mrs. McIntire."

Anne's mouth opened in an astonished O. Her hands curled into fists. "Neither, Mr. Hook, I assure you. But you are certainly the rudest man I've ever met."

His mouth slid into a taunting grin. "Then I guess you wouldn't want to eat dinner with me, would you?"

"Certainly not," she snapped.

"Fine," he said. "I'll walk you over to the restaurant, and I'll wait outside while you have your meal."

When he reached for her arm, she jerked away, prompting the stagecoach driver to call from the other side of the street, "Everything okay, ma'am?"

"I can take care of myself, thank you very much," Anne declared. "Fool man," she added under her breath, grabbing up her skirt once more to tramp after Sam Hook, who was already halfway to the door of the little café.

He put her bags down, then reached in the pocket of his chambray shirt for the makings of a cigarette. "Have a nice dinner, Mrs. McIntire," he said, flicking her a quick glance, then turning his full attention to his tobacco and paper.

"Thank you, I will." Anne flounced through the open door, not quite certain if she had struck a small blow for freedom or been struck herself by some huge, invisible hand.

The interior of the café was as rough-hewn as the dozen or so men who were seated around several tables. Their heads, which had been lowered over their plates, lifted as she came through the door. Anne walked to the first empty chair she saw, still propelled by the ire Sam Hook had ignited in her.

"May I?" she asked the young man who already sat at the table. It came out less of a question than an ultimatum, and the young man rose several inches from his chair as Anne planted herself across from him.

She drummed her fingers on the rough planks of the table for a moment. Deaf? She'd heard every word that rumbled from Sam Hook's throat. And how dare he call her stupid? She wanted to eat dinner—was that so much to ask? Anne grabbed the handwritten menu, glaring at it. Scrawled across the top of the page in vivid red letters were the words *No Injuns Welcome*.

"Oh," she said softly, feeling her heart twist. No wonder he hadn't accompanied her. She raised her eyes from the page to see all the other customers staring at her with unbridled curiosity. Most of them were dirty and unshaven, and looked as tough as New Mexico itself. The sort who would be only too happy to put down their knives and forks to help throw an unwelcome Indian out the door.

Why hadn't the man just come out and told her? she wondered. But what could he have said? What words could he have possibly used that wouldn't stick in his throat when he uttered them?

"What can I bring you, ma'am?" grated a voice just behind her.

Anne turned to look at the greasy apron and the grizzled beard of the cook. She placed the menu facedown on the table, then pushed back her chair. "Nothing, thank you. I seem to have lost my appetite."

She could feel the stares that followed her to the door.

Sam Hook was leaning against the side of the adobe building when she emerged. He took a final drag on his cigarette, then flicked it into the dirt as he pushed away from the wall with one shoulder. "Quick dinner," he said, eyeing her keenly.

Anne stood before him, sucked in her breath and lifted her chin. "I'm not deaf, Mr. Hook, so I guess that must make me just plain stupid. I apologize. I—I didn't know."

His full lips slid into a warm grin. "Welcome to New Mexico, Mrs. McIntire." He picked up her bags once more. "Come on. I'm sure Mrs. Thiel is expecting you for dinner anyway."

He seemed to shorten his long strides then, for Anne noticed she no longer had to trot to keep up with him. She noticed, too, that the stage had pulled out, and she was grateful there was no driver to check on her well-being and insult her cousin in the process.

Sam walked up to a door and hitched one of her bags under his arm to knock. The door inched open finally to reveal a woman who was nearly as tall as he, and very nearly as heavy, but with pinkish flab rather than bronzed muscle. Gray hair framed her face in molded waves and her mouth was a sour line.

"Oh, it's you," Doris Thiel said when she saw Sam.

"Evening, Mrs. Thiel. I've brought your boarder. This is Mrs. Anne McIntire, my mother's niece from New York."

The big woman gave Anne a long, hard look. Like a thrifty housewife appraising a cut of meat, Anne thought. Then the female giant nodded curtly to Sam. "All right. She can stay."

Anne didn't know whether to be grateful or appalled. Sam Hook's countenance gave her no clue at all. His face was as expressionless as stone.

"This way, Mrs. McIntire," the woman said. She snapped her fingers at Sam. "Just put her bags down there inside the door. I'll take them the rest of the way myself."

Once more Anne sensed tension snaking through Sam as he did as the big woman bid him, placing the bags precisely where she pointed. He straightened up then, and gazed down at Anne, hooking his thumbs in the waist of his buckskin pants.

"I'll have a wagon come around to pick you up about seven tomorrow morning," he said.

"I'll be ready. Thank you, Mr. Hook." Anne extended her hand.

His huge hand was warm and dry as it enclosed hers. "Good night, Mrs. McIntire," he said.

He had barely let go when Doris Thiel shoved the door closed on him.

"Well," she sniffed as she threw the bolt, "so much for that." Her face widened in a blowsy smile and she turned toward Anne. "Now tell me, dear, have you had your supper yet?"

Anne shook her head, unbalanced by the woman's quick change of mood.

"Come along then. I've made my special rabbit stew."

Before she turned to follow her hostess, Anne glanced at the bolted door, wondering where Sam Hook would be spending the night and if he would be eating any dinner at all.

"More, Sam, more," the little boy squealed.

Sam lifted him up to touch the ceiling again. "That's it, squirt," he said, setting the child's small bare feet on the hard dirt floor of the orphanage's central room. "Padre José says it's time to go to bed now." Sam gave the brown-robed priest a wink.

"No," the boy wailed. "*Más!* More!"

"*Basta, niño,*" the young priest said sternly. "That is enough. Tell Sam good-night. It is time to go to bed."

The small child raised his coal black eyes. "*Buenas noches,* Sam," he said obediently.

The tall man squatted down so his equally dark eyes were level with the child's. "*Buenas noches,* Benito." He stroked the boy's black hair softly. "*Te amo,*" he whispered as he bent his head to place a kiss on his forehead.

"*Te amo,* Sam." Benito pointed to the ceiling once more. "*¿No más?*"

Sam shook his head. "*Mañana.* Go to bed."

The boy shuffled toward the small room he shared with the other children.

"He is doing well, no?" the curly-haired priest asked Sam as he walked him to the orphanage door.

Sam scowled. "Benito told me one of the big boys kicked him and called him an Apache bastard." He stopped just shy of the door, folded his arms over his chest and eyed the slightly built priest. "Is that true, Padre?"

Father José rubbed his chin. "*Sí,* my friend. It is true. Benito was kicked." The priest sighed and met Sam's stony gaze. "It is also true that he is an Apache bastard."

Rage kindled in the big half-breed's black eyes. The priest put a hand on his arm. "And it is also true, as I try to teach my children, that the Lord loves us all the same whether we are white or brown or red. I cannot shelter him from prejudice, Sam. You of all people should realize that."

Sam shrugged off the hand. "He's just a baby. He doesn't deserve—"

The young priest cut him off sharply. "He doesn't deserve to live in a jewel box, to emerge when he is fifteen only to discover that he is not a pearl after all."

Shaking his head, Sam asked, "What did Benito do when the boy attacked him?"

Father José laughed. "I am sad to say he did not turn the other cheek."

"He's a tough little bastard," Sam said proudly.

The priest smiled. "Yes. Hardly a pearl, our little Benito."

As he walked down the street toward Sally Mendoza's cantina, Sam was grateful it was a Thursday night and there were no drunk cowhands spoiling for a fight with an Indian. He was able to lose himself in thought rather than keep his senses finely honed for trouble. That was one more thing Benito would soon learn, he thought bleakly.

The baby had been abandoned at the mission six years ago. Nobody had seen who left him, but judging from the color of his hair and skin, they'd figured him for a half-breed. Father José had been new at the mission then. He was told that Emma Hook had already raised one half-breed and maybe she'd be interested in doing it again. Sam had brought his mother into town. Emma had held the baby, her tears falling on his tiny swarthy face. At fifty-four, she was too old, she'd said, to do it again.

But Sam found himself coming to town more often after that, and his visits lengthened. Before Benito's arrival, Sam had come to town for one simple, urgent reason—to take his pleasure with Sally Mendoza. He usually got in a fight or two before going back to the ranch, for he, like little Benito, failed to turn the other cheek.

The boy had changed his life. Or maybe, Sam thought, at the age of thirty he was just getting too old to drink and whore and fight. His body was more than willing, but his mind no longer savored such pursuits. His heart, God knew, had never been in it.

He walked into Sally Mendoza's now, nodded to her surly barman and took his usual table in the back of the dimly lit cantina. Buxom, dark-eyed Sally, in a thin *camisa* that left nothing to the imagination, brought him a bottle and a glass, then straddled the chair beside his. She filled his glass to the brim with the good whiskey, not the rotgut her barman served to 'breeds.

Sam downed half the whiskey and began rolling a cigarette.

Sally cocked her dark head. "I saw you walking with that little *gringa.*"

Instead of answering, Sam licked the edge of the thin paper and struck a match with his thumbnail. He sucked in the pungent smoke, taking the edge off his hunger. He hadn't eaten since he'd had an early breakfast with Benito in the orphanage.

"You hungry?" Sally asked.

He shook his head and took another swig from his glass. Yes, he was hungry, but it wasn't a hunger food could satisfy. Yes, he was aching and longing, but it wasn't anything dark Sally with her lithe, experienced limbs could slake. Most of his dissatisfaction centered around Benito. His love for the boy lodged in the pit of his stomach like a rock. And also, surprisingly, it involved Anne McIntire, the *gringa,* with her pale hair and her ivory skin and her wide, sky blue, intelligent eyes. He had held her for only a moment when she toppled from the coach, but he could still feel her body in his arms, could still smell her flowery fragrance. And her fear.

Sam blinked and looked at the bruise beneath Sally's right eye. He touched it gently with his thumb. "What happened?"

"*Nada.*" Sally pushed his hand away.

His fingers curled around her wrist and his voice was sharp as the edge of a knife. "Who was it?"

She wrestled away from his harsh grasp. "Leave it alone, Sam. It didn't have anything to do with you, and the son of a bitch is long gone anyway."

He gazed at the mottled bruise, thinking he should have noticed it sooner, that he should be feeling more—more anger, more jealousy, more something. This woman, after all, might be his wife one day. They had talked about it once or twice, halfheartedly. Neither was exactly eligible—Sam, the half-breed; Sally, the whore.

Tonight, with Benito tugging at his heart, Sam was tempted to slide down on one knee and beg her. The padre was adamant—no wife, no son. Case closed. But Sam didn't want to be an uncle to the boy, or a friend who visited every other week. He wanted to be his father, to teach Benito all the things his own father had taught him. He wanted to just plain love him and let him know he was loved by somebody in this hard, twisted, unforgiving world.

Marry me, Sally, he thought. But the words wouldn't come to his lips. They welled in his throat, nearly choking him.

"You're in a black mood tonight," she said, fussing with the ribbons on her *camisa* the way she always did when she was cross. Her dark gaze swung to his. "Are you staying?"

Sam reached under the table and ran his hand up her thigh. It was all he could do. There was no place else to go. There was no one else. Benito was asleep on a straw mattress with five other little boys. Anne McIntire was asleep across the street and as far out of his reach as if she were on the moon. For Sam, this night as on so many other nights, there was only the bruised and willing Sally.

Anne bolted upright in the narrow bed, hugging the damp sheet to her bosom. The same dream had been torturing her ever since she left Syracuse. She would find herself alone on a dark street. Then the footsteps would come. Anne would run, and the footsteps would quicken behind her.

In the dream, she never knew who was trying to catch her. She never dared turn to identify her pursuer. But awake, she knew it was her husband, Daniel. And she knew full well that if she ever turned, she would see the damage the pistol had done.

Tonight's dream had been different, however. As she ran away from Daniel, someone had grabbed her. Two massive, dark arms had wrapped around her. Whether it was to pull her to safety or to a new, different danger, Anne wasn't sure. But she knew whose arms they were. Sam Hook was already in her dreams.

Where was he now? she wondered. Close enough to collect her in the morning. Far enough away to satisfy the prejudiced demands of the people of San Miguel.

Over dinner, Doris Thiel had informed Anne she wasn't in New York anymore and that she'd best watch her step. "Especially where the half-breed is concerned," the big woman had said. "You needn't have shaken his hand. It only embarrasses him. One thing I'll say for Sam Hook—he generally knows his place and stays in it."

Anne imagined it was the feel of his big, warm, enveloping hand that had worked its way into her dream. If Sam Hook "stayed in his place," as Mrs. Thief so grimly put it, Anne suspected it was only because he wanted to.

As she drifted into a light, dreamless sleep, Anne wondered if Sam's wings were as stiff and useless as her own.

Chapter Three

The morning sun washed the adobe walls of the buildings with a muted gold-pink, a far cry from the harsh red brick and stark white clapboard of Syracuse, Anne thought as she stood on the street with her bags behind her. But the warmth of the architecture belied the cold prejudice in the hearts of the people.

Mrs. Thiel's parting words had been, "Don't feel obliged to talk to that half-breed any more than you have to, honey. I wouldn't even smile at him if I were you. Lord only knows what it might set him to contemplating." The fat woman had leaned close to her then, her breath a cloying mix of cloves and coffee. "Those savages are particularly partial to white women, if you catch my drift."

The rattling of a wagon drew Anne's attention down the street. Her heart sank when she saw that it was being driven by a portly, bearded man. A long-robed priest walked beside the wagon, kicking his brown cassock out of his way with each step as he chatted with the driver. Had there been a change of plan? she wondered. Were these men to accompany her to the ranch rather than Sam? Had someone deemed him unfit to escort her to his own home?

"Good morning, Mrs. McIntire," the priest said cheerfully as the wagon drew up. "My name is Father José."

Anne smiled pleasantly. "Good morning," she said, her glance sliding to the bearded driver in the wagon seat. "I was waiting for Sam Hook. He was supposed to drive me to his family's ranch this morning."

The driver tipped his hat, then spat over the opposite side of the wagon before he spoke. "Morning, ma'am."

She acknowledged his greeting with a slight nod, hoping she wouldn't be spending the whole day with him. "I was waiting for Sam Hook," she said again. A twinge of worry intensified to a wave of alarm. Anne turned to the priest. "Is Sam all right? Has something happened to him?"

Father José put a gentle hand on her shoulder. His hazel eyes twinkled. "No, Mrs. McIntire. Sam is fine. He was ... um, well ... detained." He raised his eyebrows to indicate the driver. "George has hitched up the wagon and he will take you to collect Sam just down the street."

"Down at Sally Mendoza's," George added with a knowing grin, which made the priest frown.

Father José picked up Anne's bags and, with some effort, put them in the rear of the buckboard. Then he offered her his hand. "Let me help you up, Mrs. McIntire."

With the driver pulling and the priest pushing, Anne managed to haul herself and her voluminous black taffeta skirts up into the seat. "Thank you, Father José," she said. "I'm happy to have met you."

"I'll walk along with you," he said as the wagon began to roll. "Just to make sure everything goes as planned." His voice was calm and full of goodwill. He smiled up at her. "Are you intending to stay in New Mexico long, Mrs. McIntire?"

"I haven't decided yet, to be quite honest," Anne replied. "The landscape and the weather are so different from what I'm accustomed to. And I'm not so certain I care for the inhabitants."

Father José's eyebrows knit together. "Someone was unkind to you?"

"No. Not to me," she said curtly, fidgeting with a fold of her skirt. "To someone else. To my cousin."

"Ah," the priest sighed. "So you have already run into the adobe wall of prejudice in San Miguel."

Anne's eyes narrowed with anger as she looked down onto the top of his curly head. "I think it's shameful, Father. A disgrace. I'd like to—"

He pursed his lips and raised a hand to silence her. "You have only just arrived, Mrs. McIntire. This problem has very deep roots in the community. Perhaps it would be best if you did not express your feelings so vividly for a while."

She glared at him. For a moment she'd thought she had discovered an ally, but now she sensed that the priest, like Sam, accepted the shameful situation and was not moved to do anything to correct it.

"Perhaps you're right," she said with a faint shrug of her shoulders. It wasn't, after all, her problem. But anger coursed through her again when the wagon pulled up in front of a small, crumbling adobe structure and a man lounging there called over his shoulder, "Hey, 'breed. Your wagon's here."

Sam Hook appeared in the doorway then, his wide shoulders filling the frame. He was still wearing the blue chambray shirt, and buckskin trousers with a length of soft fringe down each long leg. His dark hair was tied at the back of his neck with a leather cord and a tan Stetson dipped over his dark eyes. He took a last gulp from

a steaming mug, handed it to someone behind him, then
walked slowly, almost gingerly, toward the wagon.

The springs groaned and the seat canted as Sam
climbed up to take George's place. The pungent aroma
of whiskey and cigarette smoke wafted toward Anne.

"Good morning, Mr. Hook," she said brightly.

Sam tried to focus his bloodshot eyes on her lovely face
while his head pounded like a smithy's anvil. "Good
morning," he rasped, then flicked his gaze to the priest,
who was still standing beside the wagon. "Padre."

"*Buenos días,* my friend," the priest replied. "I have
just been telling Mrs. McIntire what a fine day it is for
travelling."

Sam merely grunted and slid down in the seat, tipping
his hat over his eyes. Without even looking at her, he
passed the reins to Anne. "Here. You drive," he said.

Anne was about to stammer a reply when a small
sneeze came from the back of the wagon.

"Aw, hell," snarled Sam. "Here we go again, Padre." He tilted his hat back on his head, turned, and with
one swift motion whisked away a tarpaulin and hauled
Benito over the back of the seat. "*¿Qué pasa,* Benito?"
he asked threateningly. "What are you doing, squirt?"

"I want to go with you, Sam," Benito's big, black,
tearful eyes gazed up into the half-breed's glowering face.

Sam sighed roughly. "Not today."

Father José reached up. "*Vámonos, niño.* Sam must
leave. And you will go back to the orphanage and get
another whipping for hiding in his wagon again."

Sam shook the boy gently. "You hear that, Benito?
When are you going to learn?"

Tears cascaded down the little boy's cheeks.

"Stop it," Sam growled. "No crying."

"Oh, for heaven's sake," said Anne, gathering the child to her arms and smoothing his black straight hair. "You just go ahead and cry, little one. It's all right." She rocked him and his thin little arms slid around her shoulders.

Sam simply stared, marvelling at her effect on the tough little boy, who trusted few and rarely let anyone but Sam or Father José touch him. Now this beautiful, delicate, ivory-skinned woman was cooing softly and comforting his wild, beloved, red-skinned little boy. The fact nearly took Sam's breath away, filling his heart with incredible warmth—and unspeakable dread.

He pulled the child roughly from Anne's arms and tossed him to Father José. The priest held the struggling boy tightly against his hip.

"*Silencio,*" he snapped. "Sam will be back in a few weeks. You will see him soon."

The boy raised his big, wet eyes to Sam. "*¿Es verdad?*" he asked. "Is it true?"

Sam smiled. "I'll be back, squirt. Don't I always come back?"

Benito nodded hesitantly. "Will you bring *La Viuda de la Luna* back to see me?"

Sam glanced at the woman his boy had just named "the moon's widow." Her translucent skin glowed in the morning sunlight. Her silver-blond hair tumbled over the shoulders of her black jacket. "*Sí,* I will bring her back."

The boy turned his moist gaze on Anne. "You will come, señora?"

She nodded. "I will come."

Satisfied that he was not forsaken, Benito looked up at the priest. "I will go back and take my beating now, Padre," he said solemnly.

Sam's black eyes narrowed on Father José. "You go easy on him," he cautioned.

The priest smiled and sighed, "*Sí*, I will go easy on your pearl, my friend. We will see you soon." With a hand draped over Benito's shoulder, the priest guided the boy away.

Sam picked up the reins, which Anne had dropped. Without a word he handed them to her once more, then settled down in the seat with his hat over his eyes and his arms crossed over his chest.

She had never even driven a one-horse hansom, let alone a buckboard, but Anne had no intention of letting Sam Hook know that. Driving a wagon, she thought, was as good a way as any for learning how to fly. When she whacked the reins over the horses' backs, the wagon jolted forward, nearly pitching Sam out of his seat.

He caught his flying hat with his right hand. With his left hand he grabbed the reins from her and pulled the racing horses to a halt.

"What the hell do you think you're doing?" he yelled as he slapped his Stetson back onto his head.

"Don't curse at me, Mr. Hook," Anne snapped.

Sam shook his aching head. His voice was low and smooth as snakeskin. "We're going home, Mrs. McIntire. Not to a fire." He pointed to the horse on the right. "See that white stallion? That's Blanco. He hates pulling a wagon about as much as I hate riding in one. But he'll get us home with just a bit of gentle encouragement."

With that, Sam made a soft click with his tongue and the stallion stepped smoothly forward, pulling his roan teammate with him. The wagon moved slowly and steadily. Once more, Sam put the reins in Anne's hands.

When she grimaced, he said, "Just hold them. You don't have to do anything. Blanco knows the way home." Sam settled down again, his head slumped into his shoulders.

After a few minutes, he glanced to his left. Anne's delicate fingers had relaxed on the leather reins. Her spine had become less rigid. He could even see that her knees had separated slightly under her black skirt. Sam squeezed his eyes closed. Don't even think about it, he told himself.

He'd already thought about her half the damn night— the half before he'd passed out, anyway. He'd never even made it up to Sally's bed, but woke up this morning, his head on the table, when Sally tossed a glass of cold water in his face.

La Viuda de la Luna. Her effect on the boy had been immediate and powerful. Sam had seen it happen. But while her pale, delicate beauty had had a soothing effect on the child, Sam found it far from soothing.

Silently, he chastised his mother for inviting her to the ranch. They had enough problems already. There was enough bad blood between himself and Jay to last a lifetime. Now there would be Anne McIntire, *La Viuda de la Luna,* who had hair like spun moonlight and blue eyes as big and deep as a mountain lake. Her bones were as tiny and delicate as a baby bird's. His hands ached to touch her soft, creamy skin. Along with his head, his whole body throbbed at the thought of this woman—this woman who was as forbidden to him as the master's wife to the lowest cotton-picking darkie on a plantation. It occurred to him then that she was Jay's blood cousin and equally forbidden to him.

Sam sighed quietly. He could foresee the summer clearly. Jay would grow surlier day by day. Their mother would grow quiet and grim-lipped under the strain caused by her warring, tightly strung sons. Sam would cart the widow back to San Miguel in a month or two and put her on the stage to Albuquerque. Adiós, Anne McIntire. But he'd still have Benito. And there would still be Sally.

He drifted into sleep, thinking that maybe if he got really drunk enough, he'd be able to ask Sally....

Anne's eyes roved over the wide landscape, from the snow-capped mountains in the distance to the tall grasses and sagebrush nearby. Having lived her entire life in the city, she'd rarely been able to see farther than a block or two. The last five years she'd hardly gone beyond the walls of her own home. Now it was as if her eyes were using new muscles, new abilities she never knew they possessed.

The rugged landscape had frightened her yesterday, but now it had a strong, almost magical appeal. This was a country made for wings, with its wide, unobstructed vistas. If she were ever going to fly, she thought, this was certainly the place to do it.

She was glad she had come. Glad that in her panic last evening she hadn't jumped back into the stagecoach and hightailed it home to New York, never having known this magnificent country or, she thought, looking at the man peacefully sleeping beside her, this magnificent man.

With his hat over his face, all she could see were his wonderfully sensual lips, now slightly slackened. As the horses trotted along, Anne found herself wondering what it would be like to feel those beautifully carved lips on her own. Or those warm, dark hands on her skin.

Pleasure stitched through her like a bright silver thread. She had to remind herself that she was a new widow. Not that finding a man so physically attractive was a taboo to her under the circumstances, for it wasn't. But she had just discovered her own freedom and was in no rush to abandon it too quickly.

Suddenly she felt as giddy as a schoolgirl on her first ride in the countryside with a young beau. She smiled to herself. At twenty-three, she was more the age of schoolmarm than schoolgirl. And the man by her side was hardly a young beau, but a bronzed and weathered Apache. His innocence, if he'd ever had any, had probably been lost long ago. He had been tried and tested not only by the hard land he lived in, but by the hard people who surrounded him. He was a man who had made adjustments. Plenty of them.

And yet, under that calm and accepting demeanor of his, there was passion smoldering, along with a kind of rage. Anne decided she wouldn't mind seeing the depths of his passion, but she hoped she would never have to witness the release of its darker companion.

Just then, a strange bird raced across the trail before her. Anne stood up in the seat to watch it as it darted into a clump of sagebrush, and wished Sam were awake to tell her what kind of bird ran rather than flew. Out of the corner of her eye, she saw something else lash out at the hoof of the big roan. The animal reared back in its traces, then bolted forward, forcing Blanco, Sam's horse, to run with it. The reins flew out of Anne's hands as she fell back onto the seat.

Sam jerked awake as the buckboard jolted over the rutted plains. Anne was clutching the seat for dear life as each bounce of the wagon nearly pitched her over the side.

With one sweep of his dark eyes, he took in the situation. "Just hold on," he said, rising in the seat, his long legs spread wide for balance in the runaway wagon.

Anne's voice was high and tight with fear. "What are you doing?"

"What does it look like?" Sam replied as he leapt forward and landed on the white stallion's back. He clasped his arms around the horse's neck, leaning forward as if whispering in the animal's ear. But the roan was still running full-out, forcing Blanco to keep pace.

Anne's hands hurt from her tight grip on the wooden seat. "Be careful, Sam," she called out just as the front left wheel dropped into a deep rut. There was a resounding crack as the rim broke, and the wagon pitched hard to the left. Sam jumped off Blanco's back to the right, while Anne, along with the wagon and both horses, tumbled down the steeply pitched side of a gully on the left.

He sat for a while, stroking the great white head of the horse he had just shot. Tears streamed from Sam's dark eyes, trailing down his dirt-covered cheeks. He kept wiping them away, but they wouldn't stop.

Sam slammed his fist into the hard, dry ground. He'd had to shoot horses before, for chrissake. Horses he'd raised and loved. There had always been a tightness in his throat, even a mist in his eyes, but he'd never blubbered like a baby before. He wasn't sure what was happening to him. The emotions he'd always had so tightly under control seemed to be defying his will now.

He wiped away a last tear, then rose. He had to return to the woman he had carried to the riverbank and left only when he was certain her injuries weren't serious. On his way back, he opened one of her bags and pulled out the first piece of clothing he found that seemed as if it would make decent bandages. A nightgown, from the look of it—white and soft and ruffled. Sam pressed the cotton fabric to his face, drawing in the sweet scent of her.

You're quite a man these days, he berated himself. Passing out on saloon tables, crying like a baby and now sniffing women's clothes. He looked over his shoulder—one last, long look—at his dead horse, then loped back to the river.

Sun glinting off the water was the first thing Anne was aware of. Then the little breeze that set the cottonwood leaves above her to shimmering. And, after that, the hand softly stroking her forehead. She lurched up, yelped with pain and sank back down.

"Lie still," Sam said, pressing a firm hand on her shoulder to reinforce his command. "Where do you hurt?"

"Everywhere," she groaned.

"I can't fix *everywhere*," Sam replied gruffly. "I know your right ankle hurts and your right leg's torn up, but it isn't serious." He smiled down at her, as warm a smile as Anne had ever seen. "But you're going to have to be more specific for me to help you, Mrs. McIntire. Where else do you hurt?"

"What happened?" she asked.

"We'll talk about that later. Tell me where you hurt. Your head?"

She nodded, then raised her hand to feel a lump just above her hairline.

"Is your vision all right? Blurred or anything like that?"

"No." She could see him clearly, his bronzed, sculpted face hovering over her like some dark guardian angel.

He raised a big hand in front of her face. "How many fingers am I holding up?"

"Twelve," Anne said, grinning weakly.

Sam's lips thinned and his black eyebrows drew together. "I think that knock on the head made you a little giddy, Mrs. McIntire."

"I was just teasing you," she said. "Actually, I think I'm all right." She tried to sit up again, winced, then sagged back down. "Well, maybe not one hundred percent."

"Your ribs?" Sam asked, still scowling.

"Yes. I believe so."

He got up on his knees above her. "Just hold still," he commanded, placing his hands on her rib cage beneath her black jacket. He moved across her torso slowly, his fingers pressing slightly. "I can't feel anything that seems to be broken," he said at last. "You're probably only bruised. Let's get all this off and wrap you up, just to be on the safe side."

A vision of the massacre she had seen the day before flitted through her mind. Much as she had dreamed of being touched by this incredibly handsome man, she couldn't completely forget the blood that ran in his veins. "No, I..." Slowly she became aware of the cool wet cloth that covered her right leg from ankle to hip. She blinked. "You bandaged my leg?"

"Washed the grit off, mostly," he said, one eyebrow raised now as if questioning her sudden suspicion.

Anne could feel the hot flush of color on her cheeks. "Then you—my leg, I mean—you saw..."

He could barely suppress his grin. "Your leg, Mrs. McIntire? I saw the whole blessed limb, from ankle to hip."

Her blush deepened. "Oh, my goodness," she breathed. "Well?"

"Well what?"

"I—I don't know," Anne stammered. Even Daniel had never seen that much of her.

His dark eyes bore into her. "What is it you want, Mrs. McIntire? An appraisal or an apology?"

Anne's blue eyes widened and a nervous laugh escaped her lips. "You've embarrassed me. You caught me being much too coy for my own good, I'm afraid."

"That's a fact," he said. Then with a glimmer in his eyes he added, "What I saw of your leg while I was tending it was quite shapely. I don't think any of the cuts will leave scars."

Anne raised up tentatively on one elbow. She took in a deep breath. "It isn't too bad now," she said, sitting up farther, gazing around at the sun-dappled river and the trees. "Where are we?"

Sam walked to the water and squatted down to fill a canteen. "Judging by the sun when the wagon went over, I'd say we were about two hours out of San Miguel. You have a choice, Mrs. McIntire. It's a day's walk back to town, or about a two-day trek to The Hook. We'll do whichever you want."

"The horses?" she asked softly, knowing one of them was special to him.

He rose from the riverbank, the canteen dripping from his hand. "They didn't survive the fall." Standing above her now, he offered the canteen to her.

"Thank you," she said, drinking deeply of the cool water. "I'm sorry about Blanco. Something frightened the other horse. I don't know what it was."

"It happens," Sam said. "It wasn't your fault."

"I was the one who dropped the reins," Anne said, suddenly unable to meet his gaze.

He bent his knees, then took her chin in his big hand, forcing her to look at him. "I was the one who gave them to an inexperienced driver in the first place. Forget it. Please.''

He meant it, she knew. He didn't blame her for the death of his horse. ''All right,'' she said, feeling regret when his fingers drifted from her face.

''Ready to try your ankle?'' he asked.

''Why not?''

Sam had her up on her feet in a second, his strong hands cupping her elbows. ''Easy now,'' he cautioned as she took a small step.

The pain in her right ankle shot up her leg, and as she began to fall, Sam held her fast.

''That's what I figured,'' he murmured, stroking her arm.

''Now what are we going to do?'' she asked bleakly.

''Like I said, it's your choice. San Miguel or The Hook?''

Anne stared at the man who towered over her. ''But I can't walk!'' she exclaimed. ''What do you propose to do, Mr. Hook—carry me for twenty or thirty miles?''

He bent slightly, slipping one arm under her knees and another around her shoulders, then lifted her high against his chest. ''That's exactly what I propose, Mrs. Mc-Intire. Which way do you want to go?''

She tilted her head in order to meet his dark eyes. ''I'd say that since you're the one who's going to be doing all the work, you ought to be the one to decide.''

''Fair enough,'' said Sam. He bent once more and hooked a basket over his arm just beneath Anne's rump, then bent again to sling a rifle over his shoulder. After shifting her slightly in his arms, he began walking.

Anne let her eyes rove over the hard line of his jaw and his firmly set mouth. ''What did you decide, Mr. Hook?'' she asked.

"I've had just about all I can take of San Miguel for a while," he replied. "We'll just head for home. And it might help if you'd put your arms around my neck, Mrs. McIntire. I notice you don't quite know what to do with them."

He was right, of course. And that was what she wanted to do, but she'd thought it would be much too bold. She looped both arms around his neck, snuggling her cheek against his powerful shoulder.

"Better?" he asked softly.

"Much."

Chapter Four

Sam stayed as close to the river as he could, figuring the woman would feel more comfortable with plenty of water available. It wasn't the way he would have gone if he had been alone. Staying by the river added a good five or six miles to their journey, but Sam thought water was important.

Deep in his heart, however, he knew that wasn't his only reason for lengthening the trip. She felt so damn good in his arms. When he'd finally gotten her weight and the basket of food and his rifle distributed just right, it was an easy walk. He knew this country so well he could have gotten home blindfolded—by sense of smell and the feel of the earth beneath his moccasins. She was no burden at all, but light as a little girl, especially when she finally relaxed against him and allowed the tension to flow from her body.

What he was doing wasn't wrong—though he knew there were plenty of men around who'd be eager to horsewhip him just for looking at a white woman, not to mention hugging one close to his chest for hours. It wasn't wrong, but it was foolish. Sam knew he could have rigged a travois from the lumber of the wrecked wagon and hauled her behind him back to San Miguel. Foolish, just to want to be close to her, to spend a few stolen moments alone, looking into the wide skies of her eyes and the moonlit color of her hair. Foolish. He'd pay for it, too; Sam knew that. If not physically, by being horsewhipped or even lynched by a mob of whiskey-riled cowhands, then emotionally, by holding so close what he could never hope to keep.

This was probably the damndest, stupidest thing he'd ever done, he thought, glancing down at Anne's sun-flushed cheeks, her finely shaped nose, her petal-soft lips. Her blue eyes fluttered up to meet his. With a little heft of his shoulder and a slight dip of his head, he could have kissed her. Instead, he put her down.

"You must be tired," she said, her arms sliding from around his neck.

Sam put the rifle and basket down in turn, then handed her the canteen. "Just thirsty," he said.

After taking a long swig, she handed it back to him and watched as he drained it, his head tilted back and his eyes closed. He walked to the river then and bent to refill it.

The sun had climbed high overhead, and, without a cloud to interfere, its rays had been beating down on them relentlessly. Anne shrugged out of her black silk jacket, then undid the top two buttons of her white silk blouse. She was exhausted, and she hadn't done anything but cling to Sam's broad shoulders and solid neck all morning.

He stood by the river now, his head tipped back as he downed another canteen of water, looking as if he'd done no more than take a pleasant stroll. But how pleasant could it be to lug well over a hundred pounds of female, food and artillery over this rugged terrain? Why, her skirts alone must weigh ten pounds.

Well, she could take care of that easily enough, she decided, yanking up her black skirt and unfastening the waistband of one of her underskirts. When she had wriggled out of that one, she set about ridding herself of the other.

Sam came back from the river to find her tangled in yards of white muslin. "What are you doing?" he asked, his mouth turning down in a scowl.

"I was trying to lighten your burden," Anne said, "but I got my heel caught somewhere in this confounded mess." Her gaze flitted up to his. "Can you help me?"

Sam sighed. This was worth a lynching and a half, he thought. But he bent his long legs, sat beside her, and freed the heel of her black leather shoe from the seam of her petticoat.

Anne tossed the garment aside. "There. Now I'm ten pounds lighter."

"You didn't have to do that, Mrs. McIntire. You weren't heavy in the first place. It's just a matter of balance."

"And I'm ten degrees cooler, too," she added, skewering him with her blue eyes. "It wasn't totally for your benefit, Mr. Hook."

Sam swallowed hard, hoping she didn't plan to take off anything else for either of their benefits. With her voluminous petticoats removed, it was evident how tiny and delicate she really was. The open neckline of her blouse revealed more ivory skin than he was prepared to deal with at the moment.

He nearly shoved the canteen into her hands. "Drink up. I'll refill it, then we'll get on our way."

She took a long sip, then splashed a handful of water on her face and neck. "What time do you suppose it is?" she asked idly.

"It's two-fifteen," he said, not supposing at all, but reading the sun and the angle of the shadows from the trees around them. In all his life he'd never been more than a few minutes off. Jay used to test him when they were children.

Anne arched an eyebrow. "Not two-twenty?" she asked with a grin, thinking that any other man would have looked at the sun, shrugged helplessly and replied "Oh, two or three, thereabouts." Sam Hook seemed to know the time as if he had just consulted some mystical timepiece.

Her playful grin summoned one from Sam. "Indians tend to know things like that," he said. "I'm half Apache, Mrs. McIntire. Or did that escape your notice?"

Anne's hand flew to her mouth in mock horror. "No! I hadn't noticed. Oh, my gracious!"

Sam laughed in spite of himself, in spite of the fact that there was nothing funny about being a half-breed in New Mexico.

Anne gazed at his face. "You have a wonderful laugh, Sam Hook. You should do it more often." Without even realizing it, she had taken his hand in a spontaneous display of affection.

But she realized it quickly enough when his laughter ceased abruptly and his face returned to its customary expressionless mask. He pulled his hand away as if her touch had burned him. Then he got briskly to his feet. "I'll get some more water and we'll go," he said.

From the granite set of his jaw and the ebony hardness of his eyes when he returned, Anne never would have believed this was a man capable of laughter. And yet he had laughed—a warm, happy burst of joy. She was de-

termined to make him do it again. Sam Hook needed her,
she decided. If only to make him laugh.

As he picked her up and settled her against his hard,
warm chest, she was well aware of her need for him. And
it wasn't merely as a means of transportation. There was
a deeper need, one she had never experienced before. A
need she couldn't even identify with a name. But it was
there all the same—nameless, and vague, and very, very
real.

The sun was touching the peaks of the mountains and,
on the ground, long afternoon shadows began to blend
sagebrush with sand.

Anne had fallen asleep, lulled by Sam's long, rhythmic strides. She had one arm around his neck, the other
curled delicately against her breasts.

He was loath to wake her, knowing sleep gave her respite from an ankle that must hurt like the devil. She
hadn't complained about it for a minute, though. He was
still worried about her ribs, hoping she wasn't hurting
there and just not letting him know. Anne McIntire had
a stiff pride he admired, annoying as it was.

He loosened the rifle from his shoulder, slid it down to
the ground, then let the basket drop. Finally, Sam folded
his legs beneath him, keeping Anne in the cradle of his
arms as he sat. He rested his cheek for a moment against
the crown of her head, but lifted it quickly when she
stirred. He could feel every muscle in her body stretch
just a little as she woke. Fleetingly, he wondered what it
would be like to have her wake beside him in a big, warm
bed. Wake and turn to him, opening those huge blue
eyes.

Anne blinked and smiled sleepily. She rubbed her eyes. "I can't believe I fell asleep," she said. "How long was it?"

"Two hours."

She grinned. "Is that two hours give or take a few minutes, or two hours precisely?"

"Give or take," he said, his lips quirking to reveal his white, even teeth.

Anne made no effort to get up. Sam made no effort to release her.

"Aren't you exhausted?" she asked while she studied the faint blue shadow of stubble on his chin.

He rolled his neck slightly. "Just a little stiff. I'm hungry, though. How about you?"

"Starving."

Still, neither one of them moved. Their reluctance to end their quiet closeness became obvious. All too obvious. And embarrassing. Anne's face flushed.

He released her the instant she started to get up.

"Well," they said at the same time.

Sam stood and helped her up. "Why don't I take you down to the river and you can freshen up?" he offered.

"Thank you. That would be nice."

Self-consciously now, Sam picked her up, avoiding looking into her eyes. Anne hesitated before raising her arms to encircle his neck. When she did, she was careful not to touch his skin, but only the soft collar of his shirt. By the time he set her down on the riverbank, the air between them had stopped crackling.

After Sam left her, Anne managed to hobble on her bad ankle, take care of nature's call, then rinse as much of herself as she could, fully clothed, in the river. When she was done, she sat watching the mountains darken to the west.

A mere two weeks ago, she thought, she had been secretly packing her bags in Syracuse, preparing for her flight. She hadn't even stayed for Daniel's funeral. Now, for the first time since that night, she wondered what it had been like. She fingered the fabric of her black skirt. What was it the little dark-skinned boy had called her this morning? *La Viuda* something. Her school Spanish was rusty, but she thought it meant "widow." How strange, she thought, to be known as a widow when she had hardly been a wife.

There was a soft footfall behind her. Sam stood there, shirtless, his hair loose, just grazing his broad shoulders. A tiny gasp escaped Anne's lips, not because he had frightened her but because, outside of statues in picture books, she had never seen a male body so magnificent in its hard contours and perfect proportions.

He looked sheepish. "I thought I'd clean up a little, too," he said, "before our feast."

He slipped out of his moccasins, then rolled up his buckskin pants before he walked out into the water. "How's your ankle?" he called to her as he splashed water on his face and rippling arms and smooth, muscular chest.

"It could be a lot worse," Anne called back.

Sam turned toward her, water dripping silver from his chin and hair. "Don't be braver than you have to be, Mrs. McIntire. How about your ribs? Any more pain?"

Anne shook her head. There was this funny feeling in her chest, though—a fluttering in her heart as she watched him wade toward the shoreline, his skin glistening in the last of the light. Good Lord, he was beautiful. She wondered if he'd jump out of that bronze skin if she pressed her hand over his heart the way he had jumped when she'd inadvertently clasped his hand—as if she'd held a lit match to his flesh. Too much the gentleman to take advantage of the situation? she wondered. Or was it because of her "widow's weeds"? Or perhaps, heaven forbid, the man simply didn't find her attractive. Perhaps he already had a woman he loved. Sam Hook was a man who would be faithful—she sensed that in him. How sad, she thought, if he were already spoken for. Sad for her, not for Sam. He ought to be with somebody who loved him with her whole heart. Somebody who made him feel complete while everyone else was calling him a half-breed.

He swung her up against his damp chest. She slipped her arms around his neck without a second thought. Their gazes met.

His dark eyes glittered as they searched her face, pausing on her slightly parted lips. Anne's heart lurched. Her fingers wove through his long, black hair. She felt the strong surge of his heart against her breast.

What in tarnation was he thinking? Sam asked himself. What in the world was he doing, standing here with this moon-haired white woman in his arms, his mouth just inches from her inviting lips, his whole body aching for her? This was insane. It was suicide. It was—

She arched her neck, closing the distance between their lips, placing a soft, tentative kiss on his stunned mouth.

"What are you doing?" he whispered. He felt like a fool. Like a dolt of a schoolboy. Like an Apache man who'd just been kissed by a white goddess.

"I kissed you, I think," she stammered, as surprised by her boldness as he was.

He shook off his bewilderment, lowering his arms so her mouth was well out of reach. "Don't do it again, Mrs. McIntire," he said gruffly. "This is a long enough trip as it is. I don't need any of your white witchery along the way."

Anne stiffened in his arms. She closed her eyes as she felt a hot flush suffuse her cheeks. It was the first time she had ever done anything so brazen, and now she was ashamed and mortified . . . and rejected. "Rest assured it won't happen again, Mr. Hook," she said, fighting back the tears that were ready to spring to her eyes.

Silently, almost grimly, they sat by the fire Sam had made and ate what was supposed to have been their lunch—salty ham, cheese and a round loaf of bread.

Ravenous before, Anne found her appetite had dwindled to nothing. After a few bites, she brushed the crumbs from her skirt. Her mortification had slowly but thoroughly turned to anger. It was one thing to find a kiss offensive, which he quite obviously had, but quite another to have made her feel so cheap.

She glared at Sam across the campfire. The incident hadn't seemed to impair his appetite, she thought. He was wolfing down his portion of the food like a man who hadn't eaten in weeks . . . and as though nothing had happened between them. She knew she should bite back her ill feelings, but she couldn't. Dammit, she wouldn't.

"You truly are the rudest man I've ever met, Sam Hook," she said, rearranging her skirt over her folded legs.

"Then I don't suppose you'll be wanting to kiss me again, Mrs. McIntire," he replied coolly, gnawing a chunk of bread.

Her shoulders shook with rage. If she could have, she would have gotten up and kicked him. "If you think I'm such a brazen hussy," she spat, "why don't you just get up and go? That way I won't tarnish your sterling morals."

Sam swallowed the bread, then took a long draft of water from the canteen. "Don't think I haven't been considering it," he said, his black eyes piercing hers.

Anne fussed with the folds of her skirt. "Go ahead. Leave. Just tell me what direction the ranch is and I'll get there by myself."

"It's east," he said.

After a moment she asked nonchalantly, "Which way is east?"

Sam slammed what was left of the loaf of bread into the basket and slapped the lid shut. "You'd do it, too, wouldn't you?" he snarled, lunging to his feet. "Or you'd try. Die trying." He stalked around the fire toward her and stood towering over her like some enormous tree. "Look. I'm sorry. You just surprised me, that's all. I thought you had a little more sense than that."

"Than what?" she growled.

"Than to kiss a man flat out like that," he said. "You could get into a lot of trouble, Mrs. McIntire." Sam shook his arms toward the dark night sky. "We both could get in a lot of trouble!"

"Both?" Anne looked up at him innocently. "You mean you wanted to kiss me back?" Her voice wavered as she looked down at her lap. "I—I thought you found me repulsive."

Sam dropped to one knee beside her. He took her face in both hands. "Repulsive! My God, Annie, you're the most beautiful, most desirable woman I've ever seen in my life."

The tears she'd kept in check finally welled in her eyes. One of them coursed down her cheek. Sam brushed it away with his thumb.

"Don't cry," he said softly. "I didn't want to hurt you. I never meant..."

He didn't finish his sentence or even his thought, for Anne's tear-wet face and trembling lips were finally too much for him. He kissed the salty corners of her mouth, then softly covered her lips with his. She seemed to melt beneath him then, all warm and wet and trembling, her lips giving way to the ravishment of his tongue, her own greeting him and then joining in an exquisite mating.

When he finally broke the kiss, his black eyes were burning. She gazed up at him, trembling, dazed, her fingers drifting through his hair. For a moment Anne wasn't even sure where she was. She only knew she had never felt this way before, had never been kissed that way before, and she was shaken to her very core. It was like...like flying. And she wanted to soar higher, farther. "Love me, Sam," she whispered.

Even as Sam's hand skimmed her delicate ribs, a voice hammered in the back of his brain, "Don't do this." His breath was ragged as he worked the tiny buttons, and his mouth drew taut as he parted the halves of her blouse. "Tell me to stop, Annie. Tell me now. Or I won't," he rasped. "I won't be able to."

Her blood was racing, and her heart pounding. It felt as if a storm had taken possession of her body, with lightning flashing and thunder rolling through her, and a shimmering heat she'd never known before. She felt a stunning desire she couldn't—wouldn't—deny. "Don't stop," she whispered. "Oh, Sam. I—I want you."

The last thread of his control snapped. With one swift tug, he freed her lush ivory breasts from the thin cotton camisole, and feasted first on one and then the other as Anne's fingers combed restlessly through his hair.

Her nipples were alive, like sweet raspberries on his tongue. Sam's head was swirling, for he was drunk on the wonderful taste and scent of her, the soft feel of her, the sound of her tiny moans.

He couldn't wait. She'd have to have her pleasure later, Sam thought as he wrested her skirt out of his way and used both hands to strip her of her pantalets. He raised up to unfasten his trousers, and as he did he saw her face clearly in the firelight. Her eyes were squeezed shut and her teeth were clenched, her lips drawn tightly over them.

His fingers stilled on the lacings of his buckskin pants, and he froze, as if someone had just tossed a bucket of icy water on him. This couldn't be. She was a widow, wasn't she? *Una viuda.* Widows weren't virgins.

"Annie," he demanded. "Look at me. Open your eyes."

She did so slowly, as if her lids resisted her will.

Sam closed his own eyes briefly, seeking control. "You've never done this before, have you?" he asked, trying not to sound gruff and impatient. "You've never been with a man."

Her bosom heaved with a sob and her eyes flooded with tears. "I'm sorry," she wailed. "I'm just a little frightened."

Sam sat back on his heels. He didn't know what to do—just what he had no intention of doing now. He couldn't even put two words together to comfort or console her, so, with a rough curse, he got to his feet and stalked to the river.

He stood on the bank a moment, his breathing and heartbeat returning to normal but the rest of him still stoked with a hard, hot passion. A virgin! To his knowl-

edge he had never even kissed a virgin. He wasn't sure
he'd ever seen one over the age of thirteen, for that matter, except for the sisters at the mission.

What a fool he was. He'd thought, when she'd kissed
him, that she was a widow grown restless, a woman who
was taking full advantage of their isolation to have her
needs met. He'd thought, when he was able to think at all
after touching her, that maybe they could both get what
they wanted so desperately and then be done with it. The
widow would have her cravings taken care of, and he
would possess the white goddess who was driving him
mad. But a virgin!

All he could think to do now was throw back his head
and howl at the moon. Which he did—a long, wild,
painful cry. Then he shucked off his clothes and dived
into the cold water of the river.

When he came back, Anne was sitting quietly by the
fire, poking at the flames with a stick. Her eyes were
puffy. It was obvious to Sam that she had been crying.

He sat beside her, his arm just touching hers as he
reached into the wicker basket for his tobacco and cigarette papers. He said nothing as he rolled a cigarette, lit
it with a burning twig from the fire, inhaled and let out a
long stream of smoke. While he was swimming, he had
thought about what he was going to say to her. There was
too much to lose and too little to be gained from a night's
wild fling. He wasn't sure he could make her understand, though.

Anne spoke first. "Sam, I'm so sorry," she said,
calmly and flatly. "I truly intended to make love. I
wanted to. I just got a little frightened."

"More than a little," he said, slipping his arm around
her shoulder, squeezing it, then withdrawing from her.

She had had every right to be frightened, he told himself. He had gone at her like a savage. It was just plain luck he'd looked at her face long enough to realize how terrified she was.

"I want you to know I wasn't teasing you," she continued. "I wasn't leading you on."

"You don't have to tell me that," he said softly. "A man knows the difference."

She angled her head in order to see his face. "Then do you know I still want you?" she asked, her voice barely above a whisper now. "I don't mean right this minute, or even tonight. I just mean—"

"I know what you mean," Sam said, cutting her off before she said things that would haunt her later. "But it isn't going to happen." He sighed roughly. "I made some assumptions about you I shouldn't have."

She poked at the fire again. "Because I'm a widow, you mean?"

Sam nodded. "Yes. Because you're a widow. *La Viuda de la Luna.*" He turned toward her, took a strand of her pale hair and let it flow through his fingers. "I lost my head a while ago, Annie. It won't happen again. I promise you."

"But, Sam, I—"

He held up his hand. "Hear me out. I could count at least a dozen reasons why I shouldn't make love to you. But the biggest reason of all is that I plan to marry someone else." There, he thought. He'd said it. The one reason she couldn't argue with. If he had told her it was frowned on, or that there could be trouble or even violence, she'd have argued endlessly, trying to convince him she didn't care. So he'd decided to end it once and for all—for both their sakes—by telling her he already had other plans for his life. Plans that didn't include her. Just the thought made his stomach knot.

"Oh," was all she could manage to say. She was utterly ashamed of her behavior earlier in the evening, but more than that, she was bitterly disappointed. It was as if she had lost him. How could she lose something she'd never even had? she wondered. How could she possibly feel so bereft and downhearted? Anne tried to smile.

"Well, congratulations, Sam. Tell me about your future bride." She hoped she sounded brighter than she felt.

He feigned a yawn. Sally Mendoza was the last thing he wanted to talk about right now. He took a long pull on his cigarette, then tossed it into the fire. "Maybe later. We should get some sleep, Anne. There's another long day ahead of us."

Anne gazed around at the bare ground. "How will we sleep?" She shivered, suddenly aware that the night had become chilly.

"Best keep you close to the fire," Sam said, looking at her billowy skirt. "On second thought, I'd best stay between the fire and all that silk."

She lay down, curling on her side on the hard ground, one arm pillowed beneath her head. Sam put a few more sticks on the fire, then stretched out between Anne and the crackling flames. There was half a foot at least between her back and his front.

"Comfortable?" he asked quietly.

"No," she said with a chuckle. "But if I ignore it long enough, maybe I'll fall asleep." She shivered, drawing her knees up more tightly and wrapping her arms around her.

"Aw, hell," Sam gritted. "Scoot back."

"What?"

"I said scoot back. I can't let my cousin freeze to death, can I?"

She inched back until she felt his warmth against her. Then he placed one arm over her and tucked his legs into the bend of hers.

"Lift your head up, Anne," he ordered.

When she did, he slid his other arm beneath her cheek. "How's that? Warmer now?"

"Much," she said. "Good night, Sam."

"Good night, Annie." He stared into the blond waves of her hair, knowing he'd be lucky if he slept for two minutes.

She was on a dark street. It was just after a rain, and the cobblestones glistened under the street lamps. Her ankle hurt and she couldn't run. And Daniel's footsteps echoed loudly in the night as he splashed through puddles, coming closer and closer.

She didn't know she had screamed until Sam pulled her more tightly against him and his warm breath fanned over her ear.

"Hush, Annie. Hush. It's only a dream. You're safe. I've got you. You're safe with me."

He stroked her hair and lulled her back to sleep. When her breathing evened again, Sam fell into a fitful, ragged sleep of his own. In his dream he was undressing Annie with excruciating slowness, letting his eyes rove hungrily over her—the long, soft line of her neck, her creamy breasts swelling for the touch of his hands and his mouth, her slim, elegant legs.

"Love me, Sam," she commanded dreamily.

He was her willing and obedient slave. Whatever she wanted, he would happily do.

"Touch me here."

Oh, yes.

"Kiss me there."

Yes, love, yes.

All night long in his dreams he loved her. Deeply and completely.

As dawn broke, Sam dragged his eyes open. He was instantly aware of two harsh facts—the woman was gone and the cold muzzle of a gun was pressed against his temple.

Chapter Five

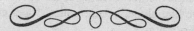

"Wake up, 'breed," a rough voice said.

Without moving a muscle, Sam took a slow, deep breath. "I'm awake," he said. "Where's the woman?"

"Woman?" The rough voice laughed. "You got a little squaw out here with you, 'breed? Out gettin' a piece of tail in the moonlight, was you?"

A second voice giggled nervously. "Where d'you s'pose she went, Sims?"

"Damned if I know, Charlie." He pressed the gun more firmly into Sam's head. "Maybe she didn't like what this Apache has to offer."

Behind Sims, Charlie giggled once more.

Sam recognized the voices of the hired hands from The Tenedor, the ranch just northwest of The Hook. These two had stirred up more than their share of trouble in the last few years. Sims was as mean as a snake. Charlie, the other one, was just plain crazy. He'd do anything Sims told him to.

The only saving grace so far was that they hadn't gotten their hands on Annie. But where the hell was she? As if in answer to his question, Sam heard her lovely voice singing as she came from the direction of the river.

"Well, lookee there," said Sims.

Charlie's breath whistled through his teeth. "The 'breed's out here with a white gal, Sims."

"Looks that way, don't it?" Sims sank his knee into Sam's back, pressing the gun even harder against his temple. "What you been up to, Injun?" he asked. "Got yourself a little white meat, did you?"

Sam heard the distinct cocking of his Spencer carbine.

"You leave him alone," Anne called. "Get away from him or I'll shoot you."

Sam groaned inside. There went his plan for getting himself out from under Sims's sharp and bony knee.

"Leave him alone," she called again. "Don't you know who this man is?"

Yes, they know who I am, Annie. Why the hell do you think they're doing this? He broke out in a cold sweat. She was going to get them both killed. First him, with a bullet through his head, and then herself, after Sims and Charlie had their way with her.

"Whyn't you just put that rifle down, little lady?" Charlie cooed. "We're just havin' us a bit of fun with the half-breed here."

"I don't like your idea of fun," she said. Then a shot rang out.

"Lord almighty, Sims!" yelped Charlie. "She just shot off the heel of my boot."

Sweat beaded on Sam's forehead and poured off his chest as he heard Anne call, "Your foot's next. Then your knee, and then . . . "

"She means it, Sims," Charlie groaned. "That shot weren't no accident."

The gun muzzle at Sam's temple wavered. Sims called out to her. "Why's a white gal like you out here with a damn half-breed?"

"Mr. Hook is escorting me to his ranch to pay a visit on his mother. He's been a complete gentleman."

Liar, Sam thought.

"I'll just bet," Sims said.

"If you don't move that pistol away from Mr. Hook's head, sir, your friend is going to lose his foot. His left heel's going now."

She fired again. And Charlie yelped again, louder.

"Lord have mercy, Sims. She did it! She did it! I ain't got no heels left on my boots."

The cold pressure of the gun disappeared from Sam's skull and the sharp knee eased up.

"What do you want to do now, Sam?" Anne called.

He rolled out from beneath Sims's leg and rose to his full height, his shirt drenched with sweat and his face glistening. Then he grinned. "You're doing a fine job all by yourself, Annie. Why ask me?" Having said that, Sam drew back his fist and slammed the unsuspecting Sims in the belly, then caught him hard on the jaw as the man bent forward to grab his gut.

Charlie stumbled backwards, tripping in his heel-less boots, as Sam stalked toward him, then passed him and continued toward the men's two horses, where he reached for a rope coiled on one of the saddles. He walked back to where Sims lay on the ground.

"Get over here," Sam ordered the wide-eyed and now leaderless Charlie. "Now."

Charlie shambled over to him. "We was just havin' some fun, Sam. Never meant you no real harm. You know that."

"Like the lady said, Charlie—I don't much like your idea of fun." Sam plunged his fist into the cowhand's face. Blood gushed immediately from his nose as Charlie sank to his knees, blubbering.

"Hooray, Sam!" Anne cheered as she hobbled up to him. If she was expecting a hero's welcome, she was quickly disappointed, for he glared at her.

"This isn't a game, Annie," he snarled as he knelt down to tie the men's arms and legs together. "You almost got us killed."

"I saved your ungrateful hide," she retorted shrilly.

Sam grunted and continued to tie the two men back to back. When he was done, he stood up and held out his hand. "I'll take my rifle back now."

She thrust it into his waiting palm. "Be my guest," she said, then limped a few yards away and slid to the ground, giving in at last to the fierce quaking in her knees.

Sam was beside her instantly, his arm around her. "Anne McIntire, you're the most—the most...the damndest surprise of my whole life. Where the hell did you learn to shoot like that?" He held her head to his chest as she snuffled.

"In Syracuse," she said. "My butler taught me."

"Your butler!" Sam echoed, shaking his head in amazement.

"Rumsey was a corporal in my husband's artillery brigade before he was our butler." She smiled weakly. "I learned to shoot with a gun exactly like yours."

"And you shot the heels off a man's boots," Sam marvelled.

"I wanted to shoot his eyes out," she said, scraping the last of her tears. "I'm considering yours next, Sam Hook, you ungrateful—"

"I apologize," he said quickly.

"And?"

"And what?"

Anne sniffed. "How about a little gratitude?"

Sam sat back, holding her by the shoulders. "You're not going to leave me with a shred of manliness, are you?" he asked, his mouth sliding into a wide grin.

"I doubt that anyone could take that away from you," she said stiffly. "I'm waiting."

Sam splayed his big hand over his heart. "Thank you, Mrs. McIntire, for saving my worthless red hide."

"You're welcome." She smiled then. "For the record, Sam, I would have shot their eyes out if they had harmed you."

"If that's your attitude, and you stay around here very long, you're going to have your work cut out for you, Annie."

Her eyes opened wide. "Things like this have happened before?"

"My whole life!" Sam exclaimed. Why couldn't she grasp the situation? What more proof did she need? "And unless the peace that passeth all understanding happens real fast, things like this are going to keep on happening to me." He held out his hands, palms down, so she could see the deep bronze skin etched with scars. "I'm half Apache, Annie. Get that through that thick little skull of yours, will you? I'm not like other men. Or at least I'm not treated like them."

She traced a fingertip over a jagged scar. "Well, you should be," she said.

Sam whipped his hand back. "Fine," he shouted, getting to his feet. "You just go on back to San Miguel and tell everyone to start treating Sam Hook like a white man. Tell Mrs. Thiel. Tell the folks in the café. Tell every damn soul in town. I'd appreciate that, Annie. I really would." He stood there glaring at her, his big hands clenched, his black eyes smoldering with rage.

Anne clambered up and hobbled to him. She fit her arms around his trim waist and pressed her cheek to his chest. "I'm sorry, Sam. I'm so sorry. God, I hate this place."

He sighed raggedly. "Well, then, go back to New York, Anne. You're not going to change New Mexico. You can't shoot the heels of everybody who thinks I'm a cross between a dog and a wolf."

"I would if I could," she said, clinging tighter.

Sam stood silently for a long moment, knowing she meant it, feeling grateful for her affection and loyalty, but haunted by it as well. She didn't have a clue about the danger she was courting. He rested his chin on the crown of her head.

"Go home, Annie," he said softly.

"Go to blazes, Sam," she replied.

Sam's long legs covered a fair amount of ground the first hour in order to put as much distance as possible between them and the two cowhands. They would figure out how to undo his complicated knots eventually, and Sam hoped they would just continue into San Miguel, reluctant to trade a wild Saturday night for "Indian chasing." He had acquired two vicious enemies, though—that he knew for sure. Next time they crossed paths, Sims and crazy Charlie would be playing a deadlier game.

That was the main reason he hadn't taken their horses. The pounding he'd inflicted on them was a matter between men. They wouldn't be relating that part of the encounter in town. But if he took their mounts, they'd have the law on him quicker than buzzards on a dead steer. Tom Atkinson, the sheriff, was a decent enough man, but he had his hands full trying to deal with all the violence that flared between whites and browns and reds. More times than he could count, Tom had locked him in jail just to let the town cool off. Just once, Sam thought, he'd like to see the sheriff lock up a white man while Sam cooled off. He never expected to see it though. Never.

And then there was Annie. This was his last chance to be alone with her, to feel her in his arms. He grinned to himself, wondering what other surprises this woman held in store for him. A widow who was a virgin. A city girl who could handle a Spencer carbine like a cavalry marksman. A warm woman who could comfort and enchant a forlorn little boy. A hot witch whose soft moans could fill a man with savage lust. A frightened innocent whose tears wrenched his heart and made him howl like a wolf at the night sky.

It tore at his gut to think of her with another man. It nearly killed him to know it would be somebody else who took her the first time, who would claim all that passion and heat. Sam didn't know a man who was worthy of her. He only hoped the lucky bastard who finally made Annie his own would truly appreciate her.

But it wouldn't be Sam Hook. He had told her he already planned a life without her. It followed—as surely as trouble followed him—that her life would not include him. Not that he wanted it that way. But Sam had learned to play the hand he was dealt, how to make do with losing cards. That was the way it had always been, and the way it would always be for him. Who knew? With luck, understanding and the passage of time, life might be sweeter for his little Benito. The boy might be dealt a better hand, might have more choices than Sam had had. But for Sam Hook, a half-breed in New Mexico Territory in 1870, there was no choice. He couldn't have his beautiful Annie. He held a losing hand and all he could do was fold.

Today, though ... today while her arms clung around his neck and her lovely face rested against his shoulder and her blue eyes lifted every once in a while to meet his and her perfect mouth composed a beckoning smile ... today she was his.

At last, a good five miles away from the two cow-hands, he set her down. She fidgeted with her skirt and her hair while he opened the picnic basket.

"I'll bet you're famished," he said. "You didn't eat a thing last night." He didn't mention that he had felt her stomach rumbling against him while he walked. He handed her what was left of the loaf of bread.

Anne broke off a third, then passed the lion's share back to Sam. "You need this more than I do."

He didn't want to argue with her today—not on this last day to pretend she was his—so he took the bread with a grateful nod.

She sat, chewing thoughtfully awhile. "You know, Sam," she said, "I've read that in some oriental lands, when a person saves another person's life, they become their slave out of sheer gratitude."

He uncapped the canteen, took a swig, then handed it to her. "You're not satisfied with having me as a simple beast of burden, I guess," he said with a smirk.

Anne sipped from the canteen. She had spent the whole morning clinging to Sam's neck, feeling the solid beat of his heart, glancing up into his sculpted face and remembering the feel of his mouth on hers, and the shocking warmth of that mouth on her breast. The memory alone had sent tremors through her.

She wasn't sure of the exact moment she had made up her mind about him. It might have been when she limped

up from the river and saw him on the ground with a gun
to his head. She'd known then that she wanted this man
with a passion she'd never dreamed she could feel, that
she couldn't lose him—not to some filthy cowhand with
a pistol in his hand, not to some woman who couldn't
possibly appreciate him or desire him as much as she did.
He had told her that he planned to marry someone else.
No. Absolutely not. Sam Hook was just going to have to
change his plans.

Two weeks ago, if anyone had told her that she would
have such feelings for any man, much less one she had
known only a day and a half, Anne would have laughed
and said it was absurd, impossible. Hadn't she just bar-
gained with the devil himself to end her five-year marriage? Wasn't it freedom she wanted—wings to fly, not
arms to hold her down? Totally absurd. Absolutely impossible. And a virtual stranger, to boot!

But it wasn't absurd. It wasn't impossible. And Sam
Hook was no stranger. Maybe she didn't know everything there was to know about the man. But she knew
what she needed to know—he was strong and good and
warm and intelligent, and there was laughter lurking in
him that longed to be set free. Perhaps more than anything else, Anne wanted to do that. She wanted to free
him—as she had freed herself two weeks ago in Syracuse.

In contradiction to her thoughts, she said, "I think
you'd make a fine slave."

A dark eyebrow quirked as Sam leaned on one elbow
with his legs stretched out. "Picking your cotton and
chopping your wood, Miz Annie?"

"Perhaps. Driving my carriage. Or—" Anne whisked
her black skirt halfway up her calf and angled her foot
toward him "—massaging my poor ankle."

Sam's eyes travelled down the pale, shapely limb. "At your service, madam," he said, unlacing her shoe and slipping it off before he unwound the bandage he had wrapped around her ankle after the accident. His strong fingers pressed the tender underside of her foot. "Just squeal if it hurts," he said.

Anne closed her eyes and smiled. "No. That feels wonderful." She leaned back on her elbows, savoring his touch, feeling only slightly guilty about her ploy. "I'm the one who should be rubbing your feet. You've been doing all the walking."

"I'm used to it," Sam said as his thumb slid along her instep. "Anyway, it wouldn't be proper for the mistress to pamper her slave."

"I'd be a very benevolent mistress," she said, her eyes still closed.

"You wouldn't beat me?"

"No. Never."

He chuckled. "Or shoot my heels off?"

Anne shook her head.

His grip hardened. "What would you do?"

Her forehead furrowed in thought. "I'd have you work in the mansion, I believe. Yes, definitely. You'd be my personal slave."

"Personal," Sam echoed.

"Uh-huh. Quite personal. I'd have you doing all sorts of very special little tasks for me."

"Such as?"

"Hmm. Such as laying magnolia branches on the grate and lighting the fire in the fireplace each afternoon. Bringing me camomile tea in the most delicate little cups. Carrying hot water for my bath." Her eyes opened then. They held his. "Warming my bed," she added huskily.

His thumb worked deeply into her foot. "Only warming it. Leaving when you were ready to retire for the night," he asserted.

"Oh, naturally. Mistresses and slaves would never—"

He gripped her ankle brutally and Anne winced. "That's right Annie. Your slave knows his place. You understand that, don't you?" His voice was low and threatening now. His expression was rock hard.

"That hurts, Sam," she said.

He continued to exert the same pressure. "There are worse hurts," he said coldly as he eased his punishing grasp and began wrapping the bandage again.

Silenced by his harsh warning, Anne watched as he finished binding the cloth around her now-throbbing ankle. How was she going to make him understand that she didn't care about pain, or danger, or even propriety anymore? She only cared about him.

Emma scanned the horizon again, hoping to see a buckboard jolting along behind Blanco and a rented horse from town. She saw only sagebrush and dirt.

She was worried—about her niece, and about Sam, too. She always worried when Sam went into San Miguel, and she didn't stop worrying till he was safely home again.

Maybe he had gotten into trouble, she thought. Nine times out of ten he did. And nine times out of ten it wasn't his fault. If only people would just leave him alone. Maybe Tom Atkinson had tossed him in jail again, and Anne was just biding her time at Doris Thiel's.

Emma frowned as she took one last look toward the horizon. Maybe after lunch, if they still hadn't arrived, she'd ask Jay if he could send out a few of the hands to look for them. On second thought, it would only give him an excuse to rant and rave about Sam. These days, though, Jay hardly seemed to need an excuse to rip Sam up one side and down the other. It was about all he did anymore.

Anne gnawed the last bit of rabbit from the bone. She couldn't recall ever having been so hungry. Granted, she hadn't eaten much since her dinner at Mrs. Thiel's, but she couldn't help wondering if her voracious appetite for Sam hadn't somehow increased her other appetites.

It was evident he no longer trusted her to behave herself. He'd been quiet and grim all day as he carried her. She would have given anything to get behind those black eyes of his and know what was going on in his head. The man was absolutely inscrutable. She watched the firelight play over the hard contours of his face now as he gazed into the dark distance, smoking quietly.

"Talk to me, Sam," she said.

"About what?" The flames from the campfire leapt in his eyes as he slowly turned in her direction. The sight made Anne's heart pick up speed.

"Tell me about you. About your past. Your future. Where Sam Hook has been, and where he's going." She pointedly didn't ask about the present—the here and now with her.

He blew out a thin stream of smoke. "I've been here. I'm staying here."

"With the woman you're going to marry?" Anne couldn't stay away from the subject any longer.

"That's right," Sam said, taking another deep drag on his cigarette.

"What's her name?"

Sam raised an eyebrow. "Why?"

"Don't be so argumentative," she said. "I'm curious, that's all. I want to know you better."

"Knowing her name won't help you know me, Annie. What was your husband's name?"

She crossed her arms defensively. "Daniel," she said, realizing it was the first time she had spoken his name aloud since that final night.

Sam's eyes bored into her. "Why did he let you stay a virgin?"

She flinched. "That's none of your business."

"Fine," Sam said, flicking the remains of his cigarette into the fire. "Good night." He lay down on his side, one arm crooked under his head, his eyes closed.

Anne glared at him from across the campfire. He was impossible. But Lord Almighty, he was beautiful. She flopped down onto the hard ground, imitating his pose, with one arm beneath her head. It was horrible. At least last night she'd had his body for warmth and comfort. She feigned a shiver, which evoked absolutely no reaction from him.

"Brr," she said with a whimper, hugging her arms around her, peeking through the flames of the fire to see if he reacted. He didn't, so she shivered again dramatically.

"Settle down, Annie," he said through gritted teeth.

"I'm cold."

"Get closer to the fire," said Sam. "Just watch your skirt."

She scooted toward the campfire. "You watch my damn skirt," she snapped. "Maybe if it goes up in flames, it'll help keep me warm."

Sam opened his eyes to see how close she was to the fire. Too close. A rough curse issued from his lips as he got up and walked around to her side of the fire. "Move over, you little witch," he said roughly, sliding down onto the ground behind her. He drew her into him and cradled her head in the crook of his arm. "Now go to sleep, dammit."

She did, and in the middle of the night awoke with his big gentle hand curved over her breast, his warm breath on her neck and the evidence of his desire for her hard against her backside.

You're mine, Sam Hook, she thought. You know it as well as I do. This is how I want to spend the rest of my nights. And I will, I swear to you, I will.

Emma stood on the front porch. In the past two days, she had entertained every possible reason for Anne and Sam's delayed arrival. Every possible tragedy had been played out in her head, every potential disaster, every act of God or man. She was limp with worry when she finally thought she saw something on the horizon. But it wasn't a wagon.

She strode into the parlor for the spyglass. When she peered into the distance again, one gray eyebrow rose, then fell, then rose again. "Sam," she breathed as she lowered the spyglass to wipe a tear from her eye.

Chapter Six

"Looks like a welcoming party," Sam said as they watched his mother rush toward them in a whirl of sleeves and petticoats.

Anne felt him hug her a little more tightly to him. Could it be, she wondered, that he was a bit reluctant to let her go? She knew she was sad at the prospect of being released. Their time together had been all too brief. Still, a special bond had formed between them. Anne was certain of that.

She looked up at Sam's impassive face now, the last time she would see it from precisely this angle. "Thank you, Mr. Hook," she said with mock formality, "for escorting me back to civilization."

"My pleasure, Mrs. McIntire." His lips quirked to reveal a flash of even white teeth.

Anne curled her arms more tightly around his neck. "It was nice, Sam, wasn't it?" she murmured at his ear.

"Uh-huh." His reply was low and warm and lazy. Then he shrugged and said, "But it's over," as he set her down on the ground to meet the happy, tearful Emma Hook.

After hugs and kisses and scores of questions, Emma finally said, "Sam, you take Anne on up to your old room. And you be real careful of her now. She looks like a little china doll.''

"Oh, yes, ma'am," drawled Sam with a sidelong smirk at Anne. "She's a real delicate creature." He swung her back up into his arms. "Aren't you?" he whispered for her ears alone.

He carried her upstairs into a bright room with a narrow brass bed. After putting her down gently on the mattress, Sam backed away as his mother, uncharacteristically chattering like a finch, joined Anne on the bed. Anne tried to respond to all of her questions while still keeping an eye on Sam, who was edging toward the door.

"I'll just leave you ladies to yourselves," he said finally.

His mother joined him at the door, her hand on his arm. "You'll have lunch with us, won't you, dear?"

Sam shook his head. "I think I'll just get a little shut-eye, Mama," he said, bending to kiss the top of her head.

"Dinner then," she insisted.

Sam's eyes flicked to Anne before he answered. "All right."

"You go on then," Emma said. "You look about wore out."

Anne wanted to run after him, to follow wherever he was going as he turned and sauntered down the stairs. It was practically the first time her "beast of burden" had been out of her sight in two days, and she felt a keen loss at his absence. How long was it, she wondered, until dinner?

Anne enjoyed an enormous lunch, knowing that Rosa, the dark-haired and diminutive Mexican maid, was boiling kettle after kettle of water to prepare the big copper tub that sat in the middle of the kitchen floor. When

Anne finally entered the kitchen, Rosa closed the wooden shutters on the window and communicated to Anne in a mixture of Spanish and English that she would wait outside the back door to prevent anyone from entering.

Anne slipped out of her borrowed pink wrapper and climbed into the wonderfully warm tub. Someone, probably Aunt Emma, had laced the water with lilac bath salts, and the heady fragrance wafted up and tempted her to sigh aloud. With her pale hair pinned on top of her head, Anne slid down to her chin in the big tub. She closed her eyes and tried to empty her mind of everything but the pleasure of her bath.

Moments later, she jerked awake when she heard Rosa's high-pitched babbling just outside the door. What in the world? thought Anne. When she heard a deep, familiar voice, she had a pretty good idea just what in the world was going on.

Sam was trying to come into the kitchen, and Rosa, the five-foot-tall terror, was doing everything in her diminutive power to prevent it. Anne watched as the door opened slightly, then slammed shut.

"No, Señor Sam," Rosa cried shrilly.

The door opened and slammed shut again.

"Out of my way, woman," Sam yelled.

"No."

Anne laughed. "It's all right, Rosa," she called out. "You can let him in."

There was silence for a moment, and then the door swung open and Sam's wide shoulders filled the frame.

"Tarnation, Annie, your bodyguard was about to beat the tar out of me. All I want to do is find a bite to eat." Still wearing his dusty buckskin pants, along with a clean chambray shirt, he stood there just gazing at her. Then he grinned. "I hardly recognize you without all the trail dust."

She had slipped down as far as possible in the water while draping a washcloth over her chest. "Did you have a nice nap?"

Spying a fresh loaf of bread on the table, Sam strode toward it. "Two blessed hours," he said, "then my stomach rumbled me awake." He angled his hip onto the table and ripped a chunk out of the round loaf.

"Your mother and I are having a wonderful time getting to know one another," Anne said, touching her hair to make sure it was still pinned securely atop her head. "She's a lovely woman, Sam."

"That she is," he agreed, biting off another chunk of bread.

"I haven't met your brother yet."

His eyes darkened perceptibly. "You will."

"Hand me that cake of soap, will you?" she asked, pointing to the yellow bar on the table where he sat.

When she took it from his hand, she tilted her head to the side and asked, "Are you still my personal slave?"

His gaze was wary. "That depends."

"Wash my back?" *Brazen hussy!* she admonished herself, hoping Sam would think the crimson blush on her cheeks was from the temperature of the bathwater and not from the delicious prospect of having his soapy hands sliding over her skin.

He edged off the table with a sigh of surrender, but his voice had a peculiar gruffness to it. "Give me the soap. The washcloth, too."

Her eyes flew up to his as she clutched the cloth to her chest. "That's all that's preserving my decency," she said, not nearly so brazen now.

He stood over her, touched a corner of the wet cloth. "Little Rosa was preserving your decency, Annie. And she's gone now." He pulled the cloth away, then just stood there and stared while Anne did the best she could to cover herself with her hands.

"God, you're beautiful," he breathed as he rolled up his sleeves, moved behind her and began to rub the cloth up and down her spine.

Anne closed her eyes, revelling in the warmth of his touch. "That feels good," she sighed.

His fingers gradually replaced the rough cloth, and the tempo of the scrubbing slowed to a massage. Anne's head lolled back as she relaxed. Her eyes were still closed.

There was that inviting mouth again, just inches from his, Sam thought. He was tempted to slide his hands up and wring her pretty little neck for luring him into this. No. He was tempted to kiss her. And she wanted him to, the little witch. He watched, enchanted, as her tongue peeked out to lick a bead of perspiration from her upper lip. He couldn't help himself. He leaned down and did the same, tasting the saltiness of her.

Her eyes opened slowly. "Oh, Sam," she murmured.

Oh, God! Sam thought before coming to his senses. "Out!" he stormed. "Your bath is over."

"What?"

"I said get out. The water's still warm, and I need to take a bath, too. Get out, Annie."

"But, Sam . . ."

He stalked to the opposite side of the table, shook out a large bath sheet and held it toward her. "Here. I'll close my eyes. Just get out."

Through the screen of his dark eyelashes, he savored each glistening white curve, while gritting his teeth at the hard tug of his loins. When he finally opened his eyes, she was standing there—pale hair piled high on her head, face rosy and moist, the bath sheet wound around her slim figure like drapery around a Greek goddess. He pointed to the door. "Out," he ordered.

"Just let me dry my feet a little so I don't slip on the floor," she protested.

"Be quick about it. The bathwater's cooling by the second." He tried to ignore her as he began to unbutton his shirt, but he felt like a wolf trying to pretend he wasn't a whisker away from a succulent prairie hen.

"I'd be happy to stay and scrub *your* back," Anne offered with a grin.

Sam aimed his index finger in the direction of the door.

"All right. I'm going. Have a nice bath, Sam."

"I will," he answered gruffly.

As Anne closed the door behind her, she noticed the large keyhole beneath the cut-glass doorknob. Nobody was around—Aunt Emma had gone upstairs to take a siesta after lunch—so she clutched the towel around her and bent down. With her eye to the keyhole, she held her breath.

Sam's shirt was already off. His back was to her and his hard muscles rippled as he slid off his buckskin breeches and then his long underwear. His legs were so long, so perfect, as if cast from bronze. He stood still for a moment, stark naked, his black hair just grazing his massive shoulders. Through the keyhole, Anne's gaze roved to his trim waist and his sleek posterior. A strangled little gasp escaped her throat when he turned in her direction.

Sam cocked his head toward the door and one brawny arm reached out and clutched his shirt. Holding it so the soft chambray fabric draped from his waist, he walked slowly—as slowly as a big cat stalks a field mouse—to-ward the door.

Anne swallowed hard. She was mesmerized. She couldn't move. He was all the way to the door now. Oh, Lord! He was going to open it and— Suddenly her view was blocked. Sam had hung his shirt on the doorknob on the other side. She could hear him chuckling softly as he walked back to the tub.

Blast that beautiful man, she thought.

Warm from her bath, oddly relaxed and restive at the same time from her encounter with Sam, Anne slid between the sheets and sighed. She hadn't really planned to nap, but it was as if her long journey finally caught up with her in a single swoop. She slept deeply and dream-lessly, despite the sun coming through the open window and the sounds that drifted in—the nickering of horses, the brusque shouts of cowhands, the ringing of ham-mers and the slamming of doors.

She woke at a soft rap on the door, and her aunt came into the room with yards of fabric crushed in her arms. Anne sat up and stretched contentedly.

"You slept well, I see," Emma said. She sat on the edge of the bed. "When I was a new widow, I slept as often as I could. It was the only way I could find any peace."

Anne nodded agreeably, though it wasn't true in her case. Her dreams were anything but peaceful.

"Well, since your clothes are temporarily missing, I hunted up an old dress of mine." Her aunt patted the rose-colored mound of taffeta on her lap. "From my thinner days," she said with a chuckle. "Still, I took it in quite a bit more for you. I'm not the world's best seamstress, but I think it will do until we can get your luggage for you."

"Thank you, Aunt Emma. You didn't have to...."

"Nonsense. It isn't black. I hope that won't make you feel awkward, dear, considering you're in mourning," she said apologetically.

Her aunt was taking her widowhood quite seriously, Anne thought. But then, that shouldn't have surprised her, considering her letters to New Mexico had been replete with the pain and sorrow of her loss. Pretended pain and conjured sorrow for Daniel, who wasn't even dead then. "I don't think it would be too indecent," Anne said, "under the circumstances."

While she helped her niece into the petticoats and dress, the Widow Hook talked sadly about her own husband's death two years before. "John was just my age," she said wistfully. "I gathered from your letters that Colonel McIntire was quite a bit older than you."

Anne lifted her arms as Emma pulled the dress down over her head. When her face emerged from the ruffled rose taffeta, she said, "Daniel was thirty-three when we married. I was eighteen."

Emma tugged at one of the corset stays. "You wrote that he had been ill, Anne, but I don't believe you mentioned what was wrong."

"It was his heart," she said, realizing it wasn't exactly a bald-faced lie. Daniel had been heartless, after all. Cold and cruel.

"So young," Emma murmured. "And so young to be left alone."

"It wasn't so much being alone that bothered me. It was being left with nothing to do. I envy you, Aunt Emma. At least you have this ranch to run."

Her aunt frowned as she pressed a ruffle between her fingers. "I wish that were true," she said. "John left the ranch to Sam and Jay, and they made it clear they expected me to become a lady of leisure. I'm hardly the type, to tell you the truth, but they are adamant. You've met Sam already, so you know how stubborn he can be. And Jay..." She paused. "Well, Jay is another matter." Emma stood back. "You look lovely, dear."

The older woman watched as Anne brushed out her long hair, then twisted it in a fetching knot at the nape of her neck. Her niece was a beautiful young woman. Perhaps the rose dress wasn't the best choice, Emma thought, as she noted the dipping neckline and the amount of snowy cleavage it displayed. Well, it was almost time for dinner and too late to do anything about that now. Her sons would just have to grin and bear the lovely vision who dined with them tonight.

"Welcome to The Hook, Anne," said Jay, rising from the ornately carved chair at the head of the table. His light hazel eyes took her in from head to toe, lingering finally on the pert and snowy breasts so deliciously displayed by the dark rose dress. He then raised an eyebrow in his mother's direction, as if to say, "Well done."

He was thinking *well done, indeed.* His mother had imported a beauty. A widow, too, who appeared to be quite ripe for the taking, judging from the little flush on her cheeks and the secret smile on her lips as she greeted him. Yes, indeed. It might prove to be an interesting summer after all. The fact that she was his cousin didn't concern him. He had no intention of marrying the wench.

Jay was wondering just how long it would take to get the widow into his bed when Sam walked into the room.

Jay saw his brother's eyes lock momentarily on the woman with a fierce, possessive gleam in their black depths.

In that unguarded second, Jay Hook had seen all he needed to. It was going to be a very, very interesting summer.

What an insufferable ass, Anne was thinking as she listened to Jay go on at great length about the recent Indian attacks. He took every opportunity to depict the Apaches as savages. Her aunt was clearly uncomfortable with her son's ranting, but she sat quietly eating her roast beef and boiled potatoes. So did Sam, for that matter. Why didn't somebody just tell Jay to shut up?

"What do you think, Anne?"

She lifted her gaze to his green-flecked eyes. "I beg your pardon? I'm afraid I wasn't listening." She heard a low chuckle from Sam as his brother drew in a deep, frustrated breath.

"I asked whether you considered that sort of behavior to be natural—in-born, so to speak. Or if, in your opinion, it was something learned." Jay pointed his potato-laden fork down the table at his brother. "Take our Sam, for example. Do you suppose, as a half-breed, he's capable of such atrocities? Half capable? What do you think?"

Emma lowered her eyes to her lap.

"Go ahead, Anne," said Sam. "Don't be afraid to answer. This is just normal dinner conversation at The Hook. You'll get used to it."

Anne studied him as he spoke. Once again she saw that rage in his eyes. In spite of it, though, he leaned back in his chair, seemingly relaxed, to all appearances a man without a care in the world.

She shifted her gaze back to Jay. "Your brother is a gentleman," she said stiffly.

His green eyes glittered like a hunter watching his prey fall into a carefully prepared trap. "A gentleman, yes." Jay's thin mouth twitched. "But is he a gentle man? There's a difference, you know. Our Sam has learned the manners of a white man. He knows how to dress like a gentleman, how to use a fork and spoon, even how to waltz. All the gentle, refined behavior of the whites. But what do you suppose lurks under all those acquired skills?"

Green eyes met black. "You wonder yourself, don't you, big brother? About what's beneath your white veneer?"

Anne couldn't believe her ears. Nor could she believe the quiet that prevailed at the table. Her aunt still stared into the folds of her skirt, Sam glared across the table at Jay, but nobody said a word. Aunt Emma didn't come to Sam's defense. Nor did Sam himself.

"Excuse me," Anne said, folding her napkin and placing it on the table. "I need a breath of fresh air." She pushed her chair back and walked out of the dining room.

An oil lamp sputtered on the front porch, where Anne flopped down in a ladder-back rocker, detesting her own rudeness, but detesting Jay Hook's more. She began to rock furiously.

Moments later a black-booted foot on the curved slat of the rocker brought her to a halt. "I appreciate the gesture, Annie." Sam's voice was gentle, but stern. "But I don't need you to defend me in my own house."

Her eyes skimmed up his long black pant leg, his black frock coat, his snowy white shirt and dark string tie. "I don't understand this at all, Sam."

"I know you don't. It's a little like falling into a nest of rattlesnakes, isn't it?"

"A little," she agreed. "Is that what I've done?"

"More or less."

Anne sighed. "I'd appreciate an explanation then, so I know how to behave."

He reached for her hand. "Come on. I'll walk you around the place. Is your ankle up to it?"

She stood up. "I think so."

He led her down the two steps from the front porch onto the bare dirt of the front yard. "You can't see too much in the dark." Sam pointed. "That's the bunkhouse over there. And the corral over there. Back there is—"

"Sam," she said. "I can't see a blasted thing. Will you stop this nonsense and just tell me what's going on here?"

"I'm not exactly my brother's favorite person," he said.

Anne snorted. "Tell me something I don't already know. Jay made that perfectly and obnoxiously clear."

Sam lifted his shoulders and let them fall. "It's a long story."

"I'm listening." Anne took his arm and leaned forward, forcing him to stroll along with her.

"Jay was born less than a year after my father brought me here. We grew up side by side. But I was always bigger, taller, faster, stronger. It didn't matter what we did. I was just better at it than he was. He never got to win, so he learned to hate me at a very early age."

Anne stopped and looked up at him, her eyes flashing. "You're excusing his horrendous behavior?"

"I'm trying to explain it," Sam insisted.

"Oh, I see. Well, explain to me, please, why Aunt Emma just sat there with her hands folded in her lap, not saying a word."

Now Sam's eyes flashed. "Don't hold that against her. You don't know the whole story."

They had arrived at the wood-railed corral. Sam leaned against the fence. He reached into his coat pocket and withdrew a pouch of tobacco and a paper. In the pale wash of light from the bunkhouse, Anne watched as his dark, graceful fingers fashioned the cigarette. Once more he reached into his pocket, this time for a match, which he lit with his thumbnail, then touched to the end of the rolled paper.

"Maybe I don't know the whole story," she said, "but Aunt Emma could have at least—"

That black rage seemed to focus on her now. "I don't need you or my mother to defend me. Believe me, I've learned to do it pretty well myself after all these years."

"But not with your brother," she said quietly.

His mouth drew into a taut, unyielding line. It was an answer of sorts, she thought, although she still didn't know why Sam chose to suffer his brother's indignities in silence. She stared up at the wide, dark sky.

"How long are you going to take it, Sam?" she asked softly.

He didn't say anything for a long while. Their arms touched as they leaned against the fence. Anne could feel his hard warmth. How she ached for him, for this man who couldn't find a measure of solace even in his own home. She repeated her question.

"How long can you take it?"

"I don't know," he answered.

Chapter Seven

Sam left The Hook at dawn, in a buckboard pulled by the big dapple gray he hadn't even bothered to name yet. That was all right. He'd take the horse into town one day and let Benito name him. It was the boy who had named his white stallion Blanco. Sam smiled to himself, hoping Benito would be a little more creative this time.

Long before he reached the wrecked wagon he saw the buzzards circling in the sky over the site. Sam's immediate instinct was to fire a shot, if only to keep them away from Blanco's flesh while he was there. But he didn't. The birds, after all, were just doing what they were meant to do, picking the horses' bones clean.

It didn't take him long to transfer Anne's bags, his saddle and the supplies for the ranch from one wagon to the other. He turned the big dapple gray around and headed for home, forcing himself to stay awake. The white stallion would have taken him home while he snored in the back of the wagon. This one needed a few trips into town before he could be trusted not to stray.

Sam's thoughts wandered to Anne. She haunted him like a pale-haired, moonlit ghost. A week ago he hadn't known she existed. Now she was the center of his universe. His every waking thought swirled around her silver hair and deep blue eyes. His every dream centered around her delicate, virginal body.

He'd known Sally for years now, and he never gave her a thought once he walked out the door of the cantina. Maybe once in a while he'd find himself trying to imagine what their marriage would be like. He couldn't. But now he found himself imagining how it would be with the three of them—himself, and Annie, and the boy. An impossible dream, he knew, and yet it pleased him to call the vision forth in his head. Benito had been drawn to her immediately. It wouldn't take him long to call her Mama. And maybe there would be other children—his and Annie's. Maybe...

Sam shook his head in the twilight. Don't, he told himself. He tried hard to summon Sally's tawny visage in place of Anne's. It wouldn't come. There was no room for it in his bewitched head. There was only pale hair, ivory skin, cream-colored breasts with delicate pink nipples, long and slender legs. Only Annie.

It was dark when Anne heard his soft, moccasined tread on the stairs. She heard him put her bags down just outside the door.

"Sam?" she called softly.

Her bedroom door, already open a few inches, opened wider. He brought the bags in and set them down by the foot of the brass bed.

"I missed you today," Anne said, raising up on her elbows. She could just make out his large silhouette. "How was your trip back to the wagon?"

"Uneventful," he said.

In the life of Sam Hook, Anne knew now, an uneventful trip was an event in itself. "I'm glad."

He grasped the brass railing. "How's your ankle?"

"Better. Don't go yet, Sam."

"I have to, Annie." He sighed. "I have to get some sleep."

"Where do you sleep?" she asked.

"Out in the bunkhouse."

She sniffed. "Was that Jay's idea or yours?"

"It doesn't matter," Sam said, turning toward the door. He paused with his hand on the knob. "Is Jay treating you all right?"

"What would you do if I said no?" she asked tartly.

Sam's voice was a low growl. "Don't push me, Annie."

"He's treating me like a cousin. In fact, he's almost pleasant when you're not around."

"That's good," Sam said. "Good night, Annie." He closed the door quietly but firmly behind him as he left.

Anne didn't see Sam again until two days later, when Emma drove her out to the south pasture, where the men had rigged a temporary corral and were branding the young strays they had rounded up.

The wagon was quickly surrounded by hot, dusty cowhands, who knew from experience that Emma's visits always meant some of her cool lemonade. While her aunt went to the rear of the wagon to begin ladling out the refreshment, Anne undid the top buttons of her dress and blotted herself with a linen handkerchief. It wasn't a land for widows, that was for certain. She was forever sweltering in her black clothes, which seemed to keep in the heat as dependably as a warming oven.

When she caught sight of Sam ambling toward the wagon, her temperature shot up another few degrees. He was as hot and dusty as the cowhands, but on him it looked wonderful. Her heart quickened when she saw his drenched shirt and slick, dirt-streaked face beneath the shade of his hat, and as he approached she realized he was wearing boots with spurs. He jingled like a Christmas ornament with bells.

He whisked off his hat and wiped a ropy forearm across his brow. "Annie."

"Hello, Sam." She bunched up her skirt in order to climb down from the wagon.

Sam reached up, his big hands encompassing her waist, and easily lifted her down. Then he tilted his head and gave her a blazing grin. "You've put on a pound of two, Mrs. McIntire," he said.

Anne laughed. "It's Rosa's good cooking. All those tortillas and sopaipillas. She keeps telling me I need more meat on my bones."

"Your bones are perfect just the way they are," he said, thinking not about her bones at all but about the sumptuous flesh that covered them.

That was one of the reasons he'd ridden out here with the men. The more distance between himself and the Widow McIntire, the better. But here she was, little pearls of perspiration on her face, the sun bringing her skin to a high flush. And here he was, wanting her again, aching for her. "I think I'll get some of that lemonade to cool off," he said. "Can I bring you some?"

Anne nodded, then listened to the music of his boots as he walked back to his mother. Blotting her face and neck, she strolled toward the makeshift corral and watched the young calves nuzzle one another. Sam came back in a long, lazy stride. He handed her a tin cup of cool lemonade.

He took a drink from his own cup, then stared off toward the mountains. "How are you and my brother getting along?"

"Fine." They were barely on speaking terms, Anne thought. For the most part, she and Jay saw one another only at the dinner table. He spent most of his time with his nose in a book and his hand around a glass of whiskey. She wasn't going to tell Sam that, however. There was no reason to make things worse between the brothers. She cast about in her head for something to say on the unpleasant subject of Jay Hook. "He mentioned something about going to San Miguel for the fiesta."

Sam swung his gaze to her face. "Just the two of you?"

"Aunt Emma isn't sure she wants to go."

"I don't want you making that trip alone with him, Annie."

She didn't relish the notion herself, but she did relish the flare of Sam's nostrils and the hard black glint in his eyes. He was jealous! That wasn't the emotion she wanted from him, but at least it was better than his calm, cool, "cousinly" behavior. Not that he had any right to forbid her, though. Especially when he was going to such great lengths to avoid her.

"That's not for you to say, Sam. I'll go with Jay if I want."

His dark eyebrows drew together as he studied the stubborn tilt of her chin and the bright defiance in her eyes. A vision of Annie lying in his brother's arms by the light of a campfire pricked at his heart, and the urge to shake her was so strong his fingers twitched. "You failed to seduce one brother, so you're aiming for the other one—is that it?" he snarled.

Her jaw dropped in disbelief. It wasn't possible that he truly believed that, was it? What sort of woman did he think she was? Before he could reply, however, Aunt Emma was standing there with a bucket of lemonade in her hand. And it didn't take the woman more than a second to read her son's expression.

"Gracious! Didn't I put in enough sugar, Sam?" she asked.

"What?"

"You look like you just bit into a lemon, son."

He fixed Anne with a bitter look as he said, "Or got hit by one." Then he turned on his heel and stalked away.

With a bemused frown, Emma appealed to Anne. "What was that all about?"

Anne shrugged helplessly. "Just a little squabble between cousins, Aunt Emma," she said. The trouble was, she thought, it had become three cousins now, rather than two. The lovely circle she was trying to draw around Sam was suddenly sharpened to a triangle.

After they returned to The Hook, Anne went into the house, while Emma drove the wagon into the barn. With most of the hands gone, she planned to see to the horses herself. "I never get to do anything anymore," her aunt had said with a twinkle in her eye.

The house was cool despite the afternoon heat. Thinking a bath might be in order, Anne stuck her head into the kitchen, searching for Rosa. There was no sign of the little Mexican servant there or in any of the other rooms downstairs. Faced with the prospect of heating her own bathwater, Anne decided a siesta sounded better, and she began to climb the stairs to her room.

When she was halfway up, she heard a strangled cry, followed by the slamming of a door. Rosa ran past her then, hastily finger combing her dark hair and pulling at the neckline of her *camisa*. The girl looked as if she had just seen a ghost, Anne thought. And then she heard Jay's voice.

"Slut!" he raged. "Who are you saving it for? The half-breed?"

Anne hurried up the remainder of the stairs and slipped into her room rather than encounter the man whose voice roared through the house like a cold north wind and sent shivers along her spine.

Sam spent the next two days riding down, roping and branding strays. He pushed his men hard and pushed himself harder. Still, he couldn't get Annie out of his head. Especially at night, when he stared up at the white moon and tried to pretend that he didn't give a damn where she went or with whom. Let her play her dangerous little game with Jay if she wanted to. Let her squander herself on his weakling brother. Sam had made it clear he had other plans, hadn't he? Why shouldn't the passionate little witch turn to Jay?

Because Jay would hurt her, that's why. Jay would delight in hurting her, because he was a vicious human being who would know instantly that by hurting Anne he was inflicting hurt on his brother. Anne had no way of knowing how bad things were between the two of them. Hell, his mother didn't even know, and she probably wouldn't be able to comprehend that one of her sons hated his brother so much that murder wasn't out of the question.

Sam had seen it clearly in Jay's eyes the day their father's will was read. His brother had always been so certain he alone, as the natural son and heir, would inherit The Hook. More than once, in fits of anger, he had told Sam he'd better watch his step or he would throw him off the place when he was in charge. Having his half-breed brother receive an equal share of the inheritance seemed almost more than Jay could bear. He hadn't done anything yet, but his moods were blacker than ever, his tongue sharper and his drinking more intense. Sam knew it would be only a matter of time until something set him off, like a bolt of lightning to a drought-stricken forest. Jay was a tinderbox waiting for a match.

Maybe that's what Annie would prove to be. He had to prevent her from being hurt by Jay's malice. Much as Sam tried to convince himself he was only thinking of her well-being, he knew at heart that he simply couldn't bear the thought of his woman in his brother's arms, or, God help him, anyone else's.

By the time he decided to stir himself, it was too late to return to the ranch. Anne and Jay were probably already on their way to town for the fiesta. All he could do then was hope that his mother had changed her mind and gone along with them.

Sam lifted the boy onto the big horse's back, holding him so he wouldn't slide right off the other side.

"What do you want to call him, Benito?" he asked.

Deep in thought, the boy fingered the horse's thick gray mane. *"El Cano,"* he finally said.

Sam laughed. "The gray one. That's what I thought. Okay, squirt. *El Cano* it is."

As if on cue, Father José stepped out of the church's front door and asked, "Have you named Sam's horse yet?"

"Sí, Padre. El Cano," said Benito.

The priest patted the dapple gray's nose. "A logical choice," he said, grinning at Sam. "Are you staying for the fiesta tomorrow, my friend? The children are all very excited about it."

Benito looked down from his high perch with big, expectant eyes.

"That's why I came to town," Sam said. "We'll have ourselves a fine old time, won't we, Benito?"

"*Sí,*" the boy said. "Did you bring *La Viuda de la Luna?*"

Sam shook his head. "No. Not this time, sprout."

Sadness flitted across the little boy's face and then was replaced by happy anticipation. "Take me for a ride, Sam," he begged. *"Por favor."*

Sam looked to the curly-haired priest for permission.

"Just up to the end of town and back," Father José said. "Then it is time for you to go to bed, *niño.*"

As expected, when Sam rode him back, Benito pleaded to go one more time. It took a black scowl from the priest and a swat on the rear from Sam to get him to join the other children for bedtime prayers.

"Where will you go tonight, Sam?" asked the father after Benito left them.

"Same place as always," Sam said.

"I wish we had room for you here."

"Thank you, Padre. To tell you the truth, a shot of whiskey's sounding pretty good right now." He wasn't sure how he felt about the prospect of sharing Sally's bed, however. His needs and desires seemed to have parted company lately.

"How is Mrs. McIntire enjoying her stay at The Hook?"

"Fine, I guess." Sam gazed down at the priest. "The boy took right to her, didn't he?"

Father José nodded, fingering his crucifix. "That he did. I have never seen Benito do that, not even with any of the women who take care of the children here. He seemed to feel a special bond with...what was it he called her?"

"La Viuda de la Luna," said Sam.

The priest chuckled. "The moon's widow. The boy is better at naming women than he is at naming horses, Sam. That might cause trouble for you down the road. You will have to keep him on a short tether when he comes of age. Have you spoken to Sally Mendoza yet?"

"Not yet." Sam's eyebrows edged together in a hard line. "I'm not sure it would work, Padre."

"You've decided to visit the Apache reservation to find a bride, then?" the priest asked.

Those were his choices, Sam thought. The priest knew it as well as he did. Half-breeds married their own kind, or whores nobody else would have. The rule was not written anywhere; it wasn't law. But it existed all the same, chiselled in people's hearts. Half-breeds did not marry pale and delicate widows newly arrived from the East. Not the breeds who had a lick of sense, anyway.

"I don't know yet, Padre. I don't know what I'm going to do."

Father José patted El Cano's smoky gray flank. "It would be good for Sally to get away from the life she is living. The woman has many good qualities, Sam."

This wasn't a conversation that made Sam comfortable. He busied his hands by tightening the cinch on his saddle. "I'm aware of that," he said. "It's just that ... well, hell, I don't love her, Padre."

Silently, Father José nodded. "Perhaps love would come," he said quietly.

"I doubt it."

The priest put a gentle hand on Sam's arm. "Do not let a misguided passion sway you from what you had planned to do with your life, my friend."

His second shot of whiskey went down easier than the first. The third, Sam thought, would begin to blur the

edges of his mind. The fourth would allow him to pull
Sally onto his lap, slide his hand beneath her *camisa* and
find a taut, brown nipple, then whisper in her ear that he
wanted her. He wanted to want her. Maybe he'd never
loved her, but at least she had always been able to stir his
blood. Even that wasn't happening now.

He had taken the priest's advice to heart. What he felt
for Anne McIntire was more than misguided. It was a
passion that threatened everything he had worked so hard
to achieve.

It hadn't been easy finding his place in this rock-hard
land. John and Emma Hook had loved him and raised
him as if he were their natural-born son. His parents had
given him what Jay so coldly referred to as his "white
veneer." He dressed and ate like a white man. He thought
like a white man. He felt he deserved to take his place in
white society as John Hook's son.

Still, Apache blood ran in his veins. He was as much
Indian as he was white. It was a fact he had tried to ignore for a long time as he yearned to belong—to his
family, to the hands at the ranch, to the people of the
town.

Cruel and arrogant as his brother was, Jay knew
something about him that no one else was aware of. Jay,
perhaps because of his bitter temperament, sensed that
part of Sam's desire to be accepted by whites was his
deep-rooted fear of his Indian blood. There was a rage
that burned like a hot flame in Sam's heart, and he was
never sure if that flame was because of the way he was
treated, the indignities he'd had to suffer over the years,
or if that fiery rage was his Apache self—a brutal, savage flame that might one day leap out and burn fiercely.

Jay never let an opportunity pass to remind him of it.
It was really the only way he could feel superior to Sam.

And it was his most effective weapon. Because he was right.

Sam had learned to be quiet, to be humble, to lower his eyes when he passed a white woman like Mrs. Thiel, to endure the punishing games of drunk cowhands. He had learned to take his pleasures with dull-witted whores. He had learned to contain his passions, because he was terrified of them. But for a quirk of fate, he could be riding with Raging Owl now, stealing cattle, burning ranches, raping and scalping whites.

Up until last week, Sam had guided his passions carefully. Since then, however, his grip on himself felt tenuous at best. It took Father José's caution to make him see the true danger in his feelings for Anne McIntire. His passions were indeed misguided. And if he wasn't careful, that savage flame might burn out of control.

He wanted only two things in his life. Sam wanted to fulfill the promise he had made to his father, to see that The Hook remained a vigorous and prosperous ranch. And he wanted to be a father to Benito. Nothing else mattered. He wouldn't let anything else matter. He would use all his strength to impose that control over himself again. To resume his life as it had been before the arrival of *La Viuda de la Luna*.

Filling his glass a third time, Sam swore under his breath. All he needed to do was stop thinking about her. Stop thinking about the bright, intelligent glint in her eyes. Stop thinking about the feminine curve of her neck. Stop thinking about the swell of her soft breast beneath his mouth. Stop wanting to bury himself in the sweet and velvet depths of her body.

It was a Friday night before a fiesta, so the cantina was unusually crowded. Sam saw Sally refilling glasses at a table across the smoky room. As she leaned to pour from

the bottle of whiskey in her hand, her *camisa* dipped to
expose a tempting portion of her tawny cleavage.

Sam lurched up from his chair. He would toss her over
his shoulder, carry her upstairs and ask her to marry him.
He would get his life back on track. Now. Tonight. Before it was too late.

As he wove through the crowd toward her, his foot ac-
cidentally kicked the leg of a chair.

"Watch where you're goin', 'breed," a drunk cowhand sneered.

"Sorry," Sam gritted.

"You damn well better be, you Apache bastard."

The white blood in Sam—the blood that was aching to
belong, the blood that urged him to turn the other
cheek—ran cold. Annie's words rolled like thunder
through his head. *How long can you take it, Sam?*

The flame of rage that had been smoldering in him for
so many years flared. It flashed in the depths of his black
eyes. It ignited in the pit of his stomach.

Sam's red Apache blood had at last boiled over.

Chapter Eight

Most of the people attending the fiesta were camped under wagons and in makeshift tents on the edge of town, but Doris Thiel was more than glad to rent her spare room to the women from The Hook.

"Real nice to see you again, Mrs. McIntire," she said as she showed them to the room where Anne had slept on the night of her arrival. "I see that Sam got you back to the ranch all right." The fat woman waited expectantly for complaints.

"Yes, he did," said Anne.

Mrs. Thiel waited another moment before she realized that was all the answer she was going to get. "There's only this one bed in here," she announced then. "You'll have make do. No other beds in town. Not for proper ladies, leastways."

"This will do nicely," Emma Hook said. She handed the heavy woman a five-dollar gold piece, overpaying her to silence her on the subject of Sam, Anne surmised.

Emma closed the door as soon as Mrs. Thiel's big skirts had cleared the threshold. "Good riddance," she said sighing.

Aunt and niece both dropped onto the bed. The trip into town had been a grueling trek under a hot sun, with

Jay complaining all the way about anything and every-thing. The horses hadn't been hitched properly. There wasn't enough water. The meat Rosa sent for lunch was spoiled. The tortillas were tough. And where the hell were his brandy and cigars?

By the time they arrived in San Miguel, Anne and Emma were worn down by Jay's foul temper. All they wanted was a good night's sleep. And silence.

They didn't even bother to undress, but lay on the bed with their eyes closed and their ears adjusting to the blessed quiet. Then, after a brief respite, there was a knock on the door.

"Yes?" called Emma.

"Sorry to disturb you, Emma," said Mrs. Thiel. "Tom Atkinson's here. Says he needs to see you."

Emma sat up. "The sheriff? What does he want?" she asked, rising and rearranging the folds of her skirt.

"I'm sure I wouldn't know," replied Mrs. Thiel in a tone that indicated she did know and highly disap-proved.

"It must be Sam," whispered Emma with a slight quiver in her voice. When she called through the door once more, however, her tone was calm. "Tell Sheriff Atkinson I'll be right there."

Now Anne rose from the bed. "Sam? What do you mean?" she asked, searching her aunt's pale and wor-ried face.

"Sam probably got into some trouble. I can't think of any other reason the sheriff would be looking for me." Emma bit her lower lip. "I'll just go see what he wants."

Anne followed her out to Mrs. Thiel's sitting room, where a great, grizzled bear of a man stood with his hat in his hand. He wore denims and a plaid shirt that strained over his belly. There was a gun holstered at his hip and a tarnished tin star pinned to his breast pocket. "Evening, Emma," he said.

Emma stood with her hands folded in front of her. "Good evening, Tom. Is there a problem?"

Noticing that Emma's hands were trembling as she clasped them over her skirt, Anne moved closer and gripped her aunt's elbow.

"Well, yes, ma'am. I've got Sam over at the jail, and he needs a bit of tending to."

Emma gasped, and the sheriff quickly held up his hand.

"Don't go getting all fluttery now. It's nothing serious. Cuts and bruises, mostly. I was on my way to fetch Doc Lopez when I ran into Jay. He didn't want to have anything to do with it. Said I should come talk to you. So I thought I'd just let you know the situation."

Emma Hook's quiet calm seemed to return once she knew her son was all right "What happened?" she asked.

The sheriff tugged at a sprig of the gray hair that strayed over the collar of his shirt. "I don't really know, Emma. Twenty fellas have told me twenty different stories. But all of them said Sam went wild over at the cantina. Smashed some fella's face into a table. Pitched a couple others out the plate-glass window. Did a fair amount of damage before they brought him down."

"Good Lord," breathed Anne.

Emma stiffened her shoulders. "I'd like to go see him, if that's all right," she said.

"We'd both like to see him," Anne added quickly.

The burly sheriff settled his hat back on his head. "Suit yourselves," he muttered. "Don't know if Sam's up to a hen party, but we'll find out soon enough."

Emma Hook bit back her tears as she walked across the dark, dusty street to the jail. She was almost sixty years old, an age when most mothers were able to relax, to feel peaceful about their children and the lives they had chosen.

But Emma had known the moment she took that robust, dark-skinned boy into her arms that she would never be able to relax, never feel peaceful, because her Sam would never feel peace. From the day she had committed herself to him, she gave up that dream.

But her worries multiplied now. Anne had been more than a little anxious about Sam's well-being. The young woman had looked absolutely stricken at the news. Thinking back, Emma recalled the looks the two of them had exchanged, and she wondered now if perhaps she had deliberately chosen to ignore their significance. After all, Sam and Anne had been alone together for two long days. Once again, she pictured her niece in her son's arms as he carried her toward the house. She should have known then that their feelings for each other were more than cousinly.

Not that it surprised her that someone with the spunk and wits of Anne McIntire would find her Sam a worthy match. It was a miracle to her that this problem hadn't arisen before with some of the young women in town. Too much prejudice, Emma supposed, for a local female to overcome. But Anne had arrived from the East, free of the bigotry that existed in New Mexico.

If it were up to her, Emma thought, Anne was just the sort of woman she would choose for her older son. It wasn't her choice, though. And with things being the way they were in the territory, Sam had no choice, either. He knew that. He had spent thirty years walking a narrow path between the two parts of his divided self. She had watched him grow into a careful and controlled man.

And Emma thought she had a fairly good idea how difficult that control was and what it cost him.

As she approached the door of the sheriff's office, she wondered now what price her son might be willing to pay for the love of the young widow who hurried along by her side.

An oil lamp burned on Tom Atkinson's desk, its glow barely illuminating the cell at the rear of the office. A dark-haired woman in a ruffled calico skirt and a blood-stained blouse was reaching through the iron bars, dabbing a handkerchief at Sam's head, speaking to him in soft tones, when the sheriff entered with the two women on his heels.

Sheriff Atkinson dug a key out of his pocket and handed it to Emma. "I'll go hunt up Doc Lopez now," he told her, glancing toward the dim cell.

"I don't need him, Tom," Sam shouted.

"Yes, you do," Sally Mendoza spat. "Go," she said to the sheriff. "You get him." Then her dark, smudged eyes moved from Emma to Anne, where they lingered.

"I am leaving now, Sam," Sally said through the bars as she rose from the floor. "I am going to put back together what you tore apart. I will see you later."

Sally Mendoza walked up to Emma Hook. "He is hurt," she said bluntly, and then shrugged and walked out the door.

Unable to wait a moment longer, Anne took the key from Emma's hand and jammed it into the lock. The cell was bare, and Sam sat on the floor, leaning against the wall. One of his cheeks was puffy and bruised, and blood trickled down that side of his face, soaking the collar of his torn shirt.

The door's dry hinges squealed when Anne yanked on the bars. Afraid she might cry if she spoke, she knelt silently beside him and took his hand. The knuckles were scraped and raw.

"You shouldn't be here, Annie," he said, his voice low and gentle.

"You shouldn't, either," she answered. "But here we are."

He attempted to push himself away from the wall, then winced as his breath whistled in through clenched teeth.

"What is it, Sam? What have they done to you?"

"Nothing. I'll be fine." He strained to focus through the bars of the cell. "Mother!" he called.

Emma came into the cell. Her lips trembled as she leaned over and touched his cheek.

Sam's eyes sought hers, mother and son trading pain and sorrow and love in a single glance. "Just get Annie out of here, will you?" he rasped.

Emma nodded. "All right, son. If that's what you want. We're staying over at Mrs. Thiel's tonight. I'll be back first thing in the morning."

Sam's eyes were closed, but he nodded.

Emma's eyebrows lifted in Anne's direction then, as if to ask, "Are you coming?"

"I'll be along in a minute," Anne said as her aunt turned to leave.

"Get out of here, Annie." Sam wiped the back of his hand across his bloody cheek. "Can't you see I don't want you here?"

"I don't care what you want, Sam Hook. I'm staying with you until the doctor arrives, so you might as well save your breath."

Sam raised his dark eyes to his mother in an appeal for help, but Emma merely shrugged. "Seems Anne has made up her mind, Sam," she said as she left the cell.

He glared at Anne then.

She reached under her black skirt to tear off part of the ruffle of her petticoat, which she dabbed at the gash on his scalp. "Your mother's a very perceptive woman," she said.

"My mother bit off more than she could chew when she took me in," he gritted. "Don't repeat her mistake, Annie."

"I think if I asked her, she'd say she'd done just what her heart told her to do." She pressed the cotton ruffle to his temple again.

"You women should start using your heads instead of your hearts," he snarled.

"Is that what you were doing tonight, Sam? Using your head? Looks to me like you were using your fists. And if you used your head at all, it was only to stop a punch." She gently brushed back a hank of black hair in order to inspect the cut, clucking her tongue softly at the sight of the deep wound.

He twisted his head away. "That was a bottle, as I recall. Do you think you could have shot off enough heels to make any kind of difference, Annie?"

The office door opened then, and the burly sheriff stepped inside, followed by a short dark man with a huge mustache, whose striped nightshirt was tucked into a pair of baggy pants. Dr. Lopez, Anne surmised.

The Mexican doctor walked directly into the cell. "You need more of my fine needlework, I see, Sam." Without another word, he pulled open the last two buttons that were holding Sam's bloody, ripped shirt together. He slid it deftly off Sam's shoulders to reveal several large bruises on his rib cage.

"It hurts to breathe, no?" Lopez asked as he poked and prodded.

"Not as much as your damn hands," Sam answered through clenched teeth.

"I will wrap you tight and then it will feel better. Then I will stitch up your head." Lopez pulled some folded linens from the battered leather bag he had carried in with him, then turned to Anne. "I could use your help, señora. Will you tear these into long strips, please?"

As Anne took the cloths from him, she peeked into his satchel. After nursing Daniel for five years, she had a good idea what physicians carried in their bags. But she found herself frowning at the contents of this one.

Sam was watching her, keenly aware of the lines etched in her forehead. Damn her, he thought. What did she expect? "He's a vet, Annie," he snarled. "They don't get real doctors for half-breeds."

When he saw her stricken expression, he regretted his harsh tone. He wasn't angry with her, only ashamed of having her see him in these circumstances. All of his anger was focused on himself. His anger and his shame and, yes, his fear. Never in his life had he lost control the way he had in the cantina. Over what? Some whiskey-besotted cowboy telling him to watch his step. As provocations went, that was probably one of the mildest. Yet a fire had flashed through him and Sam had been powerless to stop it. It had consumed him—mind, body and soul. And it scared him. It scared the living hell out of him.

Dr. Lopez was rummaging through his bag now. "Perhaps it is a compliment, Sam, in a land where animals are valued higher than most human lives." The mustachioed man winked at Anne.

"He'll be all right, won't he, Dr. Lopez?" she asked.

"That depends on what you mean, señora. If you mean will he survive, the answer is yes. If you mean will this happen again, the answer is also yes." He laughed. "How many times have I sewn you up, Sam?"

Tom Atkinson, who had come to lean against the iron bars, laughed now, too. "Nobody in town can count that high," he said. "You ought to move away, Sam. Take that little kid right out from under the padre's nose and hightail it for someplace where everybody'd just leave you be. You and the kid."

Sam only nodded grimly.

Anne watched in silence as the doctor wound the bandage around Sam's bruised ribs. Then, as the doctor stitched, she thought about the sheriff's advice. If Sam was still here after all the abuse he had taken, it was clear that he intended to stay. Nothing was going to drive Sam away from The Hook, she thought. Not Jay's abuse. Not the abuse of all the cowhands in New Mexico. He'd stay till his entire body was a crazy quilt of stitches.

And so would she.

The fiesta closed like a bright flower at one o'clock in the afternoon. The busy street, jammed earlier with vegetable and candy vendors and musicians, was nearly deserted now as everyone retired for a siesta. Emma had gone to the jail to see to Sam's release, while Anne reluctantly accepted Jay's invitation to join him for lunch. She did it only for her aunt's benefit. Jay had actually seemed like a warm human being when he'd asked them to accompany him to the café, and Anne had seen the mixture of surprise and happiness on his mother's face. Anne was afraid if she turned him down he would revert to his usual poisonous self, and she couldn't bear to have

Emma in any more pain. The woman had suffered enough for one day.

Having made up her mind to be civil to Jay, Anne had little choice but to enter the same horrible restaurant, where once again she read the words *No Injuns Welcome* scrawled across the menu. Feeling Jay's cold stare, she looked up.

"We're forthright in our likes and dislikes out here," he said, noting the menu in her hand.

"That doesn't make them right," Anne replied curtly, turning the menu facedown. She let her gaze stray to the window, hoping to catch a glimpse of Sam and Emma coming out of the sheriff's office.

"I'd be careful about flaunting my opinions if I were you, cousin dear. People will start to believe you're an Indian lover." Jay's eyebrows arched suggestively. "A woman could get in a lot of trouble with a reputation like that."

She met his acidic green gaze. "Is that a threat, Jay?"

He didn't deny it as he leaned forward and spoke in a low, oily tone. "I'm only telling you for your own good, Anne. Don't waste your time—or anything else, for that matter—on Sam. I doubt if he'd have the courage to bed you. I know he'd never marry you. For all his faults, my brother knows his place."

"Where's that, Jay? Under your boot?" she sniped.

Jay held up a soft, manicured hand. "He doesn't have to stay. Sam can leave any time he pleases."

"Why should he? The Hook is his home."

His narrow lips slid into a feral grin. "For now," he said. Jay lifted his menu then in a leisurely fashion, as if he had just been discussing fine wines or the cultivation of roses. "I recommend the beef steak," he said. "They can't do too much to ruin it."

The way you were ruined, Jay? Anne thought. Was it just because Sam outran and outrode you that you turned into such a vile man? Were you pushed into viciousness or was it always inside you? Do you hate your brother so much that you wold bring the world down upon your own head as long as Sam suffered, too? And does anyone truly know how dangerous you are?

When the waiter stood with his pencil poised for her order, Anne said, "Nothing for me, thank you. I'm afraid I've lost my appetite."

Not Jay. She sat and watched him devour a bloodred beef steak with enormous gusto, like a man whose plans were all falling perfectly into place.

Emma stood with Sam outside the sheriff's office, regarding his bruised face. "What happened, son?" she asked him.

He squinted in the bright light. "The usual, Mother. Only I didn't handle it the usual way." His gaze took in the street, with its closed shutters and quiet stalls. Siesta time. He suddenly pictured Annie curled in sleep upstairs at Mrs. Thiel's, her golden hair drifting over the pillowcase. "Where's Anne?" he asked.

"She and Jay are having lunch."

A muscle twitched in Sam's cheek as his mother put a gentle hand on his arm. "I suspect she went with him just to keep what little peace remains in this family. Anne seems to care a great deal for you, Sam."

The grave concern in his mother's face touched him. She knew as well as he did that any feelings between them would only lead to trouble. "Try to discourage her, will you, Mother?"

A woeful little laugh rose in Emma's throat. "The women in my family aren't easily put off, Sam. I'd say

Anne's going to follow her heart anywhere it leads her and damn the consequences."

"Not if I can help it," he said.

"Damn!" Sam drew in his breath sharply, straining his injured ribs as he reached up to set Benito down from his shoulders. The fiesta was coming to life again, and the two of them were wandering down the crowded street in search of a puppet show, roasted corn, sweet tamales and candy.

"*Más caramelos*, Sam," Benito pleaded now, looking longingly at a woman with a basket full of the brown, sugary treats.

"*No más*," said Sam. "You're going to get fat and your teeth will all fall out."

Out of the corner of his eye, Sam saw Sally sauntering toward them barefoot, her hips swaying under her calico skirt. He smiled and held out his hand to her. He could feel Benito withdraw, his little arms circling Sam's knee and his face pressing into his leg. Sam ruffled the boy's hair.

"Say hello to Sally," he told him.

Benito didn't answer, but clung more tightly to Sam's leg.

"That's all right," said Sally, looking slightly relieved not to have to deal with the youngster at all. She raised her eyes to Sam's. "You are better now, I see. All sewn up."

"I'm fine," he said. "I—I'm sorry about last night, Sally. I want to pay for the damage. You're going to need to order a new window."

She shook her head. "No. No more windows. They get too broke. I asked Tula, the carpenter, to make shutters for me. It only makes sense."

Sam's hand was still on Benito's head. What made sense to him was to ask her now. Forget the shutters, Sally. Marry me. Come with me and the boy. Now. Today. Then he looked down the street, and his heart stood still. Annie, with Jay close at her elbow, was emerging from the café. The sunlight lit her hair nearly to silver as it streamed over her shoulders. She wore a black dress with white lace shimmering at the throat and wrists. Even at that distance, she dazzled him.

"La Viuda," exclaimed Benito, letting go of Sam's leg and beginning to run down the street toward the restaurant.

Sam dropped Sally's hand and went after him.

As Benito approached Anne, his arms were waving wildly. *"Hola, Viuda,"* he called. "Remember me?"

Jay caught him by the scruff of the neck. "Get away, you filthy little Indian bastard."

"Let him go, Jay," commanded Anne. "I know this child. He's Sam's special friend."

Jay sneered. "That figures," he said. "He's probably covered with fleas and lice. Damn half-breed kid." He cuffed Benito on the ear just as Sam strode up.

"Don't do that, Jay," he said, his voice low and lethal.

Jay's hazel eyes gleamed "Don't do what? This?" He cuffed Benito again.

Sam grabbed his brother's wrist. "Touch my son one more time and I'll break your arm, little brother."

Jay laughed. "You'd like to do that, wouldn't you, you damn half-breed? Go ahead. Show everyone what a gentle man you are, Sam. Go ahead and break my arm. Let Anne see the savage you keep so well hidden inside you." Jay's eyes were wide and wild. Spittle gathered at the corners of his mouth.

Sam dropped his brother's wrist immediately. "Just leave the boy alone," he growled.

Anne was down on her knees now, her arms around Benito, drawing the boy's head protectively into her shoulder to prevent him from seeing the violence that was brewing above him.

Rubbing his wrist, Jay said, "It doesn't surprise me to know you've sired a half-breed. Who's the bitch who whelped him? Your whore?"

From her vantage point, Anne saw Sam's hands closing into solid fists. They shook with rage.

"Stop it, Jay," she said, her hands over Benito's ears. "The child shouldn't have to endure this."

"I don't give a damn what that Apache bastard endures," Jay snarled.

Anne stood then, facing Sam, between the brothers. "Sam," she said quietly, "don't let him goad you into this. It's what he wants, can't you see? Don't let him do it to you. Not here. Not now."

"Stay out of this, Annie," he said.

"All right," she said. "Then you'd at least better give some thought to Benito. Is this the lesson you want to teach him?"

"Break my arm, Sam," taunted Jay. "Show the little bugger just how it's done."

If Sam heard anything, it was impossible to tell. His lips were drawn back in rage. His eyes burned hot. And then Benito clutched his leg.

"*Tengo miedo*, Sam," he cried. "I'm afraid."

Only that small voice seemed to pierce his savage rage. Sam blinked, then knelt down to the boy, taking his frightened little face between his big hands.

"No. *No tengas miedo, muchacho*. Don't be afraid. No one is going to hurt you." Sam held the boy close.

"I'm going to take you back to Father José now. We'll get more *caramelos* on the way. Come on." He stood, holding Benito's small hand in his.

"May *La Viuda* come with us?" Benito asked.

Sam shifted his gaze to Anne, who agreed immediately. "Walk on ahead with *La Viuda*," Sam told him. "I'll catch up with you."

Benito happily put his hand in Anne's and began tugging her down the street, but she was close enough to hear Sam's warning to Jay.

"You can call me any name you want, Jay. You can do anything you want to me. But if you ever harm that boy or call him a bastard again, I'll kill you. I swear it."

She glanced back at the brothers, to see Jay Hook respond with a smile of such viciousness Anne found it hard to believe. Then he casually adjusted a cuff link and turned his back on Sam.

Chapter Nine

Anne popped a third caramel into her mouth.

"*Cuidado, Viuda,*" cautioned Benito. "Sam says those will make you fat and all your teeth will fall out."

She grinned at Sam. "You sound like a proper mother hen."

"It's true," Sam said. "You just wait, Benito. *La Viuda de la Luna* is going to start looking like a full moon pretty soon."

"And toothless," murmured Anne. "Don't forget toothless."

"*Más caramelos,* Sam," said Benito.

"*Más caramelos,* Sam," chimed in Anne. "*Más, por favor.*"

Sam laughed, and the sight gladdened Anne's heart.

They were almost back at the orphanage when Father José walked out to meet them. "How nice to see you smile, my friend," he said to Sam. "Good evening, Mrs. McIntire."

Benito now clutched Anne's skirt, already prepared for the battle to get him to bed. Father José's eyes lifted to Sam's, communicating his concerns regarding the widow. Sam's smile faded.

"Benito, I will not argue with you this evening. The others are already in bed. Go," the padre said.

"Do as the father tells you, Benito," Anne said, placing a kiss on his forehead. *"Te amo."*

He hugged her. *"Te amo, Viuda."* Then he whispered in her ear, "Make sure Sam stays out of trouble, *por favor."*

She nodded. *"Sí,* I will."

"Good night, squirt," Sam said.

Without further complaint, Benito ran off to his room.

"You've had a good effect on him," the priest said to Anne.

She smiled. "He's a sweet child."

"Good night, Padre," Sam said, turning on his heel and leaving Anne standing there with her mouth gaping.

She nodded a quick goodbye to the priest and picked up her black skirt to chase after him. "Sam Hook, how dare you just walk away from me without so much as a fare-thee-well."

He slowed his stride enough for Anne to catch up with him. "Are you staying at Mrs. Thiel's?" He looked at her only long enough to see her nod her head before he said, "I'll walk you back to her place. You shouldn't be out on the street alone."

Anne was about to tell him that if he didn't want to stay with her, then he could damn well take her back to Jay, when Rosa rushed up to them, her dark eyes nearly wild.

"Oh, Señor Sam! Have you seen Natividad?" she asked, her breath coming in painful gasps. "He was supposed to meet me at the church this afternoon and I can't find him anywhere."

Anne and Sam both shook their heads. When Sam reached out to gently touch the little Mexican's tawny cheek, Anne couldn't help but notice how the girl leaned into his palm, much the way a kitten would. It seemed such a natural response to his virility.

"You look like a lady who's been left standing at the altar, Rosa. Were you and Nate planning something?" he asked with a warm glint in his eyes and a touch of amusement in his deep voice.

Rosa appeared shocked and guilty at once. "Oh, no, señor. We... *Aie!*" Her dark eyes flooded with tears. "*Sí.* We were going to run away together. But it is a secret. Please do not tell. Especially Señor Jay. He must not find out."

Anne thought of the incident a few days before, when Rosa had come flying from Jay's room as if the devil himself were after her. She could still hear Jay's voice, as if it had been the devil's own voice.

Sam's voice was deep and calm. "When you're looking for a man with cold feet, the cantina's always the best place to start. Have you looked in Sally Mendoza's yet?"

When Rosa shook her head, Sam began walking again, and the two women fell into step beside him, weaving through the crowds on the street. Outside Sally Mendoza's, Sam signalled for them to wait as he disappeared through the door.

Anne eyed the broken window. "Is Sally Mendoza the woman Sam visits when he comes to town?" she asked the Mexican girl.

Rosa shot her a furtive look, then bit her lower lip and dropped her gaze to her toes. It was enough of an answer for Anne.

And then, as if to answer her further, Sam strolled out of the cantina door with his arm looped around Sally Mendoza's shoulders. He paused, pulled the blowsy woman in front of him and eased both arms around her waist.

"Nate's not in there," Sam said to Rosa. "Nobody's seen him for a couple hours."

He had to speak around the lump in his throat as he stood there with dark Sally in his arms, putting on a show for the Widow McIntire. Sam forced himself then to dip his head and place a wet kiss on Sally's collarbone, tracing his tongue over the contours of her neck. *Annie, I don't know how else to discourage you,* he was thinking.

Anne stood there in flushed silence.

"Where else can I look, Señor Sam?" Rosa asked.

He rested his chin on top of Sally's head. "Why don't you try staying put and letting Nate find you?" His hands moved to Sally's midriff now and he slid one palm along the outer curve of her breast. "I'd help you look for him, but I have more, uh, pressing business here."

Sam could see Anne's blue eyes bright with tears now, but she stood there as if she were rooted to the spot, tiny and pallid in her black dress, just staring at the spectacle. *Dammit, Annie. Go. This is the smallest of the hurts I'm capable of inflicting on you. Use your head, woman. Just turn and walk away.*

And just as the tears threatened to spill, *La Viuda de la Luna* twisted around like a tiny black tornado and walked back down the street. Sam thought the sight of her proud, rigid, black-clad shoulders might break his heart.

As Sally shuffled through the cantina door, she called over her shoulder, "I didn't know you were going to stay with me, Sam."

"I'm not. I'm heading back home, Sally. I'll see you in a couple weeks."

She shook her head wearily. "Okay, Sam. You come by and see my new shutters. Tula should have them ready by next week."

Anne, dry-eyed now, joined Emma and Jay as they sat outside the mercantile, listening to the musicians who wandered up and down the street.

Her gaze kept drifting down the street to the cantina, and her thoughts followed. Sam's message had gotten through loud and clear. There was no place for her in his life. Even if he wanted her, he was choosing Sally instead.

Anne wasn't angry. What she felt was an overpowering sadness. Oh, Sam, she kept thinking. What a waste. What a terrible, terrible waste. We could have been so happy together, you and I. The two of us and the little boy. For a moment that afternoon, while the three of them strolled along, she had imagined them a family. It would have been so easy to be a mother to that child. And he needed one. Perhaps even more than he needed a father. Sally Mendoza didn't strike Anne as the motherly type, but then, perhaps she was wrong. She hoped, for Benito's sake, she was.

Maybe it would be best if tomorrow, when the wagon went back to The Hook, Anne stayed behind and caught the next stage out of town. She certainly didn't want to spend any more time with Jay than she absolutely had to. Aunt Emma would understand. And Sam? He'd breathe a long sigh of relief, no doubt, to have her out of his life once and for all.

And then Rosa's agonized wail cut through the warm evening air. High and shrill and full of pain, it rendered the musicians silent and brought everyone to their feet. Anne ran in the direction of the scream.

But it was Sam who reached little Rosa first. He had been saddling his horse, getting ready to ride out of town, when he heard her cry. He looped the reins around the hitching post in front of the cantina, and sprinted across the street and down an alleyway.

When he reached Rosa, her screams had dulled to sobs. She was draped over a prone and lifeless body. Sam immediately recognized the fine-tooled Mexican boots and ornate spurs. Natividad. Sam gathered the grieving girl into his arms, as much to comfort her as to get her away from the body so he could see what had happened. If he hadn't recognized the boots and spurs, he never would have known it was Nate. Most of his face was blown away. There was a Colt Navy pistol in the hand flung rigidly out at his side. Nate's finger was stiff around the trigger.

Sam was holding the sobbing Rosa in his arms when Tom Atkinson arrived.

"Well, hell," the burly sheriff said. "I thought we were going to make it through just one damn fiesta without any more bloody stuff. Who's this, Sam?" Tom Atkinson hunkered down beside the body.

"Natividad Valdez," said Sam. "Nate. He's been working at The Hook for about two years now." Sam sighed. "Nice young man, too."

The sheriff took off his hat, held it between his knees as he perused the bloody corpse. Then he looked at Rosa's prostrate form in Sam's arms. "This Señora Valdez?"

Sam shook his head. "Rosa works for us at The Hook. She and Nate were planning to elope today. Nate was supposed to meet her at the church. He didn't show up."

"Yeah?" The sheriff glanced at Rosa. "Don't know why a fella would kill himself when a pretty little thing like that was waiting for him, do you?"

"No."

A crowd was slowly gathering around them in the narrow alley. Anne pushed her way to the front.

"Oh, my God," she wailed. "Sam, what happened?" She was on her knees beside him then, trying to comfort Rosa.

"Nate's dead," Sam said. He raised his eyes to the lawman as he continued. "Looks as if he took his own life."

"Nate wouldn't have done that," Anne responded instantly. "He was..." She lapsed into silence, staring at the gun as the sheriff pried it out of Natividad's hand. She couldn't look at his face. Anne was afraid she would see Daniel's face. For a moment she felt faint.

There was a flurry of activity above them and an angry voice grew louder. Jay had arrived. "What's going on, Atkinson? Somebody said one of our cowhands was shot. Where...?" He looked down at Nate's body. "Good Lord! He shot himself, didn't he?"

The sheriff, weapon in hand in order to inspect it more clearly, angled his head. "How'd you conclude that, Jay?" he drawled.

Jay's face flushed and he swallowed hard. "Well, just from the look of him. He—he looks like he ate his gun." His overly bright green eyes searched the sheriff's face. "It's pretty obvious, Atkinson. Anyway, he struck me as rather unhappy lately. Seemed to be bothered by something." His gaze slid to Rosa, still sobbing in Sam's protective embrace.

Anne just stared at Jay. That wasn't true. Nate had been wildly happy. Rosa had told her. Why was Jay insisting otherwise? She was about to contradict him when she felt Sam's dark eyes on her, shooting her a cautionary glance. She kept silent.

The deputy arrived with a blanket and they draped it over Nate's body. Rosa was too distraught now even to cry.

"I'll take her home," Sam said, rising to his feet with Rosa still cradled in his arms.

"Best do that," agreed Atkinson. "When she's feeling better, Sam, you tell her I'm real sorry about this."

Anne followed Sam and Rosa down the alley. "I'll take her back home tonight," he said over his shoulder. "Anne, will you find my mother and tell her what's going on?"

"Yes. Of course." She put her hand on Sam's arm. "Just what is going on, Sam? They were going to elope. . . . Nate wouldn't have—"

"Where are you taking her?" Jay's voice was sharp as a knife as he approached them. Sam lengthened his stride. Jay shoved Anne aside and grabbed his brother's shoulder. "Where do you think you're going, Sam?"

His eyes blazed down at Jay. "I'm making sure Rosa gets home in one piece," he said.

"What is that supposed to mean?" Jay shot back.

"Whatever you think it means, little brother."

"I'll take her home," Jay said, reaching to lift Rosa from his arms.

There was murder in Sam's eyes as he looked down at his brother. "You couldn't let her go, could you, Jay? You couldn't let her be happy."

Jay flinched. He looked over his shoulder then, making certain no one else was nearby. "He was going to make a fool of me, for chrissake. You don't think I'd let him get away..." His mouth closed abruptly as Anne gasped.

"You did it!" she said, her eyes widening in horror.

"Not that anybody will ever be able to prove it," Sam said bitterly. "Right, Jay?"

Jay's lips crooked in a hideous smile and his hazel eyes glittered. "The girl was making a terrible mistake. Somebody had to help her."

"You're despicable," Anne hissed. She raised her eyes to Sam's dark face. "Can't you do something?"

His mouth tightened. "No."

"How can you just allow him to do this, Sam?" she wailed.

Jay laughed and looped an arm around Anne's shoulder, his fingers tightening when she tried to brush it away. "I'll tell you how he can allow it, Anne." He shifted his harsh gaze to Sam. "Shall I tell her, big brother?"

Sam stood in stony silence.

"The only way Sam can stop me from doing exactly as I please would be to kill me. Isn't that right, big brother?"

Hate flashed in Sam's black eyes.

"And," Jay continued, his voice diminishing to a hiss, "by killing me, he'll only prove that I'm right. That he is a savage, after all." Jay laughed. "Poor Sam. Poor, poor, Sam."

On the trek back to The Hook that evening, Sam made it plain he didn't want to talk. Every time Anne asked a question, he answered her in monosyllables, if he answered at all. When her arm happened to brush against his, Sam shifted farther to his side of the seat. Eventually, Anne drifted to sleep, lulled by the swaying of the wagon and the rhythmic clop of the horses' hooves. She woke, chin on her chest, neck aching, when Sam pulled the wagon to a halt.

"Is anything wrong?" Emma asked from the back.

"I'm just going to let the horses rest awhile, Mother. How's Rosa?"

"Asleep, thank heavens."

Sam jumped down from the seat, removed a bucket from the side of the wagon and walked toward the river. He brought the full bucket back, set it down for the horses, then disappeared again.

Anne rubbed her stiff neck, glanced behind to see that the two women were both comfortably asleep and then wrestled her skirt over the side of the wagon in order to climb down. The last time she had been on this riverbank she had returned to find Sam with a gun at his head. She shivered at the thought that he could have met the same fate as Natividad. Or Daniel.

A sliver of moon lit her way to where Sam was sitting with his back to her, knees up, arms draped over them. She could just make out the faint glow of his cigarette.

She sat beside him, listening to the sounds of the night—the throaty croaking of frogs on the riverbank, the soft hooting of owls, the warm breeze rustling the cottonwoods overhead.

After a while, she leaned against his arm. "I know what you're thinking," she said in a quiet, almost dreamy way.

He angled his head, gracing her with a small grin. "Witch!" he murmured. "What am I thinking?"

"That this is all your fault somehow."

Sam was silent for a long moment. "It is."

She leaned harder against him, feeling the taut muscles of his arm, the heat emanating through his chambray shirt. "You're wrong, Sam."

He flicked the remains of his cigarette into the river, creating a small shower of sparks over the water. "My brother is getting out of control. I should have seen this coming, but I didn't. I blame myself for that. If I had known he was this close to the edge, maybe I could have prevented what happened tonight."

"Well, if I knew what was going to happen tomorrow, you'd call me a witch. And yet you expect that of yourself. You couldn't have known, Sam. How can you possibly anticipate what someone like Jay will do?"

"I was the one who made Jay the way he is," Sam said. "It's taken me a long time to realize that, but it's true. He hates me, and with good reason."

"Because you were bigger and stronger and faster than he was? Because the two of you had to share your father's admiration and love? Sam, that happens in families everywhere and the brothers don't wind up mortal enemies. It's the natural way of things. That kind of rivalry is healthy."

Sam sighed. "You still don't get it, do you, Annie?"

"I guess not," she said.

"It wasn't Jay who was competing with me all those years. It was me, competing with him. I was the outsider, the half-breed, the Apache bastard. I had to prove, over and over, that I was better than my father's natural son. Whether it was riding a horse, or chopping wood, or shooting a gun, or figuring out how much food for how many cattle for how many days—I had to be better than Jay. Not once did I ever let him outdo me. And I took every opportunity I could to best him. Every minute of every day I was doing something that said, 'Look, Pa. Look how much better I am.' Whatever Jay is today, wherever he's wound up, I was the one who put him on that road, who drove him relentlessly down it. Me. His big bother.''

Anne had been leaning against Sam's arm. She straightened up now, smoothing out her skirt. "You're not your brother's keeper, Sam. What if Jay had bested you in all those things? Do you suppose you'd be a murderer today? Would you kill one of your employees? Would you abuse a little child? Would you mock and abuse your brother in every way imaginable? I sincerely doubt it.''

He searched her eyes in the dim moonlight, reaching for her hand. "I should never have let you get drawn into this. You don't deserve it.''

Now Anne's eyes flashed with heat. "Oh, so now you're my keeper, too! You're responsible for my happiness and well-being, too? Sam Hook, when will you stop carrying the burdens of everyone else on your shoulders and start looking out for yourself? When are you going to start just being you?''

A harsh laugh broke from his throat. "That's funny, Annie. That's very, very funny. That's the one thing I can't do.''

"I don't understand," she said.

"I'm sure you don't. And you don't understand that my brother is right when he calls me a savage. Because it's there. Down deep inside. Jay's always known that." His grip on her hand was hard now, even painful. "What do you think happened last night at the cantina, for chrissake? What do you think could happen if I truly let myself get angry with Jay?''

She touched his cheek. "Are you telling me that sometimes you feel capable of murder?" she asked.

Sam nodded solemnly, eyes downcast, ashamed.

"Oh, Sam. Welcome to the human race. Feelings aren't actions, my sweet, dear Sam. Feelings are just... feelings. You're no more savage than I am." Probably less, Anne thought. Undoubtedly less. Daniel, if he were alive, would probably testify to that.

He rose to his feet then, his hand still gripping hers, and pulled her to her feet. "Come on. The horses have had enough rest. It's time to get going."

He cupped her elbow loosely as he guided her back to the wagon, then clasped her waist to lift her up to the seat. She turned in his arms. "Do you know why I'm so sure what a good and gentle man you are, Sam Hook?"

Their mouths were mere inches apart. "Why?" he asked, his voice thick.

"Because Benito loves you so much." Anne reached up a hand to touch his bruised cheek. "And so do I."

The fragile moonlight softened Sam's dark eyes. Anne saw a profound yearning in them. Then he blinked, and it was gone. Sam had willed it away. He lifted her brusquely onto the seat, climbed up after her and spoke not one word the rest of the way home.

Chapter Ten

He slammed the shovel into the hard earth and drove it deep with his boot, then arced one more mound of dirt over his shoulder. Another footing for his house was almost ready. Sam grimaced as he looked at the low wall he had put up during the course of the past three years. If he'd worked harder, his house could have been finished by now. But there hadn't been much reason to hurry. Now there was.

The house, or what there was of it at this stage—a roped and staked outline, one low wall, a cord of piñon logs he'd cut and shaped, a stack of adobe bricks and more baking in frames in the hot sun—was laid out in the center of the piece of land he'd bought when he made up his mind to adopt Benito. He had named the land East Hook. Jay referred to it as "the wasteland."

Only a tenth the size of The Hook, the land would never be as profitable. Sam's only access to water was from a trickle that ran down from the Canadian, and that trickle tended to disappear in the hottest summer months. It wouldn't support many cattle, and whatever crops he grew he'd have to scratch with his hands out of the dry, begrudging soil. But that was all right. It was his.

And now he was in a hurry to take full claim to it by finishing his house. He had a good reason now. A couple of good reasons.

Now that Jay's bitterness and resentment seemed to be coming to a head, Sam wanted to have a place to move his mother if it became necessary. His brother was behaving so erratically, it wouldn't have surprised Sam if he'd shove them out of the house any day.

Then there was Benito. It was time to stake his claim to the boy. He was growing up fast and Sam was missing too much by letting him languish in the orphanage. Benito was missing too much, too. It was time to bring the boy home.

Which brought Sam's thoughts to Sally Mendoza. He looked around at the mess around him. Sally could do a lot better than this, he thought, but not a whole lot better. And she wasn't getting any younger. He hadn't noticed a line outside the cantina waiting to ask for her hand. He'd tell her that. If he had to pitch her over his shoulder and carry her out here, he would, and then do everything in his power to make her stay.

Last but hardly least in his rush to finish the house was Anne. The night they had brought Rosa home from San Miguel, the night she had consoled him on the riverbank and then confessed her love for him, Sam had felt dangerously close to his own admission of love.

He wiped the sweat from his brow as he leaned on the shovel. After a lifetime of trying to do everything right, of riding himself hard to rein in all his passions, he'd gone and fallen in love with a white woman. A lovely, sky-eyed white woman. In a world where a half-breed could be lynched for even giving a woman like Anne McIntire a glance, Sam had given her his heart.

The hell of it was, he believed her when she said she loved him. He knew she would suffer any indignity that loving him entailed. She was stubborn and loyal and strong. She was his perfect mate. And he was rushing to finish his house so he could bring Sally Mendoza, his less-than-perfect mate, here in order to put a final and indisputable barrier between himself and Anne. He loved her too much to let her live the life he was doomed to live.

If he had his way, he wouldn't be seeing Anne again. No, that wasn't true. If he had his way, he'd spend the rest of his life with her pale, fragile hand in his, with her languid blue eyes shimmering beneath his, with her sweet body in his arms and her warm words of love in his ear.

He squinted up at the midday sun, cursed, then drove the shovel once again into the hard and unforgiving earth.

Since returning to the ranch, Rosa had poured all of her grief into cooking and cleaning. She chopped vegetables with a fury, rubbed lemon oil into the heavy furniture until she practically wore grooves in the wood. Anne caught her doing just that in the parlor. There were tears streaming down the little maid's face as she worked.

Anne put a comforting hand on her quivering shoulder.

"I am so sorry, señora. I cannot stop my tears from flowing."

"That's all right, Rosa. It's going to take you some time, but things will start looking brighter. I promise you."

Rosa used both hands to scrub the tears from her face. "I know I was not married to Natividad," she said, "but I feel like *una viuda*." She let her eyes drift over Anne's black dress. "After your husband died, señora, did you feel a great, gaping hole in the middle of your heart?"

Anne turned her head to look out the window. No, Rosa, she longed to say, not after Daniel died. But there is a gaping hole right now. There's an emptiness in me that only Sam can fill. "It'll hurt a little less every day," she said lamely, not believing it herself.

Sam hadn't said a word to her after she had told him of her love. In fact, he'd made every effort to avoid her before he disappeared. Aunt Emma had been very mysterious on the subject of her son's whereabouts. Bewildered and hurt, Anne hadn't pressed her.

Rosa sighed tearfully. "It is my deepest regret that we did not have a child together. I would have a part of Natividad always with me then. Do you ever regret that, señora?"

"No," Anne said. For the little Mexican's benefit she embroidered the bleak truth a bit. "It has allowed me to forget a bit more easily."

"I don't want to forget a single thing about my Natividad," Rosa said, weeping softly as she resumed her housework.

Funny, Anne thought, she remembered very little about Daniel. Had he been dead only a month? It seemed a lifetime. Her wish to leave her past behind had been granted—with a vengeance. She had an entirely new life now, and it centered around a tall, strong, bronze-skinned man. Or at least it longed to center around him. Only she wasn't doing anything about it, was she? And with each day that passed, Sam was slipping farther out of her grasp. If she wasn't careful, Anne thought, Sam was going to be married to Sally Mendoza before she even had a chance to convince him that he ought to marry her.

"Where's Sam?" she asked Rosa now, a thread of panic in her voice.

"I'm not supposed to tell, señora. He said he wanted to be alone to work on his house."

Anne's eyes widened. "What house?"

"The one he is building on his ranch, about half a day's ride due east of here. He..." Rosa swallowed. "Oh, señora! I've never been able to keep secrets. You won't tell anyone, will you? Señor Sam would be very angry with me."

"I won't tell him, Rosa. I promise."

Anne looked at the clock over the fireplace. Half a day's ride. If she left right now, that would put her there just before sunset. Then what will you do with me, Sam Hook? she thought. You can't very well send me away in the dark.

Wearing only his fringed buckskins and moccasins, Sam bent forward and poured a dipper of water over his sun-scorched neck and sweat-drenched hair. There was an hour of daylight left, but he'd reached a good quitting point. And he was bone tired.

Too tired for trouble, he thought as his eyes shifted to the faint movement of a horse and rider still far to the west. Well, hell, Sam picked up his Spencer rifle, moved to the low wall, then sat and leaned against it. He'd never had trouble out here before. But that didn't mean it wouldn't come. Judging from the pace of the horse, though, it would take fifteen or twenty minutes to arrive. There was time for a cigarette before he had to rise to meet it.

He had smoked it down to his fingers when his eyes finally picked out the pale hair and the black skirt moving relentlessly toward him. He toyed with the notion of firing a warning shot to scare her off. It would take more than that to discourage Annie, he thought bleakly. Besides, if she had a rifle, she might just shoot back and hit him smack between the eyes. Dim as his prospects were, Sam still preferred life to death.

He stood there as she rode the last hundred yards toward him, his long hair pulled back from his strong face, his bare chest burnished by the colors of the sunset, his massive legs parted slightly in a fighting stance. He cradled the rifle lightly in the crook of his arm.

Anne wasn't expecting a joyous welcome, but she had hardly anticipated being met with a gun. She was almost too tired to care at the moment. Her backside hurt like the devil himself had been kicking her all day long. If the first words out of Sam's mouth were snappish, she was going to cry or scream. She wasn't sure which.

He wasn't smiling. Anne could tell that his full, sensuous lips were pulled down at the corners in a definite and unmistakable scowl. When she got close enough for him to hear her, Anne scowled, too, and called out to him.

"Sam Hook, if you say so much as one cross word to me, I'll..." The long journey in the hot sun and the lack of food and water suddenly caught up with her. Anne swayed in the saddle, listed precariously to one side and then felt two strong arms grasp her and ease her down.

He held her against him, revelling in the feel of her slender, delicate body. Every harsh word he had planned to say had fled from his brain the instant he saw her begin to swoon. He had reacted spontaneously, without thought, and now Sam regretted it even as he held her in his arms. He might have had a prayer if he hadn't touched her, he thought grimly. But now...

Her big blue eyes fluttered up to his. "Don't be angry, Sam," she said. "I had to see you."

"I'm not angry," he said. Or if he was, it was with himself. Just touching her as chastely as he was had already stirred a fire in his loins. A fire he meant to put out with all the willpower he could muster. "You need some water, Annie," he said brusquely, leading her to the low adobe wall. "When was the last time you drank something?" he asked, getting his canteen and handing it to her.

She took a long pull. "This morning," she said. "I never thought to bring any water along. Or food. I was nervous enough about riding a horse for the first time." She shifted uncomfortably on the ground.

Sam couldn't help but laugh. "Then I've got a pretty fair idea how your backside's feeling right about now. Annie, Annie. What a fool thing to do. When are you going to learn?"

She struggled up to her feet, feeling a little dizzy, and sat promptly down on the wall. The pain in her posterior was such that she bolted to her feet again immediately. "I'm never going to be able to sit down again," she wailed.

"You will," Sam said, "but it's not going to be too pleasant for a while. Come on. I've got a jackrabbit and some beans on the fire. That ought to make you feel a little bit better."

After her second helping of succulent rabbit and beans, Anne did feel much better. Sam still didn't seem glad to see her, but at least he hadn't put her back on the horse and turned her toward The Hook. Yet.

The sun had dropped out of sight while they were eating and the sky had become black and salted with stars. Sam had put on his shirt, though he had left it unbuttoned and untucked. From one of the crates that littered the construction site, he produced a small jug. After he took a deep pull on it, he handed it to Anne.

"Mescal," he said. "Apache wine."

She took a tentative sip and felt the liquor burn all the way down her throat. "Oh, my goodness," she said hoarsely.

Sam laughed as he took another swig. "I guess you have to develop a taste for it."

"I like your house, Sam," she said. The firelight was glancing off the adobe wall and lighting up some of the roped outlines.

"What there is of it," he said. "You're smack in the middle of the kitchen right now."

"I could tell. It's cozy and warm. Where are you?" She watched him standing by the wall, one leg cocked up on it, leaning his elbow on his knee.

"I'm in the bedroom, looking out the window at the piñon tree in the front yard."

"Is there a swing?" she asked dreamily, almost picturing one.

Sam nodded. "For Benito? Yeah. There's a swing. There's a pinto pony hitched to the fencepost, too."

"What's his name?"

He chuckled. "If I know my boy, the pony's name is Pardo," Sam said. "He named my white stallion Blanco, and my dapple gray El Cano. A brown pony would only be called Pardo. Benito's imagination doesn't stretch too far."

"Oh, I don't know about that," Anne said, rising and moving to his side. "He named me *La Viuda de la Luna*, didn't he?"

Sam's eyes glittered in the firelight as he looked at her. He took a strand of her pale hair and let it drift through his fingers. "Maybe he should have called you *La Bruja*."

"I'm not a witch," she murmured softly. "If I were, I'd have cast a spell over you a long time ago. You'd be mine now. I'd snap my fingers and the walls of your house would rise around us, keeping the rest of the world out. Then I'd say some magical incantation, and Benito would appear. And Pardo, too." Anne sighed as she leaned against him. "We'd be so happy, Sam."

"Bruja!" he snarled, bringing his leg down from the wall and moving away from her. He tipped the jug to his lips once more, fully intending to drink himself into a fog, where he wouldn't even be aware of her presence.

Anne stared out at the nonexistent piñon tree with the phantom swing. "I wish I were," she murmured. "I could do with a little witchcraft now."

The mescal only made him surly. It did nothing to ease his longing for her. If he hadn't known better, he would have accused her of giving him a potent magic potion. He'd never wanted a woman more. Damn her.

Sam spread a blanket against the wall, which served as a good windbreak and held in some of the warmth of the campfire. Then he shook out a second blanket. "I'm going to sleep," he said, knowing he sounded churlish, but unable to help it as he angled his long legs under the blanket and turned on his side.

She poked at the fire awhile, casting sidelong glances at Sam. If she had come here with the idea of seducing him, she was doing a damn poor job of it, Anne thought. Some witch!

There were a few inches of blanket on the ground behind Sam. She ambled over to the wall, then eased herself down. Her breath was shrill as a whistle when her rump made contact with the hard earth. Anne never wanted to look at a horse again, let alone ride one. How was she ever going to sit on one of the wretched, trotting beasts long enough to return to The Hook if she couldn't even bear to sit on the ground? She thrashed around, trying to get comfortable.

She was cold, in spite of the heat radiating from Sam's broad back, and she was miserable. She was lying beside the man she loved, touching him without knowing how to reach him. A tear slid from one eye. Anne sniffed as she scraped it away.

Turning toward her, Sam adjusted the blanket so it covered her from shoulder to ankle. He angled his right arm so it pillowed her head. Finally, with a rough sigh, he draped his left arm over the jut of her hip. "Go to sleep, Annie," he whispered.

His breath was warm and moist on her neck. Anne was wrapped in a cocoon of mingled scents—tobacco, the fiery mescal, the musky remnants of a long day's labors. She inched back, planting her backside firmly against him. Sam didn't move, nor did he say a word, but she sensed a change in his breathing. It became a little ragged, as if the air had thinned and he couldn't quite get his fill of it. She felt the hard rise and fall of his chest against her shoulder blade.

The hand loosely flung over her hip moved idly over the curve of her flank. Anne closed her eyes as a dizzying warmth seeped through her. "I could use my personal slave right now," she said huskily. "My backside would be enormously grateful for a massage."

His thumb dug into the firm mound of her rump, working the saddle-abused muscles. Anne moaned softly at the intermingling of pleasure and pain.

"Hurt?" Sam asked softly.

"It hurts good," she murmured. "Don't stop."

As if he could, he thought, leaning his head forward to trace the pale shell of her ear with his tongue. She was a witch who sapped him of his will, who made his blood rage and his heart drum fiercely.

His tingling exploration sent a shock wave of wanting through her body. She started to turn into him, but the hand at her hip held her fast.

"Lie still," he commanded.

Perhaps, he thought with amazing control and a powerful effort of will, he could give her the release she so obviously craved and still leave her intact. It was the best of all possible strategies, having Annie all warm and wanting and quivering in his arms, yet allowing her to go on with her life after this night unscathed, still a virgin, still whole for the man who would one day truly make her his own. As his hand slid under the folds of her skirt and travelled up her slim leg, over the sweet curve of her hip, over her flat abdomen, Sam clenched his teeth so hard his head ached. The thought of someone else touching his woman was like a knife in his gut.

She tilted her head back to invite his kiss just as his fingers slipped into the waistband of her pantalets and moved to her secret, untouched place. A small cry of astonishment escaped her at the newness of the sensations his touch called forth. His slow caress kindled a flash fire of wanting in her. And his tongue, tempting hers, moved in imitation of his deft fingers.

Anne wasn't sure if her eyes were open and she was looking at the bright stars in the black velvet sky, or if her eyes were closed and the stars were sparks on her eyelids. She moaned beneath Sam's mouth, beneath his insistent hand. She shuddered fiercely. Then tears sprang from her eyes.

"Ssh. Hush, Annie," he whispered against her ear, his hand moving back to knead her firm rump. "It's supposed to feel good. You're not supposed to cry, sweetheart. I didn't hurt you, did I?"

"It did feel good," she sniffed. "I never knew—"

"Sleep now," he murmured, drawing close against her. "Are you warm enough?"

"So warm," she said as she sighed. "Warmer than I've ever been in my life."

She had turned in her sleep, her lovely face now only an inch or so from his. With a little luck, she'd sleep till dawn. Then he'd put her back on her horse and send her west, back to The Hook, away from him. He'd need all the luck that fate could grant him. Because Sam knew if she opened her fathomless blue eyes, if she reached for him, if...

Her heavy-lidded eyes opened and locked on his steely gaze. She smiled slowly, richly, like a woman who had been well loved. Her fingers drifted over his chest.

"Sam." His name welled up from deep in her throat. "Love me, Sam." Her warm hands went to his waist and began fiddling with the leather thongs that laced his buckskin breeches.

"*Bruja!*" he whispered as his mouth covered hers. "Witch!" And then he was lost, at the mercy of her small, seeking hands, a slave to her warm, sweet demands.

When he rose above her, parting her legs with his knee, and when he entered her with one mighty thrust, Sam thought his heart would explode with the love he felt for this woman. And when his body did explode in her dark, secret depths, Sam Hook—in the tight grip of passion, utterly and hopelessly bewildered, and far, far beyond help—finally surrendered.

"I love you, Annie," he murmured in the crook of her neck. "You're mine. Only mine. Forever."

Chapter Eleven

They stayed there for the next two days, working on the house by day, riding to the river to bathe and make love at sunset, riding back for dinner and more loving beneath a canopy of stars.

Sam taught Anne how to make adobe bricks. It didn't take her long to learn how to get the consistency of the clay soil, the straw and the water just right by stomping in it with her bare feet until all the lumps were gone and just the right amount of water had been forced into every part of the mixture. Sam would pour the thick brew into the wooden molds then and arrange them to dry in the sun.

Anne spent as much time working as she did stealing glances at Sam—at the way the broad muscles of his back bunched and shifted as he worked, at the way his black hair strayed from the leather thong at the back of his neck, then stuck to his glistening cheekbones, at the determined set of his jaw and mouth.

Sam stole glances in turn, berating himself for not keeping his mind on his work, especially when he'd looked at Annie too long and had to reset an entire row of adobe bricks. She was so damn beautiful with the sun picking out golden highlights in her hair and her black dress all bunched up around her pretty knees as she worked on the wet mix for the bricks. More than once he'd put down his trowel, lifted her out of the soggy mess and made slow love to her, covering her pale, delicate body with his own to shield her from the ravages of the sun.

Out here, away from people and problems, it was easy to forget that world existed. It was so easy to love her and pretend they could go on this way forever. Sam knew better, but his heart was so full of love that it lent itself to hope.

On the second day, Emma and Rosa drove over in a buckboard just to make certain that Anne had arrived safely. They brought apple cider and cold chicken and one of Rosa's wonderful rhubarb pies. The fact that Anne chose to remain with Sam rather than return to The Hook was accepted with a furrowed brow and a quiet sigh of resignation from Emma.

"I think Rosa's going to be fine," Anne said later that evening as she lay in Sam's arms, gazing up at the star-sprinkled sky.

"She's young," Sam said. "She'll forget."

Anne was quiet a moment. "What about Jay?"

"What about him?" The words seemed to be strained through Sam's teeth.

"He killed Natividad, Sam. Or he had him killed. Jay's dangerous."

"I'm not the law, Annie," he said bluntly.

"You're a very forgiving man, Sam Hook. I'm not sure my heart's big enough to include Jay."

"It doesn't have to be," he said, nuzzling his face into the crook of her neck. "But it's going to have to bend, Annie, if you're so determined to love me, and to love Benito. You're going to have to put up with a whole lot of hurting. And if your heart can't bend a little, it's going to break. That's a lesson my mother learned a long time ago."

"Well, I've learned to ride well enough. I've learned how to make adobe bricks and how to make a decent pot of coffee on a campfire. I guess I'll be able to learn how to bend."

A slow smile lit his face as his big hand roved over her soft flesh. "You've learned a few other things, too," he murmured.

Neither one expected, however, that Anne's first lesson in bending would come so soon or so violently.

They were swimming in the Canadian River after a long day's work under a relentless sun. Anne had kept her ruffled pantalets and camisole on in order to wash them while she swam. When two riders approached from the north, Sam got out of the water and into his pants, ordering her to remain in the river, well down in the water.

As the horses neared, Anne recognized the two men who had accosted Sam before—Sims and his loco sidekick, Charlie. But they were grinning now, and, to all intents and purposes, seemed bent on no harm.

"Howdy, ma'am," Sims called to her, doffing his sweat-soaked hat. "Mighty hot, ain't it?"

With the Spencer carbine resting in the crook of his elbow, Sam stood on the riverbank. "What do you want, Sims?" he asked.

"Well, now, that ain't real friendly, Sam," drawled Sims.

That was precisely what Anne was thinking as she watched Sam's stance—legs parted, shoulders squared, muscles and nerves primed like a mountain lion about to spring on its prey. She knew these men were trouble, but Sam seemed to be openly inviting it now.

"That ain't friendly at all," echoed Charlie, whose horse nervously stamped at the ground as if mirroring its rider's nervous shifting in the saddle.

"We heard you was working on that house of yours, Sam. Rode by to take a look, but you wasn't there." Sims spoke with a long, drawn-out smile on his face.

At his shoulder, Charlie giggled.

"What did you do to my house?" Sam growled, eyeing Sims and bringing the rifle up a few inches. "If you so much as touched a single brick..."

Anne could almost smell the tension, like unlit gunpowder, in the air. From her vantage point, the situation was as much Sam's fault now as it was the other two men's. They had ridden in with smiles on their faces, only to be greeted with a rifle and a scowl. Sam was right to be suspicious, she thought, but he could have made an effort at reconciliation.

"All he said was he rode by, Sam," Anne called. "I'm sure these men appreciate how hard you've worked on the place."

Sam shot her a look that could have boiled the water around her.

"Well, now you're bein' right friendly, ma'am," said Sims. "And ain't that the truth? We seen how much you done to the place, Sam. I didn't know you had it in you, as a matter of fact." He looked over his shoulder at his compatriot. "Did you, Charlie? Did you ever figure ol' Sam could build himself anything but a tepee or a wickiup?"

Charlie snickered behind his dirt-streaked hand.

So much for trying to coax a little humane conversation from these two, Anne thought.

Sims touched the brim of his hat. "Well, we'd best ride on before the sun goes down any more. You never know what's waiting out there in the dark."

"Give her the package, Sims," urged Charlie.

"Oh, yeah." Sims lifted a burlap bag that was tied to his saddle. "When we heard you was keeping company with Sam," he called to Anne, "we thought it might be kinda mannerly to give you a little present. Show you we don't hold no grudges for that day you shot at us and 'bout near took Charlie's feet off."

He tossed the bag into the water. "It's just our way of saying 'welcome to the territory.'" Sims reined his horse quickly to the side then and said, "Let's go, Charlie."

As the horses kicked up dust in his face, Sam shouted, "Don't touch it, Annie. Get back."

But she had already waded through the water toward the bag, which was floating on the quiet surface. She was thinking that the two men might be trying, in their own hardened fashion, to make amends for their behavior. It was probably easier for them to apologize to a woman than to a forbidding figure like Sam. She reached for the burlap bag.

"Annie, don't," Sam shouted again as he began running toward her.

"Oh, Sam, don't be such a suspicious goose," she laughed as she pulled the twine from the top of the bag.

She never got a chance to reach in. The rattlesnake lunged out, pausing only to sink its fangs into Anne's forearm before it coursed through the water to the opposite bank. Anne stood there, unable to move as her mouth twisted in fear and shock and her eyes widened with horror. The hammering of her heart seemed to reverberate in her ears. She was deaf to Sam's shouts, blind to everything but the two red punctures in her skin.

The leather thong from Sam's hair was already in his hand by the time he reached her. He glanced at the double-fanged wound just below her elbow before he wrapped the thong tightly around her upper arm. Her breath was beginning to come in quick, panicky jerks. Her lips were white, pressed together hard.

"The less you move, Annie, the better it will be," Sam said, lifting her in his arms and wading toward the shore. "I know you're scared, sweetheart, but I'm going to take care of this for you. It'll be over with in just a few minutes and then you'll be fine. I promise you. I've been bitten at least a dozen times."

"It—it was a rattlesnake," she said, her big eyes locked on the two-pronged bite. "They're—they're poisonous. People die."

He lowered her onto the riverbank. "Only if they don't get help right away," he said, his voice calm and quiet. "All that's going to happen to you is you'll have a fancy scar to impress your grandchildren."

Anne tried to smile, but she couldn't even force her lips upward. "I'm scared, Sam," she said. Her eyes widened even more when she saw that he was taking his knife out of its leather sheath. "What are you doing?"

He sat beside her, loosened the leather thong a minute and then tied it again. His face was as calm and impassive as his tone of voice, but there was a thin sheen of perspiration on his forehead. "I'm going to make a few little cuts around the bite and then I'm going to suck the poison out. It'll be all over then. Turn your head, Annie. It's better if you don't watch."

She let her gaze wander over to the darkening sagebrush where their horses were tethered. Sam's big dapple gray dipped its head to pull a mouthful of brush. Her horse—

Sam gripped her wrist hard and she felt the knife as it scored her flesh around the bite. Anne bit her lip and tasted her own blood. She turned to look, but could only see Sam's shiny black hair as he bent over her arm, his mouth covering the wound. He spat twice, his lips now crimson with her blood. He wiped them with the back of his hand.

"I'm sure that's got it, but I want you to sit here quietly for a while, just in case." He loosened the tourniquet once more and this time, rather than retie it on her arm, he tied back his own hair.

Her fingers trembling, Anne reached up to rub a speck of blood from his chin. "I guess this means I'm going to have to be your slave now," she said, her lips quirking into a feeble grin.

He didn't smile back. "I guess it means you'll think twice about accepting gifts from strangers."

Calm as he appeared, Sam's heart was drumming and his stomach was knotted tighter than a noose. For Annie's sake, he'd exaggerated his own experience with snakebites. He'd been bitten, all right, not a dozen times as he told her, but twice—once through his moccasin and once through his pant leg. Both times his father had been there to tend him. Neither bite had penetrated very deeply—not like Annie's deep punctures.

What he hadn't told her, and what weighed like lead on his mind, was that he had once seen a man die from the bite of a rattlesnake. One of the hands from The Hook had been alone when he'd climbed into a bedroll already occupied by a snake. It had struck him on the calf, just behind the knee. Poor Sears. When they found him on the range he was almost dead, his eyes bulging from their sockets, his tongue swollen and protruding from his mouth. Sam could still hear the man's agonized screams.

He was sure he'd done everything right. He'd used the tourniquet and drawn out the poison. It was just that Annie was so small. A little poison could do a lot of damage.

She was leaning back against him now, resting as he'd told her to. There was an ugly bruise on her arm where he'd sucked out the venom. An hour should do it. If she was all right then, she'd be fine. In an hour he'd know whether he'd have to avenge her wound or her death.

Other than some tenderness in her arm, Anne felt no ill effects from the bite. After she had rested an hour they had ridden back to Sam's house. As nearly as they could tell in the dark, the only damage from Sims's and Charlie's visit was a few shattered bricks and some missing provisions. Sam's jug of mescal was gone.

Sam kept his rifle within reach all the while they were eating their dinner of beans and bacon.

"I want to go in to San Miguel tomorrow and talk to the sheriff," Anne said, touching her arm again, testing it. "Those lunatics should be locked up for what they did."

Sam, sitting by the fire with his legs drawn up and his head pulled into his shoulders, said, "Don't waste your time. Tom Atkinson's not going to waste his. He'll listen to you, nod very politely and then just chalk it up to one more ugly incident he can't do much about."

Anne glared into the flames. "So they're just going to get away with it?"

Sam didn't answer.

"Sam?" she said, shifting her gaze to him. He was like a rock next to the fire, silent and still. "What's going to happen?"

"I don't know," he replied.

He knew that if the snakebite had been more serious, or, God forbid, if Annie had died, he'd be out now, tracking Sam and Charlie by what little moonlight there was. The two men would be dead by sunrise. Sam would give them about as much chance as they'd given her.

But Annie appeared to be all right. Now, rather than focusing his rage on the hands from The Tenedor, Sam focused his fears on Annie. What had happened today was child's play compared to what could happen.

He'd been a fool the last two days thinking he and the white woman could live and love in peace, unmolested. As much as he wanted it to be, it wasn't going to happen. They would come some night—Sims and Charlie and a mob of liquored-up cowhands. They'd string Sam up from the piñon tree in the front yard. Annie would scream, and keep screaming as they passed her around from cowhand to cowhand. And Benito would see it all. He'd see it the rest of his life—his father hanging from the tree where his swing was; his mother weeping and bleeding and half-dead.

No. He couldn't control a mob of ignorant men. It was beginning to look like he couldn't even control himself all that well anymore. But he could damn well control that small portion of the future and make sure that that blood-curdling scene would never take place. He was going to take Annie back to The Hook tomorrow. It was over between them. It had to be. Nothing she could say or do was going to change his mind.

"No," she cried in her dream. "No, Daniel. Oh, don't. Please don't." He had caught her at last. His hand had snaked around her wrist, and then he made her look at his face. Only it wasn't a face at all, but a bloody puzzle of eyes and teeth and gore. "It wasn't my idea," she moaned. "I only did it because you begged me to."

Flames leapt in the blood-colored eyes. The jagged teeth rattled. "No," she screamed again. And then she was sitting up, rocking, hugging her arms about her. As Daniel's bloody visage disappeared, Sam's brooding profile came into focus. He was still sitting by the fire, still smoking and staring into the darkness the way he had been when she fell asleep. Without his strong arms around her to shield her, Daniel had finally caught her.

"Sam," she whispered.

The tip of his cigarette glowed brighter and a wreath of smoke curled over his head. "Go back to sleep, Annie. It was only a dream."

She curled beneath the blanket, afraid to close her eyes again. It wasn't a dream, Sam, she wanted to say. It was her past trying to catch up with her. It was a living nightmare and she didn't know how she would ever rid herself of it. No matter how far away she flew, how fast or how high, it would always be with her.

The sun was warm on their backs, but a disturbing coolness had settled between them the next morning as they rode west toward The Hook. Anne had never seen Sam so grim or so determined. But she hadn't a clue where that determination was taking him. He had hardly said two words to her since telling her to go back to sleep the night before. All she knew this morning was that they were riding resolutely back to The Hook.

Her guess was that he intended to dump her on Aunt Emma's doorstep and then take off after Sims and Charlie. He wouldn't listen when she suggested they ride to San Miguel and inform the sheriff, and Anne had given up trying to convince him. It would have been easier to convince a brick wall.

It was early afternoon when they rode into the central courtyard at The Hook, and Sam didn't like what he saw there. Tom Atkinson's big roan gelding was tethered outside the front door. Sam immediately recognized the Mexican saddle with its high cantle and ornate fenders. He didn't, however, recognize the horse standing beside Tom's. All he knew was that there was going to be trouble—if it hadn't started already.

There was no point lying to Annie when she asked him about the horses. "It's Tom Atkinson's," he said with steely resignation, his assumption being that the sheriff had come to haul him off to San Miguel for some crime, real or imagined. "We'd best get in the house and see what he wants."

Anne couldn't have been happier. Now she no longer had to worry about Sam pursuing the two miscreants from The Tenedor. She couldn't wait to show the sheriff her wounded arm and give him a blow-by-blow description of the events at the river. "This saves me a trip to town," she said, sliding off her horse and walking purposefully toward the house.

"Save your breath, Annie," Sam told her again as he followed her.

"I will not," she retorted huffily, opening the door and storming inside, mad all over again that Sam didn't think the lawman would be prepared to do anything about the two human rattlesnakes, Sims and Charlie.

They crossed the clay-tiled foyer and stood in the arched doorway of the parlor. Emma was at her usual spot by the window. Jay, whiskey glass in hand, was lounging on the settee. Tom Atkinson and another man—stocky, his serious demeanor accentuated by the

Colts he wore on each hip—were standing at the big fire-place.

Jay bounded up from the settee like a ringmaster who couldn't wait for the show to get underway. "Well, well. The prodigal returns," he said to Sam. "And Anne, dear. We've all been waiting for you." Jay took her by the elbow and led her into the parlor. "You've met the sheriff, haven't you, Anne?"

"I have, and I'm glad to see you, Mr. Atkinson. I—"

"And our other guest," Jay cut in. "Anne, I'd like you to meet Horace Bray, the U.S. Marshal from Albuquerque."

"How do you do?" Anne said, barely acknowledging the man before returning her attention to the sheriff of San Miguel. "I really do need to speak to you," she said.

Sam stepped to her side. "What's this all about, Tom?" he asked.

The burly lawman dropped his gaze. "I'd best let Marshal Bray handle this."

Bray's voice was professionally crisp. "Are you Mrs. Anne McIntire, of Syracuse, New York—the widow of Colonel Daniel McIntire?"

A blunt fear pressed Anne's heart against her ribs. "Yes," she said in acknowledgement.

The marshal's gaze did not leave her face. "Mrs. McIntire, I have a warrant for your arrest."

Emma turned from the window to gaze sadly at her niece. And Jay, who had just refilled his glass from the decanter beside the settee, sat back, crossed an ankle over his knee and looked as if he were ready for the festivities to begin.

Anne's mouth went dry. She couldn't speak.

"For what?" demanded Sam, moving closer to Anne's side and placing a protective hand at the small of her back.

The marshal's eyes flicked to Sam, then honed in once more on Anne's pale face. "For the murder of her husband, Colonel Daniel McIntire."

Chapter Twelve

Hands folded calmly in her lap, Anne sat on the edge of the bed. Earlier, she hadn't fainted so much as withered at the marshal's words, and Sam had gathered her up like a rag doll to carry her upstairs. She had clung to him, to his hard strength. All her own seemed to have fled. Sam had questioned her then, but with her mind in such a blur, she couldn't put words together. Or understand what was happening to her. She didn't understand it at all.

Daniel had promised her he would leave a suicide note fully exonerating her from any guilt or complicity in his death. No one, he insisted, would think it was her fault. She had asked him again that last night as she stood by his bed, trying not to breathe in the foul mix of camphor and laudanum and Irish whiskey that always filled his room.

"Are you sure, Daniel?" she had asked, her voice quavering. "I—I couldn't go to jail."

There was an odd light in his cloudy eyes then. "Where will you go?" It was as if it had suddenly occurred to him that his wife would survive him.

"I don't know," she lied. "Somewhere."

She was accustomed to pain in his eyes, to panic and anger and fear. But Anne had seen something else that last night. Was it lust? A demonic possessiveness? Whatever it was, it had shaken her to her core.

"You could come with me," Daniel had said, reaching an ashen hand for hers as Anne shrank back. A brutal laugh had issued from his thin lips then. "Not that loyal, are you, Anne? Just get me the goddamn gun. Bring me pen and ink, too, and I'll write your ticket to freedom."

Now, despite the late-afternoon sun spreading its buttery warmth across the pine planks of the floor, Anne shivered. Her nightmare had become real. Daniel had come from the grave to pursue her. There was no escape. Not from Daniel, anyway.

With slow deliberation, she changed into the black dress with the white lace edging the collar and cuffs. As she slid her arm into its long sleeve, she checked the snakebite. It seemed to be healing nicely. The purple bruise was beginning to turn to shades of yellow and blue. There was no sign of infection. Thanks to Sam, she thought.

She sighed as she fixed the hair that she hadn't bothered to pin up since her arrival in New Mexico. Well, she'd be out of Sam's hair now, she thought. The two lawmen would undoubtedly take her back to San Miguel, to the same cell where Sam had been held. The marshal would probably take her by stage to Albuquerque. Somehow then she'd be sent back to Syracuse.

Her flight had been all too brief. But at least she had flown, had proven to herself that her wings still could carry her.

Her reflection in the oval glass over the dresser stared back. A tear slid down her cheek. Oh, Daniel, how could

you have done this to me? Anne thought. Wasn't it
enough to have me caged as your wife? Why does your
widow also have to give up her freedom? Why couldn't
you let me go?

Then a wild panic seized her. No feeble canary fluttered in her rib cage now, but an eagle, bruising its huge
wings in an effort to escape. Anne had always been obedient, law abiding. When the marshal had made his pro-
nouncement downstairs, her immediate instinct had been
to offer her wrists for the shackles.

Daniel was dead. Nothing could change that. But his
death had given her wings. And, by God, Anne intended
to use them.

She raised the window. The flat-beamed porch roof
was just below her. Her horse was still tethered to the
hitching rail. It was time to fly.

Emma maintained her post at the window, head
cocked slightly as she listened to Jay's harangue on the
subject of Indian reservations. He was, of course, in favor of them and believed they should be walled off from
the so-called civilized world. The sheriff, Tom Atkinson, sat with his hat balanced on his knee, mouthing
"yup" and "nope" at the appropriate pauses in Jay's
speech. Marshal Bray bit down on a yawn.

Sam leaned against the door to the foyer, one ear
trained upstairs toward Anne's room. He thought he
heard her moving around, but when he saw the subtle
shift of his mother's shoulders and heard the little catch
in her breath, he knew immediately what was happening.

He was out the front door in an instant, then up on the
dapple gray, digging his heels into its ribs. The bay mare
Anne was riding was no match for the gray. Just beyond

the corral, Sam reached over and pulled Anne—fists, feet and hair flying—off her saddle and onto his.

"You little fool," he snarled as she pushed against his chest. "This isn't the way to do it."

"I'm not going to prison, Sam," she shrieked. "Let me go." The strength induced by her panic seemed to leave her body then, all at once. Weak, forlorn sobs replaced it. "For the love of God, Sam, let me go."

He held her against him, his lips brushing her ear. "You can't run out on a federal marshal, Annie. Don't make this any worse than it already is."

There was a commotion now on the front porch of the house. The marshal's gun was drawn, and Tom Atkinson had a hand clamped on the lawman's shoulder. Jay stood with his arms crossed, calmly surveying the scene, while his mother picked up her skirts and walked briskly across the dusty yard toward them.

"Listen to me, Annie," Sam said, his voice urgent and harsh. "I want you to get very, very sick. Cry, moan, do whatever you have to to make Tom Atkinson believe you're too sick for the trip into town."

"But, Sam, I—"

"Don't argue with me. Just do it. Now."

It wasn't that hard, Anne thought, bending forward, clutching her stomach. Her heart was racing anyway, and she felt as if she could faint with very little provocation.

Emma reached them at that moment. "Poor dear," she said, patting Anne's leg. "What did you do to her, Sam?"

"I told her to get very sick very fast, Mother," he snapped.

"Ahh," responded Emma. She then renewed her patting of Anne's leg with exaggerated purrs and murmurs of "poor, poor dear."

Sam slid down from the big gray's back and guided Anne to the ground just as the two lawmen arrived.

Emma turned to the sheriff. "This young woman is very ill, Tom," she said, whereupon Anne sagged against Sam to demonstrate her fragile condition.

"Not too sick to make a run for it," groused the marshal. "Huh, Mrs. McIntire?"

"Yes...no...I was confused," she stammered, thinking perhaps she wasn't carrying this off convincingly enough. The marshal was going to take her away unless...

Anne turned, put her hand to her mouth as if she were going to cough, and at the same time surreptitiously stuck her finger down her throat. She gagged and retched.

"Look here, ma'am..." the irate lawman began, only to be cut off by Tom Atkinson.

"The lady's sick, Bray. Use your head, man."

Sam's dark eyes appealed to the sheriff. "I'll bring Mrs. McIntire into San Miguel tomorrow, or the next day, when she's feeling better," he said. "She can't go anywhere today, Tom. Not in this condition."

The burly sheriff rocked on the balls of his feet, sucking in his lower lip. "Fine with me, Sam, but it's up to the marshal here."

Marshal Horace Bray gave Sam a long, appraising look. "I don't know about that," he drawled.

Anne took that as her cue to cough and gag again, reasserting her presence as well as her dire condition.

Tom Atkinson frowned. "How 'bout if Sam takes her all the way to Albuquerque, Horace? No use in your hanging around San Miguel so long."

The marshal hemmed and hawed, but what swayed him finally was Tom Atkinson's statement, "If Sam

Hook says he'll do it, Horace, then he'll do it, and she'll be there.''

By the time everyone had reached an agreement, Anne was feeling as ill as she was pretending. Knowing that Sam had given his word that she would turn herself in made her feel even worse, because she had absolutely no intention of doing it.

After Emma tucked her in bed, Anne pulled the covers over her head and wept. Why had Sam made that promise to the marshal? Why hadn't he just let her go, or let them take her away? Now not only did she have to flee the law, she had to flee Sam.

When her tears subsided, she heard the sounds of an argument downstairs. Jay's voice predominated. He didn't like harboring a criminal. He didn't like Sam turning The Hook into a jail. He was angry about this, incensed about that, furious in general. Occasionally, Anne could hear Aunt Emma's voice, strained and subdued. But not once did she hear Sam. Either he was no longer in the house, or he chose not to respond to his brother's ugly tirade.

It occurred to Anne that no one had questioned her guilt or innocence. How could she answer when she was both guilty and innocent? It was true she hadn't held the gun to Daniel's head and pulled the trigger. But she had brought him the gun, knowing full well how he intended to use it. The terrible truth was that as she left his room that last time, she had prayed that he wouldn't change his mind at the last second, forcing them both to endure endless years of pain and sorrow. So, yes, she was guilty. Still, she probably wasn't being arrested for her thoughts. She was being sought by the law for murder pure and simple. And that she hadn't committed.

There was a soft knock on her window. Startled, Anne turned to see Sam's dark face and long hair silhouetted against the sunset. She scurried to raise the sash.

"What are you doing out there?" she asked as he swung his long legs through the opening.

"Avoiding my brother," he said, before pulling her into his arms.

As her arms circled his neck, Anne felt surrounded and protected by his hard warmth. "Oh, Sam," she sighed, pressing her cheek to his chest. "What an awful mess I'm in."

He buried his face in her hair, breathing in the lilac scent that always clung to her, even out on the high plains after a long day's work. Then he tipped her chin up, looking into the deep blue of her eyes. He had to ask. He couldn't help her unless he knew the truth. "Did you do it, Annie?"

His eyes held only love as they searched her face. She knew he would keep loving her no matter what answer she gave him.

"No," she said.

There was no wavering in his gaze. There was no glad sigh of relief. All Anne saw was total acceptance.

He bent his head and kissed both corners of her mouth. "You need to tell me everything so we can figure out how to get you out of this mess."

Later, Sam lay on his bed in the bunkhouse, staring into the dark, his arms crooked beneath his head. Over and over, he repeated Annie's story to himself.

She had refused to marry Daniel McIntire while the war was going on, telling him that she didn't want him burdened with worries about her when he should only be worried about Johnny Rebs. In hindsight, she had admitted to Sam, she harbored some doubts about her love for the colonel and thought their time apart would help either settle those doubts or allow her to tell him gracefully that she had changed her mind.

Poor Annie, he thought. She never got that chance. Her fiancé took a bullet in the back just three weeks prior to Lee's surrender at Appomattox. The shot that should have killed Daniel lodged too near his spine for the surgeons to do anything but bandage him up and send him home, paralyzed from the waist down.

Her blue eyes had brimmed with tears when she said, "I had no choice, Sam."

Though he didn't agree, he remained silent. Others would have felt they had a choice. Other women would have wept and agonized and then quietly disappeared. Annie, with her damned loyalty and her sense of fairness, was trapped the second that bullet struck home. And the fine Colonel McIntire had apparently known that.

It was hard to blame the man, though, when it came right down to it. Lord knew Sam was having a hard enough time trying to remove this beautiful woman from his life. And he was a whole man, with other options, other choices. McIntire had Annie. Only Annie. He hadn't let her go. The man may not have been noble, but he'd been very human.

"The pain became worse," Anne had said, "or more difficult to bear. I don't know. The doctors said the laudanum and the morphine were all they could do for him. But the drugs created their own kind of pain. Especially when we couldn't obtain them. And he kept requiring larger and larger doses."

Sam tried to imagine himself, half-paralyzed, torn as much by the physical pain as by the thought of his useless limbs, with Annie ever present, feeding him, bathing him, seeing to all his needs. Or almost all. Had the colonel's manly needs been paralyzed, too? She hadn't told him that. But the fact that she'd remained a virgin was a good indication they had.

Daniel began asking her for his gun only a year after their marriage, jokingly at first, then with more and more seriousness. She refused to listen in the beginning, leaving his room whenever he brought up the subject. Toward the end, she listened.

Annie's tears had brimmed over when she admitted to Sam that, deep in her heart, she wanted her husband dead.

"You could have walked out," Sam told her, wanting to kiss her tears away but knowing the moment wasn't right.

"No," she said simply. "I couldn't. Someone else could have, perhaps. But I couldn't."

He knew that was true. A woman capable of walking out would never have married McIntire in the first place.

"You didn't kill him, Annie," Sam reassured her, lightly touching her tear-soaked cheeks and smoothing back damp strands of her fair hair.

Her choked voice became brittle. "I know all the arguments, Sam. Believe me. Daniel used every one of them. And I made up some of my own. But the fact remains that if I hadn't brought him the gun, Daniel would still be alive."

"And you wouldn't be here," he reminded her.

"No," she sniffed. "And I would never have known you. Or had a chance to love you. Or make love to you."

He held her close, thinking of the pain and violence that had brought them together. It was true. He never would have known her if that first bullet hadn't wounded

Daniel McIntire or the second bullet hadn't killed him. But it was true as well, he thought bleakly, that she never would have been bitten by a gift-wrapped rattler if she hadn't chosen to love him. As he held her, though, all tearful and trembling and delicate, there was nothing for him to do at that moment but love her. When he took her face in both hands, he meant only to kiss away her tears, but before he knew it, he was tasting the sweet depths of her mouth and aching for her other, sweeter depths.

Annie clung to him then and the grim chill of her fears gave way to her searing needs. "Love me, Sam," she whispered.

How could he not love her? How could he not respond to her soft moans and the warm, desperate plea in her eyes? Whether it was the right time or not, they had dissolved in a welter of silk and soft cotton and buckskin, and took each other with a fierce, almost blinding passion that left them both shuddering and utterly spent.

Now, lying in the bunkhouse, his eyes focused on nothing, Sam knew he had to help her, but he still couldn't come up with a plan. From all Anne had told him about that final night, he realized her guilt or innocence would be judged primarily by the note that Daniel McIntire had been writing as Anne left his room. If he had left a suicide note, Anne would have been in the clear. No federal marshal would have come after her. Therefore, Sam had to assume the authorities had found no such note.

The question then became had Daniel McIntire written the note at all? It was possible, Sam thought, that in his drugged and beleaguered state of mind, the man had deceived his wife. God knew he had married her and made her a virtual prisoner to his disabilities. The man who would do that might also wish to keep his widow imprisoned, literally. His thinking might have been, *If I can't have her, then no one else will, either.*

But if he had written a note, then what had happened to it? When Sam asked Anne, she had no idea.

"I left the house right after the pistol shot, Sam," she said. "I never went back upstairs."

"Who did?" he asked her.

"Rumsey, our butler. And probably Pauline, his wife."

"Would anyone else have been there before the authorities were notified?"

Anne shook her head. "Daniel's family lives in New York City. And we really had no close friends. Other than Rumsey and Pauline, there wouldn't have been anyone. Well, perhaps..." She paused, her forehead creasing.

Sam pressed her. "What?"

"Well, there was Dr. Tobin. He came to see Daniel frequently. He was the one who supplied him with morphine and laudanum. Rumsey might have sent for him before notifying anyone else. I just don't know." Anne's eyes widened in horror then. "Oh, Sam. Maybe he didn't die right away. I never thought of that. Maybe they had to send for Dr. Tobin."

Sam frowned. "I doubt it, Annie. A Colt does a lot of damage at such close range. And don't forget he was a soldier. I'm sure he knew what he was doing."

Sam shifted his body on the thin bunkhouse mattress now, shifted again, then finally got up and walked quietly outside. The sky was black from horizon to horizon. At night, with no moon, it was impossible to detect the peaks of the Sangre de Cristos. He rolled a cigarette, struck a match with his thumbnail and then stared at the glowing red coal.

Everything hinged on that note, he thought. If it existed. And if they could find it. He let his eyes wander to

Anne's dark window. He hoped she was sleeping well. If
they were going to travel all the way to Syracuse, staying
ahead of the federal marshals, she'd need a good rest tonight.

Tomorrow Sam was going to take Anne home. If a
suicide note existed, he would find it, and then . . . well,
he'd deal with that when the time came.

Chapter Thirteen

Sam lifted the latch on the wrought-iron gate and swung it inward, motioning Anne through with a little sweep of his hand.

She looked up at the large three-story house where she had spent five long years. The late afternoon sun glinted on the windows. How quickly she had adjusted to the soft colors and textures of adobe, Anne thought. The red brick looked harsh, almost institutional. Like a prison. Yes, very much like a prison.

Her eyes flitted up to Sam's warm, steady gaze. "I'm not sure I can do this."

His slight smile offered her understanding, but no way out. His voice was level. "You have to, Annie."

Her own smile, in return, was tentative. How many times had he used those very words during their trip back East? Their long, arduous trip. They had started out on horseback, riding to Santa Fe, where Sam boarded his dapple gray at a livery stable and sold Anne's mare for additional cash for their journey. On the stage out of Santa Fe, when several passengers objected to his presence, Sam had had to ride on top with the baggage. On the train, he was not allowed in the dining car. Anne had almost gotten into a fistfight with the conductor until

Sam restrained her and reminded her they were better off
if they didn't attract any undue attention.

But when they were finally east of the Mississippi
River, Anne noticed a distinct difference in the way Sam
was treated. The farther east they travelled, the more
Sam's Indian features seemed to become a curiosity
rather than a threat. In Cleveland, where they boarded a
steamboat to take them up Lake Erie and eventually to
Rochester, a small boy had installed himself next to Sam
on a deck chair and quizzed him endlessly about redskins, bows and arrows and buffalo. When the boy's
mother finally tugged him away, she apologized pro-
fusely for disturbing Sam. In New Mexico, a mother
would have thought she was rescuing her child from a
fate worse than death.

Along the way they had worked out what seemed to be
a good plan. They assumed that Rumsey and Pauline and
Dr. Tobin were aware of the warrant for her arrest. In
light of that, when they reached Syracuse, Anne would
introduce Sam as a federal marshal from New Mexico
and would conduct herself as if she were in his custody.
Their plan went no further than that, however. Neither
one had any idea how to go about locating the missing or
nonexistent suicide note.

Anne sighed now, gazing at the long brick walk that led
up to the door. With Sam's hand on the small of her
back—his warm touch guiding her as it had for the past
ten days—she took one step and then another toward the
house. When they finally stood at the dark green door,
Anne laughed nervously.

"We'll have to knock, I'm afraid. I don't have a key."
Her hand trembled as she brushed a stray wisp of hair
from her cheek, then smoothed the wrinkled front of her
dress.

She watched as Sam's bronzed hand grasped the heavy circle of iron and tapped it on the iron plate. The sound pounded in her head and sent a ripple of fear the length of her spine. She bit her lower lip, once more swallowing the words *I can't do this,* for she knew Sam's answer. And she knew it was true. She had to.

The dark green door jerked open. There was Rumsey, one button left undone on his black waistcoat, his cravat askew, his eyepatch slightly off center. His narrow face was pinched with irritation and his mouth was set in a thin, defensive line as he angled his head to take in Sam's imposing figure first, and then swivelled so his good eye lit on Anne. The butler's eyebrows lifted in surprise. His skin flushed and his jaw dropped perceptibly.

"Hello, Rumsey," Anne said calmly. "I seem to have forgotten my key." And then she stepped forward over the threshold, reclaiming the house she had abandoned just two months before. As she walked into the marble-floored vestibule, the Meissen clock on the mantle in the parlor chimed five times.

Whether it was a threat or a welcome, Anne couldn't say. Everything was as it had been the night she left. She had a deep sense of the familiar, but she was keenly aware that she had not come home.

Sam lay awake in the massive guest-room bed. The second floor of the big brick house was like an oven, and as he kicked the crisp sheets off his naked body, he had a renewed appreciation of adobe architecture. The thick clay bricks always managed to keep the interior warm when it was cold out, or the reverse. Not only was he hot, he was tired from the long trip. Perhaps too tired to sleep. Or his nerves too tightly strung to relax.

In the near-dark—for the street lamp cast shadows of sycamores and elms along the walls of the room—a faint smile touched his lips. Annie was home. The first part of his plan had worked perfectly.

My God, he thought, she was so beautiful here. The dark-panelled interiors with their deep velvets and rich brocades only served to accentuate her paleness. They didn't overpower her, as he might have assumed, but set her off—a diamond on a bed of dark velvet. The fine porcelains were so like her skin; the quiet elegance of the house so like her own. She moved through its interiors with an almost liquid grace, turning down wicks, touching a finger to the edge of a frame to put it right, lifting a silver bell to summon her servant. Here, Anne was like a cool mountain stream that had finally found its true course.

Sam's smile faded into a frown. He, on the other hand, felt awkward here—not a smooth and facile stream, but rather a river that had overridden its banks, threatening to topple anything in its broad path. Not a graceless man, he was too big for the house, too accustomed to open spaces to navigate well in these elegant and bric-a-brac-dotted rooms. He was too big for this bed, he thought morosely as his feet once more banged against the massive footboard.

Not that he had expected it to be different. If anything, it should have pleased him to feel so uncomfortable, so alien in her world. That should make it easier for him to leave her here. But nothing was going to make that easy. It would probably be the hardest thing Sam had ever done, or perhaps would ever do.

Just walking away from her in the hallway had been hard enough tonight. They had eaten—leg of lamb, boiled potatoes swimming in butter and dusted with parsley, golden carrot coins—in the green-and-gold dining room. Silently. Still carrying on their masquerade of U.S. Marshal and prisoner. Rumsey had served them in chilly silence, moving like a glum, one-eyed ghost around the elegant room, from Sam's end of the great polished table to Anne's place at the other end.

There had been a flicker of disapproval when Anne requested him to bring wineglasses and a bottle of "the colonel's white Bordeaux." There had been something else in the butler's expression, but Sam couldn't quite put his finger on it. Caution, perhaps? Wariness? Sam had the overriding impression that Rumsey knew something about Anne's plight, and perhaps the missing note.

They had finished the bottle of wine in the parlor, with Sam consuming the lion's share, hoping to dull his senses as much as possible before climbing the stairs to their adjoining bedrooms. He walked behind her up the richly carpeted staircase and watched the sway of her heavy brocade skirt, the light touch of her fingers drifting on the oak banister as they passed the colonel's imposing portrait. In the hallway, lit by gold-and-crystal sconces, Sam noticed that she paused at Daniel's door, her fragile shoulders sagging just a notch, her head tilted as if listening. It was probably an old habit. When she seemed to realize what she was doing, Anne shivered and quickened her step along the corridor.

She stopped at the door of her room, turned and raised her chin. The invitation that filled her deep blue eyes was sweet and clear and direct.

He cupped her chin in the palm of his hand, then bent to kiss her forehead. "Sleep well, Annie," he said, his voice barely above a whisper. And then he strode toward the guest-room door, opened it and closed it behind him, not daring to spend another second with her, nor look into her beautiful, inviting eyes.

Not that he regretted it, Sam thought now as he shifted once more in the bed and angled his legs away from the solid footboard. There would be no more lovemaking, in spite of her silent pleas, in spite of the desire that was contributing to his discomfort, in spite of the urge to walk back down the hall and quietly turn the ornate brass knob on her door.

That would only make it more difficult to leave her. To touch her lovely body one more time might make it impossible. He had to leave her—here, where she belonged, where she was safe.

At the kitchen table the next morning, Anne dipped the miniature spoon into the crystal saltcellar, raised it an inch, then let the white grains fall back into the tiny dish. She loved being in the kitchen. It had always been her favorite room in the huge house. All the other rooms were too big, too dark, too chilly. The kitchen, even though it was belowstairs, always seemed bright and warm. And she had always enjoyed Pauline's company. For the past few years, her cook had been her sole female companion. They weren't friends exactly, but there did seem to be a quiet bond between them that surpassed their professional relationship.

"You look exhausted," Pauline said now as she placed a cup of coffee on the table in front of Anne. "If you don't mind my saying so, Mrs. McIntire, you could do with a few more pounds. You don't want to get too thin, you know. It's not good. Not good at all."

Anne watched as her cook laced her own coffee with three teaspoons of sugar. She wondered how the woman could do that and still manage to remain stick thin. Or just how thin she would be if she didn't sprinkle sugar on everything.

Anne took a sip of her coffee and found it weak by New Mexico standards. Everything back here in Syracuse now seemed weak after her stay in the rugged territory. She missed it, Anne realized suddenly. She couldn't wait to clear her name and then return with Sam. "Thank you for seeing to the house while I was away," Anne said to her cook.

Pauline's mouth flattened out as if to say, "I was merely doing my job."

"I left...well...in a rush, I'm afraid. In a—a blind haste," Anne stammered. "I appreciate everything you and Rumsey did...what you must have gone through."

The thin woman's eyes met hers directly. "There were some who didn't understand," she said. "I understood." Her voice dropped then. "You gave him five years, ma'am. That's more than most women would have."

"I don't know." Anne drummed her fingers on the table. "I only knew I couldn't stay. Not one moment longer. Not even..." Her blue eyes brimmed with tears. "Not even..."

"There was nothing you could have done," said Pauline, replying to the unstated question. "The colonel was dead. Immediately."

Anne wanted to say she was glad, but it didn't seem appropriate, somehow. "He didn't suffer any, then?" she whispered.

"No, he didn't."

It was time to ask, Anne thought. Time to begin in earnest to pursue the quest that had brought her back to this house—the quest that, when ended, would allow her to return to New Mexico. "When you went upstairs that night, Pauline, did you or Rumsey happen to find a note, anything Daniel might have written before he . . . ?''

Pauline's expression changed. No longer sympathetic, her demeanor was now cool, closed. She gazed, not at Anne across the table, but into her lap. ''You'll have to ask my husband about that,'' she said.

Anne leaned forward. ''There was a note, then?''

The cook continued to avoid her gaze. ''Ask Peter,'' she said, pushing her chair back from the table and rising. ''May I get you more coffee, Mrs. McIntire?''

''This is important, Pauline. My life depends on it. Please, tell me. Was there a note?''

The woman locked her eyes on Anne's now. ''I can't tell you,'' she said flatly. ''I didn't . . .''

''You didn't what?'' Anne pressed.

''I can't say anything more, Mrs. McIntire. Forgive me. Peter is my husband. I'm sure you can understand my situation.'' Pauline turned and walked quickly out of the room.

Anne knocked softly on the guest-room door, and when there was no reply, she quietly opened it, then stood there savoring the sight of Sam's dark, sculpted body slanted crossways on the bed. The top sheet was bunched by the footboard. One pillow was under his head, while the other one was clutched to his chest, as if he were embracing a lover. Who he was dreaming of, Anne didn't know, but she could see that his dreams had had a powerful effect on his body. She sighed, hoping it was a dream of her that had inflamed him so, that had wakened his manhood while he slept.

She hesitated in the doorway, suddenly feeling self-conscious and shy. It must be the house, she thought. She couldn't imagine feeling this way in New Mexico. There,

Sam's glorious nakedness had made her bold. Here, the sight of his bronzed manliness nearly paralyzed her. She was tempted to turn and leave, to tiptoe back down the hall to her own room. And then his dark eyes opened.

A slow grin warmed his face and his eyes flickered with desire, just briefly. Then he seemed to realize where he was. The luster of his smile disappeared and the light in his eyes faded. The pillow he'd been embracing now covered the evidence of his desire, as if he meant to snuff it out.

"Good morning," Anne said, her gaze meandering around the room—to the window, to the rose-marble top of the washstand, over the Persian carpet—everywhere but at the bronzed body against the white sheet.

Sam levered up on his elbow, the pillow still clutched in front of him. "Give me a few minutes to get dressed, Annie," he said.

Her eyes met his then, for a yearning second, before she blinked. "Yes. All right. I'll be down in the parlor."

As she waited downstairs, rocking in the same platform rocker where she had waited that last night, Anne felt as if she had never left Syracuse, as if her wings were stiff and useless again. They shouldn't have come back here, she thought. It had been a terrible mistake. Sam should have let her run away. She should have insisted on taking what little freedom she had left. Even if there was a note, and even if they found it, it didn't mean she'd go free.

The iron ring on the front door resounded through the room. Anne tensed, her knuckles whitening on the arms of the rocker as she heard Rumsey's heels clicking across the marble floor of the vestibule. Male voices floated in her direction. Rumsey's voice, hesitant and icily polite. Another voice, calm but quite insistent.

She heard Rumsey's footsteps again, then sensed him standing in the doorway of the parlor. He cleared his throat.

"There's a Marshal Bray to see you, Mrs. McIntire. He is, um, rather determined."

Anne swallowed. What would the marshal do now? Take her to that cold stone building with bars on the windows? Lock her up somewhere and throw away the key?

"Thank you, Rumsey," she said, her voice not betraying her apprehensions. "Send him in, please."

Sam made sure the leather thong that tied his hair back was tight enough. His black pants and jacket as well as his white shirt had reappeared in his room this morning, the soiled spots attended to and the wrinkles pressed out. His face in the mirror was that of a stranger, woefully out of place in the richly furnished guest room of Anne's house.

The elegant house had already begun to work on her, he thought, remembering her discomfort as she'd stood in the doorway earlier. Had he looked so out of place to her then? The savage suddenly transported to civilization? He had awakened from a passionate dream of her to find her lovely face actually there. Against his better judgment, he had been about to reach out for her, and then she had avoided looking at him, as if he were a stranger who had appeared—naked, erect and threatening—in her guest room.

Well, good, he thought now. Good. So much the better. The more she retreated from him, the easier it would be for her when he left. The easier it would be for him, too, if she looked at him with dismay and disgust rather than with longing. For, if she turned her blue eyes up to him and begged him not to go, Sam knew his heart would rip down the middle and his soul would shrivel.

He couldn't take her back to New Mexico and a life of bigotry and violence, no more than he could stay here and live like a fish out of water. Even if he wanted to, he couldn't stay here. Not with his mother back West at Jay's mercy. Not with Benito waiting for a home. Besides, he'd promised his father to see that The Hook endured and prospered. He had to go home. Alone. He had to make Annie understand.

Sam walked down the stairs slowly, dreading the awkwardness of their first few moments alone together. And then he heard the low, rumbling voice of Horace Bray. His dread vanished. There was only his love for Annie, his natural instinct to protect her. Sam took the last of the stairs two at a time.

In the parlor, Anne was just tying the chin bow of her black silk bonnet. Her black kid gloves were already on. The U.S. Marshal stood patiently by the fireplace, waiting for his prisoner, apparently in no great hurry now to take her the last half mile.

Sam met the stocky lawman's penetrating gaze as he moved to Anne's side. "Marshal," he said by way of greeting, "you're a long way from home."

The man merely nodded.

Anne raised her eyes to Sam's. "Marshal Bray is taking me to the courthouse, Sam." There was a distracted calm in her voice that twisted Sam's heart. "I've told him you had nothing to do with my leaving New Mexico. You merely followed to protect me."

Sam turned to Bray. "Did she tell you about the note?"

The lawman nodded again, chewing on his lower lip. "Yup. Until I see it, though, there's nothing else I can do.

I'm obliged to—" A commotion in the vestibule interrupted him.

Pauline's shrill voice was saying, "I won't stand by and let him take her. Do you understand me? I don't care what you say."

"Give it to me," Rumsey demanded, his voice low but resolute.

"No," his wife shouted as her pinched and panic-stricken face appeared in the doorway.

Anne, in her daze of anxiety, didn't seem to notice her wild-eyed cook, nor the butler, who rushed in just behind her. When Pauline spoke her name, Anne turned slowly.

"I was just leaving, Pauline," she said distractedly. "I don't know when I'll..." Her voice trailed off then, as if she didn't have enough breath to finish.

Pauline brought a folded piece of parchment from the pocket of her skirt. "The colonel left a note, Mrs. McIntire. We—"

Rumsey reached out to snatch it from her hand, but Sam lunged and got the folded paper first.

"Damn you," the butler hissed at his wife. "You hated him, too, just like she did. You never knew him when he was tall and strong. The colonel was a hero." He whirled on Anne now. "He would have gotten better. I saw him improving. You didn't have to give him that gun. You didn't have to do it." Rumsey's voice broke, but he stiffened his shoulders, wheeled about and left the room with military dignity.

By now, Pauline had dissolved into tears. She caught Anne's gloved hand. "Forgive him, Mrs. McIntire. He was just so loyal to the colonel. Too loyal. He thought he was doing the right thing, for the colonel's sake. He loved him so." Pauline let go of Anne's hand, then shrank back toward the door. "I'm sorry," she whispered as she followed in her husband's footsteps.

Sam opened the note, his eyes quickly scanning it, then he held it out to Horace Bray, who had regarded the scene played out before him with quiet interest. "Daniel McIntire's suicide note, Marshal," Sam said. "This is what we came for." He angled his head in the direction of the vestibule. "You can see for yourself why it wasn't with the colonel's body."

"So I see," said the lawman, taking the note and perusing it quietly as he continued to lean against the fireplace. "Looks authentic," he said. "I'll have to confirm the signature, as I'm sure you understand. Mrs. McIntire, have you seen this?" He held it in Anne's direction.

She looked at the note as if it had suddenly appeared out of thin air.

"It's your husband's note, Annie," Sam said, taking it from the marshal's hand and pressing it into hers. "It clearly states that he died by his own hand. You don't have to go with Marshal Bray. It's all over."

She hadn't realized she'd been holding her breath, but when the clock on the mantle started striking, Anne began to take in deep, raw breaths with each chime. It was as if she couldn't get enough air into her lungs, as if there weren't enough air in the house, in the whole world to satisfy her. The sharp little lights that danced before her eyes diminished to blackness, and she barely felt Sam's arm slide around her as her legs buckled.

Pauline Rumsey's thin arms were crossed in front of her on the kitchen table. She had pushed her sugar-laced coffee aside and sat watching Sam Hook finish his cup of the dark brew.

"My husband's not a bad man, Mr. Hook," she said. "When he saw the colonel with half his head blown away that night...I don't know...something just happened to Peter's good sense. He—we—never meant to hurt the Mrs. I swear to you we wouldn't have let her go to prison."

Sam drank the last of his coffee, then set the cup back into the delicate saucer and pushed it toward the center of the table, where he wouldn't inadvertently knock his hand against it and break the nearly translucent china. "What will you do now?" he asked her.

"That depends on Mrs. McIntire, I guess. I don't know if she'll keep us on after what happened." Her pale, watery eyes searched Sam's dark face. "I don't know if she'll even be staying here herself."

"She'll stay," he replied. "And she'll need taking care of."

The thin woman raised her chin. "My husband and I made a mistake, Mr. Hook. But I took good care of Mrs. McIntire for five long years. I expect I can continue to do it."

Sam offered her a brief smile, thinking he'd be damned if he'd thank the woman for simply offering to remain in her job, a job he'd have fired her from in a second if he were going to be here.

But he wasn't. And after he left the repentant woman in the kitchen, he walked out the front door of the house without even looking in on the sleeping Annie one last time. It was easier if he didn't see her again. No, he thought as he closed the door behind him, it wasn't easier. Only faster.

There was nothing easy about walking away from his heart and his soul. There was no satisfaction in knowing he was doing the right thing. There was only emptiness inside him.

Chapter Fourteen

Once again Anne was the only passenger left on the stagecoach as it rattled over the dusty plains toward San Miguel. With the side curtains rolled up, she noticed the subtle changes in the landscape since she had last seen it in midsummer. It was September now—nearly autumn—and the green that had predominated two months ago had given way to gold. All afternoon the sun seemed to cast a richer, more somber light on the vast lands that stretched out around her. All of it—the low sagebrush, the spiked yucca, the sturdy piñons and the occasional stands of shimmering cottonwoods—seemed beautiful to her. She felt as if she were coming home.

She leaned her head against the seat back and closed her eyes. Coming home, she thought. Aunt Emma's desolate letter had begged her to come back. Her aunt was so lonely without her. Jay was unbearable. Drunk most of the time, he was cruel and caustic to Emma, and on the verge of violence with Sam. Half the hands at The Hook had left because of his abuse. Sam was doing the work of six men as a result, and still trying to get his house finished.

In her mind, Anne could picture Aunt Emma's flowing script.

"Sam would never say what happened back East, other than to assure us that your legal difficulties had been settled, for which I am most grateful. But he came back changed. And not for the better, I fear. My son is quiet, and seems to be filled with a sadness so profound that it leaves no room for even the smallest joys. His determination to adopt the child, Benito, is stronger than ever, yet even that prospect does not seem to cheer him. I don't know how to help him, Anne. I appeal to you, dear, knowing how deep were the feelings that you and my son shared. Please help him, if not out of love for him, then out of warmth and kinship for me."

Anne sighed now, letting her head roll with the rhythm of the coach. Sam hadn't even left her a note that day he'd walked out of her house in Syracuse. It had been all she could do those first few days not to follow him, not to rush to the window each time she heard a passing carriage, in hopes that he had changed his mind and come back for her.

She wrote him a long, beseeching letter, which she tore up in a torrent of tears. It was no good. He loved her—or so she thought, although now she wasn't even so sure of that—but he wouldn't share his life with her. He seemed to think he was sparing her from a lifetime of hurt and persecution. He seemed to think he was doing the right thing, the noble thing, the true and loving thing. But he wasn't. Anne planned to tell him that. And more.

From the window now she could see the bell tower of the adobe church in San Miguel. The setting sun touched it with warm pink and topaz. Not far from there, she imagined, Benito was just sitting down to his evening meal with the dozen or so other orphans. She intended to

visit him before she made the trip out to The Hook, and
had brought him a brightly painted wooden train and a
bag of peppermints and lemon drops to share with the
other children.

As the stagecoach entered the little town, Anne was
suddenly overcome with memories of her previous arrival in San Miguel. She recalled her initial panic, her grim
determination to get on with her life and to try her wings.
And then, of course, she recalled her first sight of Sam—
dark, looming over her, his mighty passions all tamped
down in his heart. It seemed so long ago, and yet it was a
mere three months. How her life had changed in that
time.

She had sold the house in Syracuse complete with fur-
nishings. Well, almost complete. She'd given her Li-
moges china and her silver tea and coffee service, along
with all her linens and silver flatware, to Pauline. To
Rumsey, she gave the remainder of Daniel's wine cellar.
The butler's good eye had shed copious tears when she
bid him farewell.

"I wouldn't have done it, you know, Mrs. McIntire,"
he had told her. "I truly wouldn't. I couldn't have let my
colonel's wife go to prison."

She had forgiven Rumsey, despite the fact that she
didn't believe him. There was crime of one sort or another lurking in everyone's heart. Anne knew that now.
Whether it was murder or theft or blackmail, it only required the right circumstances to rise to the surface. If
a person wanted something—or someone—desperately
enough...

She had intimate knowledge of her own heart's crimes.
Blackmail, for instance. She was plotting again, but it
wasn't a matter of choice or will this time. Rather it was
a simple fact of life. She was pregnant. After Sam had

left Syracuse, Anne had prayed that his seed was growing in her, that she was carrying a child conceived by the light of a campfire, under a wide, starry sky. And when her monthly flow failed to appear in its usual clocklike fashion, she was overjoyed. Even without Aunt Emma's letter to spur her, she would have returned to New Mexico. It was her home now. Sam was her home. She was determined to make him understand that.

Anne was ready for all of his old, tattered arguments about why they couldn't be together. It was too dangerous, he'd tell her, and she'd only wind up getting hurt. She planned to listen patiently, even smile sweetly, nodding now and then in apparent agreement, and then she would tell him she was carrying his child.

Knowing Sam, it was easy to envision the succession of emotions that would play across his face. First there would be shock. His dark eyes would widen and a muscle would twitch in his cheek. Then his brow would furrow and his sculpted nose flare slightly as the surprise turned to anger at something he couldn't control. And finally, when he fully comprehended her news, his fierce face would soften and his mouth would slide into a dazzling, joyous grin.

Or so she hoped. Sam was a stubborn man, and he had convinced himself that his love could only bring her harm. Now she had to make him see that none of that mattered. The child growing inside her changed everything. This was their future—hers and Sam's.

If blackmail was required, so be it, Anne thought. If she had to use Sam's deep sense of responsibility to make him marry her, she would use it gladly. And then she would do whatever it took—including shooting off every heel in the entire territory—to see that they remained happy and safe.

* * *

"Welcome back, Mrs. McIntire." Father José's hand reached up to steady her descent from the coach.

The faint hope that it would be Sam welcoming her back was just that—a faint hope—but she felt the weight of disappointment in her heart. In spite of it, Anne was delighted to see the priest's curly hair and friendly smile. "Thank you, Father José," she said as she alighted on the street. "How did you know which stagecoach I'd be on?"

He smiled sheepishly. "I have met each stage for the past week. I must tell you how happy I am to see you safe and sound. There have been problems with the Apache. You must have heard in Albuquerque."

"Hi, Padre," the driver called from the baggage compartment at the rear of the dusty vehicle. "You talkin' about them renegades?"

"Yes. We've all been quite worried about your safe arrival," the priest said. "I'm happy to see there were no problems."

The driver shook his head as he lifted one of Anne's bags down from the rear of the coach. "I ain't lookin' forward to the trip back, I can tell you that. Damn bastards! Why can't they stay on the reservation with the rest of their kind?"

The priest made a noncommittal cluck with his tongue. "We don't want to spoil your arrival with such talk, Mrs. McIntire." He looked as the driver put another bag on the ground. There were a total of four—a large camelback trunk, two leather valises and a carpetbag. "It appears that you plan to stay for a while," Father José said, his eyebrows lifted in curiosity.

"A good long while, Father," she said. "How is little Benito? I'll bet he's grown half a foot while I've been gone."

"Not taller, Mrs. McIntire, but the boy's wiles seem to increase daily. The sisters have a difficult time keeping up with him."

She raised her eyes to the priest's. "Perhaps they won't have to much longer," she said. "Sam isn't in town this evening, by any chance, is he?"

The look in Father José's warm brown eyes grew cautious. Anne saw him glance briefly in the direction of Sally Mendoza's before responding to her question.

"I cannot say for sure, Mrs. McIntire. He was here earlier today to take Benito for a ride. I have not seen him since then."

The coolness in his tone was apparent. "You still don't approve, do you, Father? Of Sam and me?"

He shook his curly head. "It is not for me to approve or disapprove. I only see the heartaches that would come from such a match. I strongly urge you—as I have urged Sam—not to pursue it."

Anne's mouth tightened. "Sam agreed with you, of course."

"Let us just say he saw the wisdom of my advice."

"You're a coward, Father José," Anne said bluntly.

The priest smiled, seemingly unoffended by her remark. "I choose to call myself a realist, Mrs. McIntire," he said.

"That's the last of your luggage, ma'am," the driver said as he hoisted himself back onto the high front seat of the coach. "We're going to lay over down at the livery stable. Don't want to meet up with Raging Owl and his braves in the dark." He gave a helpless shrug, then snapped the reins over the horses' backs. The big coach creaked as it moved slowly down the street.

"Will you be staying at Mrs. Thiel's tonight?" the priest asked.

Anne nodded. She wasn't looking forward to an evening in the company of the opinionated widow. Her gaze drifted down the street toward the cantina. Did Sam know she was coming back? she wondered. Probably. There weren't many secrets in a town as small as this. And was he glad? Probably not. After all, he hadn't met her stage. Anne imagined him sitting at a table in the rear of the cantina, his dark hand gripping a whiskey glass, plotting how to rid himself of her once and for all.

"Good luck, Sam," she muttered under her breath as she followed Father José across the street.

The cantina was quiet, but since it was early on a Saturday night, that merely meant it was the lull before the storm. Soon it would be noisy and crowded, hazy with smoke and rife with curses.

Sally Mendoza slid into the chair next to Sam's, reached for his glass and poured herself an inch of whiskey from the full bottle on the table. She swallowed the amber liquid in a single gulp, blinked slowly like a cat and wiped the corner of her mouth with her thumb.

"My answer is no, Sam," she said, tilting the bottle and pouring another good-sized shot, which she pushed toward him.

He stared at the whiskey as it sloshed against the sides of the glass. A muscle twitched in his cheek. "Fine," he said, then he downed the shot and refilled the glass, this time to the rim.

Sally sat quietly for a moment, studying his dark face. "That's all you have to say? Just 'fine?' You don't even want to know why I won't marry you?" she asked.

"Not particularly," he said, about to lift the full glass to his lips.

Sally stopped him with a hand on his wrist. "Well, you're going to hear it anyway. In the first place, I like running the cantina. I don't want to sell it and move out in the middle of nowhere. What would I do all day? Sweep floors and make tortillas?"

Sam was tempted to say it might be a better life than getting beat up by drunk cowhands, but he merely gazed at her, his expression blank, his hand still curled around the whiskey glass.

"And in the second place," Sally continued, "I don't think I'd make a very good mother. Why should I give up my life for children when I don't even like them?"

He didn't answer. He had exhausted all of his arguments already when he'd asked her to marry him. It wasn't even a proposal, but a cool and rational proposition, delivered from his head rather than his heart.

"Finally," Sally said, her smudged eyes clouding with tears, her index finger tracing a line over his thick wrist, "I would like to be loved by the man I marry, Sam." She sniffed and lifted the hem of her skirt to wipe her eyes.

His voice was thick, from disappointment, from witnessing the woman's despair. "I'd be good to you, Sally. I can't promise anything more. And maybe—"

She shook her head emphatically. "No maybe, Sam."

The front door of the cantina swung open and three cowhands pushed inside. One of them, a swarthy Mexican in a freshly pressed shirt and black string tie, leaned back against the bar and signalled to Sally.

She fiddled with the ribbons on her *camisa,* then sighed. "I gotta go to work now." She touched his hand, then shifted her eyes to the whiskey bottle. "You take it easy tonight, all right?"

Sam drained his glass as he watched Sally amble to the bar, then fit her hip against the dark cowhand's. He wished he could feel jealous. He wished he could feel angry. Anything but empty.

Earlier, when the stage had clattered past the door, his heart had shuddered. Annie. Annie was coming back. Maybe now, tonight. Desperate, Sam had grabbed Sally and made her sit still while he proposed, while he tried to get the words out warm and right. Instead, he'd sounded stiff, cool and calculating, like a lawyer presenting a case. It was little wonder Sally had turned him down. It was surprising she had sat there so long without getting up and throwing her chair at him.

What now? Sam wondered as he fingered the empty whiskey glass in front of him. Why the hell didn't Annie stay in Syracuse where she belonged? Stay in her big house with the grand staircase and the Persian rugs and the velvet drapes and the crisp, snow white sheets? She was safe there. She might have been happy there if she'd given herself half a chance.

Damn her! The little fool. What was it going to take to finally scare her enough to see the brutal truth? Once coupled with his, her life wasn't worth a damn. But guns and rattlesnakes and the likes of Sims and Charlie hadn't dented her blasted courage, that was for sure. Maybe it truly would take an angry mob of whites to pound some sense into her head. Or maybe...

Maybe not a mob of whites. Maybe just an encounter with one savage Apache would do the trick.

Sam tipped the whiskey bottle over his empty glass, unable to suppress a wolfish grin. Now where was he going to find a fierce, hot-blooded Indian to scare the living daylights out of Anne McIntire?

Mrs. Thiel carried a candle as she walked Anne to her room, continuing the conversation they had been having in her parlor. The big woman kept looking at Anne over her shoulder, which caused her to weave in the narrow hallway as if she were on a ship. As she talked, she passed the candlestick from one hand to the other, which bounced her huge dark shadow from wall to wall.

It was barely eight o'clock, and Anne wasn't the least bit sleepy, but she had spent the last half hour feigning yawns in order to convince her hostess otherwise. If she had to listen to Mrs. Thiel go on any longer about "drunks, deadbeats, dirty Mexicans and useless half-breeds," Anne thought she would scream.

The woman came to an abrupt stop in the hallway now, half turning to Anne. "But when it comes to just pure meanness, Mrs. McIntire, there's nobody worse than an Apache. They're the devil's own people. That's for damn sure."

Anne remained silent, shifting restlessly from one foot to another. Doris Thiel's eyes reminded her of dark little raisins set in dough.

"I'd think twice about riding out to The Hook all by myself if I were you, Mrs. McIntire, what with that devil, Raging Owl, on the loose. Won't stay on the reservation where he belongs." She sighed. "Well, I don't know why our government bothers, to tell you the truth. They try to teach them how to farm, but those people don't know how to do anything but rape and kill and steal."

Anne wondered if it would be unconscionably rude to just yawn in the woman's face. "Mrs. Thiel, I—"

The candle came dangerously close to Anne's face as Mrs. Thiel leaned forward to make her point. "Someone has to tell you the facts, dear. I'm sure Emma Hook hasn't bothered. Not that she's not a sweet woman, mind you. It's just that she got so attached to that Sam. Her husband never should have..."

It was simply too much. Anne opened her mouth in a great, unbridled yawn. "Oh, I'm so sorry, Mrs. Thiel."

The big woman didn't seem to know whether she had been deliberately insulted or not. She made a huffing sound and then said, "Well, sorry to keep you up so late, Mrs. McIntire." She turned and waddled the final few steps to the door to Anne's room. "There's a lamp and matches on the dresser just inside," she said. "I'll say good-night now."

Anne sighed inwardly as she turned the knob on the door. "Good night, Mrs. Thiel." She slipped inside the dark room before the woman could answer, pulling the door closed behind her.

"And good riddance," she whispered, just before a large hand slid over her mouth and an ironlike arm clenched around her waist.

It had seemed like such a good idea earlier as he'd hoisted himself through Mrs. Thiel's window, then tiptoed to the room where Anne's luggage was piled high against a wall. Sam felt like humming as he stripped to his buckskins and moccasins, then took the leather thong from his hair and let the dark mass fall to his shoulders. He stood in front of the dresser, in the swath of moonlight coming from the window, and grinned in the mirror while he parted his hair in the center and twisted it into two braids, and then streaked his face with the red cheek paint he'd stolen from Sally's room. A fierce bolt of lightning on the right. Three hard lines on the left. A slash on his chin. Half-breed turned full-blooded Apache.

Then he waited by the door until he heard voices in the hall. Mostly what he heard was Mrs. Thiel's sharp, complaining voice, like a saw rasping through lumber, Sam thought. He could imagine the strained expression on Annie's face as her ingrained politeness warred with her need to speak out in his defense.

Candlelight dipped under the door, then disappeared. Sam held his breath. He closed his eyes, envisioning the scene about to take place. Annie didn't scare easily, so he was going to have to do a little more than just toss her around the room.

On the other hand, he didn't want to hurt her. And, considering the difference in their sizes, that was a fact he had to keep in mind continually. Her spirit might be tough, but her body was small and delicate. A wrong move and one of her bones could snap like a twig in his hand. The mere thought of it made him wince. The whole point of this charade was to keep her from getting hurt. What irony, Sam thought, if he were the one to seriously injure her.

But in order to sufficiently frighten her, he was going to have to subdue her, then put on a good, dress-ripping, hard-handed show of attempted rape, all the while keeping his identity concealed. Suddenly, he couldn't imagine touching Anne's soft, ivory skin without murmuring her name.

It wasn't going to work. What the hell had he been thinking of anyway when he concocted this ridiculous plan? The whiskey he'd drunk must have addled his brain. Maybe his longing for Annie had finally driven him crazy. Or maybe this was just his desperate way of being close to her, of touching her without having to admit to himself that each day brought agony when he couldn't touch her.

The voices were right outside the door now. Sam gritted his teeth. He wished he hadn't come. He was lying in wait for her like a predator, while the truth was that Annie, all unsuspecting, was the huntress. It was Sam who was trapped—wanting her, his heart battering against his ribs, his blood rushing through his veins like a hot river at flood stage.

When she slipped into the dark room, he was careful not to hurt her as he stifled her scream. Then he was nearly overcome by the feel of her in his arms, overwhelmed by the sweet lilac fragrance of her hair, staggered by his desire for her. Her small body stiffened with fear, and then she sank her teeth into the palm of his hand, and at the same time drove her heel into his knee.

Sam bit his lips to keep from yelping. Somehow, in all his fantasies, he hadn't imagined Annie fighting back so hard. It was like trying to subdue five feet of tornado without harming it.

"Annie, stop. It's me," he whispered. He felt her body slacken immediately, so he removed his hand from her mouth and brought it to his own to lick his wounds.

Anne's heart was pumping fiercely. "What in blazes got into you, Sam Hook?" she rasped as she felt across the top of the bureau for a match to light the lamp. When the wick caught, Anne looked in the mirror and saw

Sam's reflection. The thick black braids hung nearly to his shoulders. The chiselled planes of his face were accented with red paint. His bronzed chest gleamed with a light sheen of sweat. An authentic Apache warrior. A wounded warrior now, as he stood sucking the palm of his hand where she had bitten him.

Anne approached him slowly, the way she would have approached a lion with a thorn in its paw. His dark eyes were wary as she took his hand and turned it palm up. There was a neat semicircular impression. Thankfully, only one tooth had broken through the callused skin.

She pressed her lips to the wound, then raised her eyes. They twinkled with moonlight and lamplight and mirth. "You're lucky I'm not rabid, Sam," she said.

A grin touched his lips, then disappeared. He pulled his hand from hers. "You're lucky I'm not somebody else."

Her hand reached up to grasp one of the thick braids. "What in the world are you doing, all plaited and streaked like that?"

Sam twisted his head, wrenching the braid from her fingers. "I was on my way to a masked ball, Annie. For chrissake, what do you think I was trying to do?"

Anne just stared at his fierce expression. "I really don't know, Sam. Trying to frighten me, I suppose, although I haven't the slightest idea why." She couldn't resist the temptation to fit her arms around his waist. "I'm so happy to see you. Oh, Sam, how I've missed you. How I've missed holding you like this."

He lifted his eyes to the ceiling, letting his arms hang limply at his sides, reminding himself that he should never plan anything while he had a whiskey glass in his hand, warning himself not to respond to her embrace as her hands roved over his back and her lips began a tender exploration of his chest. He was loath to even grasp her to move her away, afraid that just that slight a touch would break his resolve. But he couldn't endure her soft lips much longer.

"Annie, stop," he said, lowering his head now and breathing in the sweetness of her pale hair.

Her response was to flick her tongue across his hard male nipple.

A ragged groan escaped Sam's throat as desire burned through him like fire along a fuse. His knees nearly buckled as he locked her in his embrace. And as his hungry mouth sought hers, he knew he was as lost as ever a man could be.

Chapter Fifteen

Lost. Lost in the fragrant silken forest of her blond hair. Lost in the honeyed depths of her mouth. In the snowy valley between her lovely breasts. In the only heaven he would ever know. Lost in heaven while his body flamed as if touched by the fires of hell.

His voracious mouth and insistent hands kindled a like fire in Anne, and she unlaced his buckskin trousers with deft speed, reaching for him, stroking and stoking the fire hotter still.

There was no time for gentle caresses and whispered endearments as Sam lowered her to the floor, swept her skirts out of his way and whisked off the last silken barriers to his need. No time to prepare her for the thunder of his need, but a single touch told him she was ready. And the single word she uttered. "Now."

He entered the hidden heaven of her, buried himself deep inside her, lost himself completely and never wanted to be found.

She matched him thrust for thrust, shuddered almost as violently and settled into a breathless, stunned after-glow. Her fingers drifted lazily over his slick back.

"Annie," he murmured near her ear in a voice drained of strength, drenched in only lassitude now. "Did I hurt you, love? I didn't mean—"

"Shh. You pleasured me. Completely. You always do."

He slid into sleep, so lost, so truly found.

Anne woke with her arm draped over Sam's chest, her legs entwined with his, their hair tangled together in a web of yellow and black. The pale light of dawn had replaced the fragile moonlight in the room. Sam was deeply asleep now, his chest rising and falling rhythmically beneath her arm. She splayed her hand open to feel the smooth warmth of his skin. A slow heat spread through her, like a strong and intoxicating liquor. Could she ever get enough of him? she wondered. Could they ever get enough of each other?

Her lips curved into a sleepy, honeyed smile. Heaven knew they had tried last night. They had barely slept. Their lovemaking had been fierce and fast, like a thunderstorm over the desert. Only after that first passionate coming together did Sam even begin to slowly unbutton her dress, his fingers drifting over each inch of skin he disclosed, his warm lips following in their wake.

Still adrift in the aftermath of their initial loving, Anne felt buoyant in his arms as he carried her to the bed, as if she were floating on a warm, lazy current. And then, as Sam's ravenous mouth took hers and his deft fingers teased, the current surged once more inside her and soon it was pulling them both along—through the moonlight on the white, white sheets, pale ivory limbs twined with bronze, murmuring words of love, climbing to heaven and falling back again and again.

Now, as morning light touched the corners of the room, Anne watched Sam's face in sleep. How contented he looked. At peace, briefly, with himself and the world. His black braids had come undone during the night and Anne had kissed the wild red slashes from his cheeks and chin. Her warrior had been undone, brought down at last by love.

She placed a soft kiss on his shoulder, tangy with salt now, smooth and hard. When he woke, she would tell him about their child. In the throes of last night's passion, she had withheld the news, fearing Sam would hold back, leery of hurting her. She had wanted him too much—all of him—to deny herself that pleasure. So she had kept her secret in the depths of her heart. But now it was time to tell him, to allow Sam to share the pleasure of the life their loving had brought forth.

He stirred, tensing for a moment as if he didn't know where he was or with whom. Then a slow smile warmed his face and his eyes kindled with a loving light as they opened wide on Anne's face.

"Witch!" he whispered as he gathered her against him, his hands roving over her sleep-warmed skin, his lips pressing soft kisses on her hair, her forehead, her eyelids.

So much for frightening her back to Syracuse, he thought. So much for any plans he had made that failed to include this beautifully obstinate female. He couldn't fight her anymore. It was like trying to put out a wildfire with a teacup of water. Like trying to tear out his own heart. Impossible.

He raised up on an elbow, gazing down into her round, expectant eyes. It was time. If they had a hundred years together...or only a hundred days...it had to be.

"Marry me, Annie," he said.

She smiled and closed her eyes, trying to preserve this moment for eternity. Her heart felt as if it were waltzing in time to the beat of Sam's strong heart, and, holding very still, she could have sworn she heard their baby's tiny heartbeat ticking like a little pocket watch.

"Oh, Sam. Oh, yes." She fit her arms around his neck and brought his mouth down to hers. "I love you so much," she said, kissing his mouth, his chin, his finely sculpted nose.

He stilled her with a thumb on her lips. "This isn't going to be a picnic, Annie. You know that, don't you? It doesn't matter how much we love each other. People aren't—"

"People!" she scoffed. "I don't care about people. I care about you and me and... oh, Sam, I have the most wonderful news for you."

There was a rough knock on the door, followed by Doris Thiel's voice. "Mrs. McIntire, are you awake?"

Anne's eyes widened in momentary panic before she remembered that when Sam had turned down the wick on the lamp last night he had also thrown the bolt on the door. There was no way Mrs. Thiel could get in. "Good morning," Anne called to her, forcing a heavy, sleep-laden note into her voice, and at the same time stifling a giggle as she watched Sam try to make his huge frame invisible under the thin covers.

"I didn't know how early you were planning to leave," the woman called. "I've made coffee and toast for you."

"Thank you."

After a pause, Doris Thiel cleared her throat. "Were you too warm last night, dear?"

Anne blinked, staring at the door, imagining the large woman's tiny, inquisitive eyes boring through the wood. "I was perfectly comfortable," she said.

"Oh," came the reply, followed by silence.

Sam raised the sheet and mouthed the words, "Get rid of her."

"I only inquired," Mrs. Thiel continued, "because it sounded like you were thrashing around half the night."

More than half the night, Anne thought, and what were you doing, staying awake listening, you old bat? "I tend to have nightmares," she said. "I hope I didn't disturb you."

"Not at all. Well, to be quite honest with you . . ."

Sam emerged from beneath the sheet, grimacing. As Mrs. Thiel continued to complain and quiz her guest through the closed door, he untangled himself from Anne and climbed out of the bed.

The first of their trials, he was thinking as he gathered up his clothes and got dressed. Maybe Mrs. Thiel was the person he should have accosted last night. Now that the sun was up it was going to be a neat trick climbing out her second-story window without being seen. And there was Annie—her pale hair streaming over her delicate shoulders, the sheet clutched to her delectable bosom, her attention directed toward her inquisitor on the opposite side of the door. Lord, how he loved her. He couldn't imagine ever loving anyone else.

He shrugged his shoulders into his shirt, wondering how he was going to protect her from all the perils that lay in wait, all the insults from the likes of Mrs. Thiel, all the physical threats from drunk and ignorant cowhands. For a second, he imagined Anne in her big, snow-white bed in Syracuse, wearing a white lace gown. Hell, he didn't even own a bed, let alone have a house to put one in!

Sam lowered himself beside her on the edge of the bed and ran his hand along the soft, creamy skin of her upper arm.

She tilted her head toward him. "I'll get up, Mrs. Thiel, and then I'll be out for breakfast in just a few minutes," she said, concluding her conversation with the talkative woman.

Sam traced small patterns on Anne's arm as she leaned against him, both of them listening to footsteps diminishing down the corridor.

"How will you get out of here?" Anne whispered at last.

"The same way I got in. Through a back window."

"Be careful." She pressed her lips to his ropy shoulder. "Now that you're truly mine, I expect you to take excellent care of yourself. At least when I'm not there to do it for you."

He slid his arms around her. "I don't know how I've survived for thirty years without you looking out for me, love," he said, his voice rich with warmth and mirth. "After you have your breakfast, why don't you meet me at the orphanage?"

"Benito!" she exclaimed, ashamed that in the joy of thinking of their unborn child she had momentarily forgotten about the little boy who was already born and just waiting for a home with them. "Do you think Father José will let him come with us right away?" That way, she thought, Benito would be accustomed to living with his new mother and father before his upstart young brother or sister came along.

"Slow down, Annie. Let's take this one step at a time, shall we? The padre's not exactly going to be turning cartwheels over this marriage."

Her eyebrows drew together in a frown. Not only would Father José disapprove of their marriage, she thought, but wait a few months and he'd really be clucking his tongue. By her calculations, she was nearly three months along. For the time being, her stomach was still flat. But it wouldn't be long and she'd be puffing out like a balloon.

Sam appeared distracted now as he walked to the window and looked out on the street. The tension in his body was evident, from the set of his broad shoulders to the tight grip of his fingers as he held back the curtain. His dark eyes scanned the street. She didn't even want to think what might happen if he were caught climbing out. One step at a time, she reminded herself. Sam had enough on his mind right now without the additional distraction of impending fatherhood. She'd tell him her news on the way out to The Hook. There would be plenty of time then. Time for him to savor the good news. Time for them to plan their future together.

Anne had rushed through breakfast with Mrs. Thiel, fending off her questions as best she could. She had dressed in a black velveteen riding habit and then had nearly flown down the street to the orphanage to meet Sam.

She thought now, as he squatted down with Benito on his knee, she had never seen him so content or so happy. For a man who rarely smiled, Sam was doing his fair share this morning. Father José, on the other hand, looked as if he'd eaten lemons for breakfast. Anne told him so.

The priest fingered the crucifix that hung around his neck. "I have grave concerns for you both," he said. "Your marriage will cause a great stir in this community. Not a happy stir, I am sorry to say."

"More like a tempest in a teapot," Anne sniffed.

Sam raised his eyes to the priest. "The worst of it will blow over pretty fast, Padre," he said. "We'll stay away

from town for a while. After a few months, most folks
will just ignore us.''

Father José clasped his hands together over the silver
cross. "I pray that you're right, my friend. For both your
sakes." He looked down at Benito. "And for the little
one's."

The two men exchanged dark glances then, as if they
were seeing into a future beyond Anne's ken. It frightened her. It angered her as well. All she and Sam wanted
was a chance at happiness. No one had the right to deny
them that.

"If anyone dares insult us," she said fiercely, "I'll tell
them a thing or two."

The priest laid a hand on her arm. "Do not have a
fool's courage, Mrs. McIntire. There are those who may
try to do you great harm." He lowered his gaze to Benito,
then pursed his lips. "This is not the time to say more.
Not in front of the child."

"It isn't merely a matter of approval or disapproval,
is it?" Her blue eyes widened with sudden understanding. "You're truly fearful for us, aren't you, Father?"

Sam shifted Benito onto the ground, then stood up.
"Not now, Annie," he said, his voice low and his eyes
steely.

She took a few steps away from Benito, who was ab-
sorbed in playing with the little wooden train she had
given him. "Now, Sam. I want to know why you and
Father José are both looking like you're about to go to a
hanging."

Father José pressed his index finger to his lips. "Not
in front of the *niño, señora*," he cautioned as he took her
arm and walked her away from the boy. Satisfied that
Benito could no longer hear them, the priest turned to
Sam. "You have told her nothing?" he asked.

Sam shrugged helplessly. "We love each other, Padre. We want to get married and share our lives. We want to be left alone." There was an agonized tone in his voice, as if he knew he were asking the impossible.

"What hasn't Sam told me, Father?" Anne asked.

The curly-haired priest smiled wanly as he turned his crucifix over in his hand. "You said we looked as if we were about to attend a hanging, señora. Your words were perhaps more true than you realize."

Sam held up a hand to silence the priest, but Anne caught it and clasped it. She looked up into his dark and somber face.

"I need to know everything, Sam," she said. "The good as well as the bad. I need to know just what to expect so I'll be ready for it." She clasped his hand even tighter as she nodded to Father José. "Go ahead, Father."

"There was a half-breed—part Navajo, I believe—by the name of Billy Preston, who used to work at the livery stable. The owner then was Joshua Kemp. He had a daughter named Olive—a pretty girl with hair as fair as yours, señora. Billy and Olive ran off to marry, and then they made the grave mistake of returning to San Miguel."

As the priest spoke, Anne glanced at Sam, whose face was hard and expressionless as a stone.

Father José sighed. "To make a long story short, they had been back but a few days when Billy was discovered hanged from the rafters of the stable. The men who did it forced his young bride to watch him die. Then they had their way with her. She never revealed their identity, most likely because they threatened to kill her if she did. Her father sold the livery stable and took her back to Illinois.'' The priest paused, then shifted his gaze to Sam. ''How many years ago was that, my friend? Five? Six?''

''What difference does it make?'' Sam said through gritted teeth. ''It happened. But it's not going to happen again. I won't let it.''

Anne stepped closer to Sam's side, her hand still in his. She had thought his objections to their being together were solely for her sake, for her safety. It had never occurred to her that his own life was jeopardized by their love. Her heart felt leaden with dread, but she was determined not to let him know. ''I'm not worried,'' she said. ''We'll handle any trouble that comes our way.''

''Then allow me to worry for you both,'' said Father José. ''I will keep you in my prayers. Do not think ill of me when I tell you that I cannot let Benito go into such danger. I would never forgive myself if something happened to the child.''

''Padre,'' pleaded Sam.

But the priest held up his hands. ''No. I am sorry. You may visit him as often as you like, but he will remain here until I am satisfied that he will be safe.''

As if each moment now were precious, Sam walked back to where Benito was playing, crooked his long legs and sat down on the ground with the boy. Both Anne and the priest watched the two of them—the boy who needed a father; the man who craved a son. Their hair was almost identical in color and texture, though Benito's was cut short and blunt across his forehead. Their complexions were the same rich bronze. When they smiled, their strong white teeth gleamed against their dark faces.

Anne found her hand unconsciously moving to her abdomen. They were a family—the four of them. She was determined that they would live like a normal family, laughing and loving and free from fear. But when? she wondered. And where? And, heaven help them, how?

Mrs. Thiel's face looked big and pink as a watermelon as she lugged another of Anne's suitcases to the front door of the mercantile. "There," she said as she ran the back of one hand across her sweat-glazed forehead and studied the pile of luggage. "I don't think much of the idea of you going off by yourself, Mrs. McIntire. I surely don't. A lady like you has no business..."

Grateful as she was for the woman's help, Anne hadn't asked for it. Nor had she asked for a piece of Mrs. Thiel's mind—her narrow mind. Anne walked out onto the street. Come on, Sam, she thought. Don't leave me here with this harpy too long or I'm liable to say things I shouldn't.

There was no activity down at the livery stable, where he had gone to rent a wagon. One flea-bitten nag was tethered there, too weary, it appeared, even to swish its tail at flies. Anne looked down the street in the opposite direction, her hand raised to shade her eyes. Sam was standing outside the cantina, dark hair riffling in the late morning breeze, one lean hip slung up on the hitching post. He was talking to... Anne squinted. It was Rosa, the little Mexican girl who worked at The Hook. Her thin brown arms jerked up and down like pump handles and she was pacing back and forth in front of Sam, dust swirling up around her bare feet. Something was definitely wrong, Anne thought, but before she could take a step in that direction, Mrs. Thiel waddled to her side.

The big woman looked down the street and made a harrumphing noise in her throat. "I didn't know *he* was in town," she said. "Seems like that Sam never works anymore. Always hanging around the cantina. Well, long as he's here, you can probably get him to take you out to The Hook.'' She gave Anne a look as hard as granite. ''I guess if you rode out there with him once, it wouldn't hurt none to do it again. Long as you can stand it.''

Anne bit her tongue, reminding herself that she was going to be living in or near San Miguel for years to come and that lighting into Doris Thiel was not the way to begin her long-term residence. ''I believe I'll just go see what's going on,'' Anne said, leaving the mountainous woman without a second glance.

As she neared the cantina, she became increasingly aware of Rosa's distress. The girl's voice was high and insistent. Her dark brown eyes blinked rapidly, and she kept gesturing southwest in the direction of The Hook. Sam, on the other hand, remained placid as he leaned on the hitching rail, arms folded across his chest and head bent toward the diminutive Mexican, his whole attention focused on her.

''What's going on?'' Anne asked, as she too leaned a hip against the wooden rail.

Sam lifted a hand, chewed briefly on his thumbnail. Rosa, as soon as she recognized Anne, began flailing her arms again and speaking so fast that Anne couldn't understand a single word.

''Slow down, Rosa,'' she told the girl in her own slow and careful Spanish. ''What's wrong?''

The dark-haired girl swallowed hard, as if to put a brake on her speech. She continued in a blend of both languages. ''Oh, Señora McIntire. It's Señor Jay. He has gone loco.'' Rosa touched the palm of her hand to her forehead. ''He is on his way to Santa Fe to—''

Sam shifted off the hitching rail. ''All right, Rosa,'' he said to her, at the same time looking out of the corner of his eye at the little group of onlookers loitering nearby, all of them drawn by Rosa's hysterics. He placed his large hand on the girl's shoulder. "Go inside the cantina. Tell Sally I asked her to fix you a lemonade."

"But Señor Sam..."

His grip tightened on the gathered white cotton of her *camisa* and his eyes skewered her. "No sense letting all of San Miguel know our problems, is there?"

Rosa blinked. "No, señor." Her eyes skimmed the curious little crowd and her deep olive complexion blazed crimson. "A thousand pardons, Señor Sam. I would never say or do anything to bring shame to your family."

"I know that," he said quietly, nudging her toward the door of the cantina. "I'll take care of this, Rosa. Nothing bad will happen to my mother or the ranch, I promise you. Now you go on and get something cool to drink."

As Rosa's thin shoulders disappeared through the door, Anne moved closer to Sam. "What happened? What has Jay done?" She kept her voice low and tried to impose a measure of calm in her expression as her eyes raked Sam's face for a clue to the recent events at The Hook. A fire smoldered deep inside him, flickering in his dark eyes, tightening his mouth, blanching it at the corners.

"Damn him," he hissed.

She caught his arm. "What, Sam? What is it?"

"He's going to Santa Fe to try to sell The Hook."

Anne's mouth dropped open. "What?" she exclaimed. "But he can't do that. Your father left The Hook to both of you."

"Morally, yes. Legally, he left it to Jay, to avoid any problems that might arise from my background."

"He can do it, then? He can sell it right out from under you?"

Sam nodded as a muscle worked in his jaw.

One of the onlookers stepped forward. The man spat across his shoulder. "You got trouble out at The Hook, Sam?"

Though her arm was barely touching his, Anne could feel Sam stiffen. "Nothing we can't handle." His reply was terse, uttered through clenched teeth. Then he clamped a hand on Anne's elbow. "Come on," he said, propelling her out into the dusty street.

She had to take three quick steps for every one of his long strides. When he stopped in front of the mercantile, Anne stumbled into him.

"Sam, for goodness' sake," she exclaimed as she stood in his dark shadow beneath the beady, curious gaze of Doris Thiel.

"Trouble at home, Sam?" the big woman asked, a little trill in her voice, as if there were nothing that would please her more than to hear of some catastrophe.

"Mrs. Thiel, I wonder if it'd be all right if Mrs. McIntire stayed on with you for a few days?" he asked her.

Before the woman could answer, Anne spoke out. "Absolutely not, Sam. I'm going with you. If there's trouble..." Her voice trailed off as she saw Mrs. Thiel's doughy face sharpen with interest. "I'm not staying here. That's final."

Sam sighed roughly. There she stood, her arms crossed, her lower lip jutting out, her eyes like blue ice on a mountain lake. "Where's your luggage?" he asked.

Anne pointed to Mrs. Thiel's doorstep.

"I'll get the wagon," he said, turning on his heel and walking toward the livery stable as he heard Anne let out a small but clearly victorious breath behind him.

There was no point arguing with her, he thought. He had to return to the ranch, anyway, to pick up Jay's trail. No sense starting out their life together butting heads, when all he had to do was take Annie along now, leave her safely at The Hook with his mother, and then take off after Jay alone. It was one small victory he could afford to give her. There might not be too many more. For either of them.

Chapter Sixteen

The dapple gray pitched his head as if to protest pulling in harness with a rented steed. Sam held the reins loosely in his big hands, his dark eyes focused a quarter mile ahead of the jouncing wagon. Anne leaned against him, their bodies touching from shoulder to hip to knee, then angled her head back to see Rosa, curled in sleep, the girl's dark head rolling with each rut in the hard earth.

When Sam gazed down at her, his slow smile flushed out a butterfly from the pit of Anne's stomach and she dipped her head to rest against his shoulder. She still hadn't told him about their child. The leisurely ride back to The Hook hadn't happened as she had planned. Instead they were travelling as fast as the ramshackle wagon and the mismatched horses would allow.

Damn you, Jay Hook, she thought. Not only was he interfering with Sam's life now, but with hers and her child's as well. Now was hardly the time to tell Sam her news. He'd let her win too easily back in San Miguel, loading her luggage and helping her into the wagon without so much as a scowl or an errant eyebrow. She knew Sam Hook well enough to know that he didn't lose graciously. He had something up that blue chambray sleeve of his, and Anne guessed he planned to dump her with Emma this evening and then ride out alone in pursuit of his brother.

She nuzzled her cheek against his hard arm. You don't know it yet, Sam, she thought, but you're not going alone. Her news would keep a few more days. Long enough to help him rescue The Hook from the madman's cruel plan.

"Tired?" Sam asked her now, tilting his head to touch hers.

"No," she lied.

"You should be. I didn't let you get a lot of sleep last night, Annie," he murmured.

She watched his bronze thumbs smoothing over the leather reins, wishing it were her skin beneath his touch the way it had been last night. "So I noticed," she said. "Shame on you, Sam."

Although her tone had been light and teasing, only her words seemed to register on him. His knuckles whitened as he clenched the reins. "I'm sorry, Annie. I should have put a brake on myself, shouldn't have made so many demands. It's just that..." His face darkened as if the sun had slipped behind a cloud. "It's just that you do something to me. When I touch you, I—I lose control."

A crisp little laugh issued from her lips. "Good," she said.

He looked down at her. His black eyes were stormy. They flickered as with heat lightning. "Good?" he echoed incredulously. Sam shook his head. "I took you four times, for God's sake."

She tilted a devilish grin up into his dark countenance. "Five, Sam."

His lips tightened. Anne could have sworn that she saw the rose tint of a blush on his bronzed cheeks.

"Five, then," he gritted. "I'm sorry I made you—"

Now Anne's eyes flashed. "Sam Hook, don't you ever apologize for loving me or for anything that you say or do while you're in my bed. In *our* bed." She sat up straighter as she smoothed the dark fabric of her riding habit over her knees. Her own face was flushed now, and heat suffused her pale cheeks as she recalled their tangled limbs, Sam's low voice tempting her and her own half-swallowed moans. If he was apologizing for his fierce loving, did he expect her to be sorry for her less-than-ladylike behavior?

Anne's throat was tight and her voice was just above a whisper. "I'm not ashamed of loving you, Sam, or of showing you how much."

He closed his eyes, as if trying to find the right words to say to her etched behind his lids. What he saw there instead was Annie's smooth, moonlit face, her mouth bruised by his kisses, her delicate neck arched and throbbing and slick with his own sweat. He had ridden her like some wild mare he was trying to break, again and again, and when she finally lay softly whimpering and utterly spent beneath him, he had felt more like a sated beast than a conquering lover. He had hated himself for his lack of control, for the way his body defied his better judgment.

This woman should have been wooed slowly with gentle fingertips and teasing kisses—and Sam had tried. God knew he had tried. But each time his cool, languid, white man's kisses grazed her skin a fire flashed through him. A wild Apache fire that took his blood to the boiling point and turned his soft kisses hard. When he wanted to merely taste her, he devoured her. When he meant to merely suckle gently at her breast, he nipped and gorged. He wanted to bring sweet words of love to her throat. Instead he forced urgent, husky moans.

He had yet to show her those slow, more courtly forms of loving ... gentle waltzes rather than fierce, fast mating dances. With time, Sam thought, and with patience, he would be able to rein in some of the urgency he felt. With practice, perhaps he could contain the fires she stirred in him.

He slipped his arm around her shoulder and drew her against him, gently, gently.

"I'm glad you love me, Annie," he said.

"Jay snapped. He just snapped." Emma Hook rocked on the front porch, twisting a handkerchief in her hands. Her eyes were moist and red-rimmed, and her hair seemed grayer than Anne remembered. Her aunt looked ten years older.

Sam leaned against a rough-hewn post, his arms crossed casually as he listened to his mother. The setting sun colored his face a rich gold as it threaded blue highlights through his black hair.

"What set him off?" he asked her now.

Emma dabbed at her eyes. "He saw the wire Anne sent, telling me she was coming back." Emma shook out the twisted handkerchief. "There was no reasoning with him after that. He was like a crazy man, Sam. He drank and he drank, and he kept raving about how you two were plotting to take The Hook away from him by having a child, who would eventually inherit everything. I— I could never repeat to you the harsh things he said. He took the deed with him, Sam, to Santa Fe."

Sam nodded as he calmly began rolling a cigarette. Anne noticed how rock solid his hands were while her own, like her aunt's, were trembling.

"What are you going to do?" Anne asked him.

His whole attention was focused on the shreds of tobacco he was arranging on a small rectangle of paper. He rolled it slowly and firmly, then licked the edge of the paper to seal it.

"Sam?" Anne wondered if he even heard her.

He lit a match with his thumbnail and held it to the cigarette until it caught, then he shook out the flame and stared at the blackened tip of the wooden match.

"I'm going to bring him back," he said. "I'll leave first thing in the morning."

Anne looked briefly at Emma, who was rocking and nodding her gray head in time with the chair. Her face was washed of all expression now and her linen handkerchief fell limply from her hand.

"I'm going with you," Anne said, returning her gaze to Sam and meeting his dark eyes.

He shook his head as he blew out a hard stream of smoke. "My brother's crazy, Annie. I don't want you getting in his way."

She stood up and smoothed out the gathers of her skirt. Now that Sam was truly hers, she wasn't going to let him out of her sight. His fate was hers now. "If you leave without me, Sam, I'll only follow," she said. "I'll be a lot safer riding beside you than a quarter mile behind."

He shot a supplicating gaze at Emma, but his mother only smiled wanly and said, "The girl has a mind of her own, son."

"I'll just go in the kitchen and have Rosa put some supplies together for us," Anne said coolly as Sam swore through clenched teeth. He turned then and stalked toward the bunkhouse.

Anne placed a comforting hand on her aunt's shoulder before going in the house. "Don't worry about Jay,

Aunt Emma. Maybe he's calmed down already and is on his way back.''

Alone then, Emma continued to rock, staring bleakly into the fiery red-and-orange patterns of the sunset, wondering if she should confess to Anne that it wasn't Jay she was worried about now. It was Sam. Sam, whose hands were the size and shape of his father's. Sam, who had inherited his father's strength and stubbornness. Sam, who tilted his head sometimes and sighed in perfect imitation of his sire.

She had known it the moment John brought the tawny baby home, for she had seen the intense pride in her husband's eyes. Half-breed, yes, but still John's son, John's gift to his barren wife. She never asked about the mother. Emma never wanted to know. She knew it would have hurt John deeply to be forced to admit his unfaithfulness, no matter his motives. It was John's secret, and she vowed she would never admit she knew the truth.

What would the truth accomplish, anyway? Sam's lot in life wouldn't change. He'd still be a half-breed no matter who had sired him. Worse, her beloved son might leave her to seek his natural mother.

Emma rocked in the dying light, her head muddled and her heart torn between truth and falsehoods, between her sons.

Sam pulled the cinch so hard that the dapple gray stomped its front hoof, then angled its great head back to nip Sam's elbow.

"Sorry, fella," Sam said as he eased the strap, then stroked the huge horse's flank. "Looks like I'm a damn savage with you, too."

He pulled out a kink in the saddle blanket, then looked over his shoulder at the house. It was lit up like a fiesta.

The yellow glow of the oil lamps through the windows made the chilly morning seem warmer. He could see his mother and Annie and Rosa bustling around inside, packing last-minute provisions into saddle bags.

What did they think this was, some damn picnic they were going on? His mother, of all people, should have known better after having spent so many years witnessing Jay's vicious moods and outbursts of violence. He wished she would have talked some sense into Annie instead of silently encouraging her to go. I know what you're doing, Mama, he thought. You think if Annie's with me Jay won't try anything crazy. I hope to God you're right.

Through the window now he saw Annie take the Spencer rifle from the gun rack, then fill the pockets of her jacket with ammunition. Jay's rifle, Sam had noticed the evening before, was gone. Well, hell, he thought, touching the Colt holstered at his hip. We're all armed and dangerous now, aren't we?

No matter how many times he told himself that it only made sense to take precautions with Raging Owl and his followers on the loose, Sam didn't completely believe it. He was going after Jay with a gun. Somewhere in the back of his mind he sensed that that was what his brother wanted—that Jay had finally maneuvered him into a lethal confrontation.

As he finished saddling Anne's horse, he was aware of the tremor in his hands and the hard knot in his gut. He gave a quick jerk to the horn and cantle, then pulled the cinch tighter. When he was satisfied with the fit of the saddle, Sam checked his gun for the third time that morning to make certain it was empty.

His tracks were easy to follow. Too easy, as far as Sam was concerned. Jay was riding the black gelding with the nick in its right rear shoe. The tracks were distinct, which meant his brother was setting a slow pace, not hurrying toward Santa Fe as everyone thought, but hanging back to wait for whoever was following him.

Sam hadn't told Annie of his suspicions, in part because he didn't want to frighten her, but mostly because he harbored the hope that Jay's threats were empty. Brothers could hate. Sam knew that well. But they didn't kill each other.

"Shouldn't we be going a little faster?" Anne asked him now as she nudged her horse with her knee.

"This pace is fine," he answered.

She planted a hand on her hip. "I hope you're not dawdling on my account, Sam. I'm a better rider than I used to be, you know."

"How's your backside, Annie?"

"Perfect," she snapped.

He graced her then with a warm grin, the first since they'd been on the trail. "I'd say that's a pretty good description."

Her cheeks colored, despite the pleasure she took from his admiration. "That isn't what I meant, Sam Hook, and you know it." As a little flame sputtered inside her, Anne marvelled at what this man could do to her without even trying. With a grin and a few words he was able to kindle a fire deep within her. Her cheeks flamed as she recalled what he could do when he set his mind to it.

"You're blushing, Annie." Sam's grin widened.

"Hush," she said as she urged her horse forward a few steps ahead of his.

How strange, she thought, as they continued to make their way west under a wide blue sky, that she had been married to Daniel for five years, had nursed him and known his body so intimately, yet had never felt a twinge of heat or desire. She couldn't remember now if those twinges had even been there before Daniel was wounded. Surely, she thought, she'd remember if they had been.

She looked over her shoulder at Sam now. He sat straight, but there was a relaxed quality about him. His hands rested on his thighs, reins drifting through his fingers as his thumb idly moved over the leather. His long, buckskin-clad legs appeared to extend forever before meeting the stirrups. The mere sight of him could set her heart skittering. How lucky she was to have found him. How happy she was to love him and to be loved by him. How good it felt to be carrying his child, a tawny, dark-eyed son, perhaps. She longed to tell him.

Her eyes shifted to the west, where the mountains were just beginning to darken. Where are you, Jay? she asked silently. The sooner they found him, the sooner they could go home and truly begin their lives.

A rock formation loomed directly ahead of them, a huge edifice of red boulders that appeared to rise out of nowhere.

"Ride behind me, Annie," Sam said quietly.

She reined her horse in, allowing his big gray to come shoulder to shoulder with hers. Sam's hand rested on the butt of his gun now.

"What's wrong?" she asked, her eyes following his hard gaze toward the red rocks.

"Nothing," he said, realizing she had no idea what a perfect site this was for an ambush. Why should a city girl, born and bred, even be aware of such dangers? Annie looked and just saw rocks, while he looked and saw Indians behind them. Or Jay. Right now he wasn't sure which would be worse.

The dapple gray was nearing the rocks when they suddenly came alive with Apache warriors, bows drawn and war clubs held high. A single painted brave on horse-back came around the rocks from the left. Two more rode out from the right.

"Oh, my God," breathed Anne.

Sam pulled his horse up. "Don't say anything, Annie," he cautioned. "Don't do anything. Don't even move."

How could she? she thought. Fear had frozen her muscles. She recalled the brutal aftermath of the Indian attack she had witnessed when she first arrived in San Miguel and wondered bleakly if these were the same men who had murdered the rancher and his wife.

As Sam raised his hands shoulder high, palms toward the Indians, Anne thought about reaching into the scabbard on her saddle for the rifle. But even assuming she could move quickly enough, there were too many Indians. She counted six on the rocks above them and two on the right. One more on the left appeared to be the leader. Anne noted that all the other men kept glancing his way, waiting, perhaps, for a sign or a signal. Sam, too, focused his attention on the fierce-looking warrior.

To her surprise, the man raised a dark hand in imitation of Sam's gesture. Then he gave his horse a quick little kick and rode forward, stopping only when the dapple gray stamped a nervous hoof at the approach of the Indian's mount. The man sat quietly looking at Sam's face, studying him.

It struck her then how much the two men resembled one another. Their hair was the same length and texture. Their high cheekbones matched. Even their stony expressions seemed to mirror each other as their eyes locked.

Slowly, the Indian turned his gaze on her. He urged his horse toward her, then reached out and took a hank of her hair in his hand. He studied it as if he thought pale hair ought to feel somehow different from dark hair, as if it were a strange and foreign element. Just as Anne began to wonder if she were going to be scalped, the warrior let the lock of hair fall from his dark fingers and turned back toward Sam, who sat poised as if ready to kill the man if he touched more than her hair.

This perusal seemed to go on forever. Anne could feel her heart bashing against her ribs. She had to remind herself to breathe. Then to her utter amazement, she saw the Indian's mouth crook into a little grin. He said something over his shoulder to his companions, who nodded solemnly. The warrior took one last, long look at Sam, then whirled his horse around and signalled his men to follow him.

Anne let out her breath in a ragged sigh.

"Stay quiet a little longer," Sam whispered as they both watched the Indians' horses kicking up dust. At last, when they were a half mile away, Sam eased a long leg over his saddle and sat with his knee cocked over the horn while he began to roll a cigarette.

Anne ran a dry tongue over her lips, not certain of her voice yet, not wanting Sam to suspect how terrified she had been. "What do you suppose that was all about?" she asked, watching Sam trying to control the tremor in his own fingers enough to roll a decent smoke.

Sam shrugged. "Beats me."

"He looked at you so strangely, Sam. It was almost as if he thought he recognized you."

"He probably did," Sam said, striking a match and drawing the flame into the tip of the cigarette.

"What do you mean?"

Sam exhaled a thin stream of smoke, then picked a stray piece of tobacco from his lower lip. "That was Raging Owl. It's more than likely he's my cousin!"

"Your cousin!"

His dark eyes speared her. "For all I know, Annie, he's my damn brother."

They bedded down by the red rocks. Not long after they had both given in to sleep, Anne woke with a jolt, sure she had heard something in the dark outside their small circle of firelight. Sam's arms tightened around her as he murmured sleepy endearments into the nape of her neck. She would have gotten up to take a look around, but Sam swung his leg over hers, virtually pinning her in place. When his hand curled warmly over her breast, Anne sighed and tried to find her way back to sleep.

She realized then she'd been dreaming about bronze-skinned men with harsh lines smeared on their faces. Apaches, of course. But Sam had assured her they were long gone by the time he flung out their bedrolls in the shadow of the rocks.

After his comment about being related to Raging Owl, he had refused to discuss it further and had remained quiet all evening, smoking, staring off into the darkness. Anne knew better than to press him when he retreated into himself that way, but she couldn't help her curiosity. Silly, she supposed, that she had never given a thought to his Apache origins and the probability of his having relatives.

Raging Owl had looked enough like Sam to be his brother. No doubt that accounted for the man's intense scrutiny of Sam and for his mysterious grin. It was also, she realized, why she and Sam were still alive this minute and not lying all bloody and dismembered at the foot of these rocks.

But rather than appearing glad for the encounter, Sam seemed upset by it, as if the vivid reminder of his Indian half were painful.

Anne heard the noise again. Something. Someone. Slowly, she slid an arm from beneath the blanket and stretched her fingers toward the Spencer rifle.

A shot cracked like thunder. She felt Sam's body quiver at her back and heard a soft moan issue from his lips, then everything was still. She curled her fingers around the stock of the rifle just as another shot rang out. Then a searing pain tore through her head and blotted out her consciousness.

Chapter Seventeen

Anne dragged her eyelids open. Her head felt heavy and her mind like a thick skein of black wool—ravelling, unravelling, tangling, then twisting tight. A bright disk of light from above assaulted her eyes. She closed them, letting the dark skein unwind once more.

Hands moved her, and she could do nothing but submit, caught as she was in the thick and jumbled dark. Voices spoke above her, beside and around her, but she could not understand.

The hands were gentle and the voices were kind. They were her world, her universe. Gradually, the blackness diminished to dull gray. Then the gray dispersed like smoke in the wind.

She opened her eyes to a circle of blue sky centered in a dark dome. A face, round and sweet and coppery like a rising harvest moon, moved into her field of vision. The face smiled.

"Smart Woman said you would awake today. She was right." The woman touched a cool fingertip to Anne's forehead. "The pain is gone?"

Pain? Anne searched for it in her head. There was no pain. "Yes," she said. "All gone." The sound of her own voice was like an old friend. It warmed her, made her feel more alive. She frowned then, reaching deep in her thoughts for something that eluded her. A question. A concern. Something—what was it?—just out of reach.

The woman edged closer, her long black braids bobbing on her shoulders and the deep fringe of her sleeves brushing against Anne's cheek. Her dark eyes were as warm and liquid as a doe's. "Your man is hurt," she said softly. "He cannot walk."

"Daniel?" Anne murmured, aware now that her lips were dry and cracked.

"I do not know his name. We call him Twenty-One Scars." The woman lowered her dark lashes. "Smart Woman counted."

Anne blinked. Not Daniel. It couldn't be. Daniel was dead. Her head ached suddenly and fiercely behind her eyes. "What—what did you say?"

"Your man is hurt," the woman repeated slowly.

Anne waved a weak, impatient hand. "No. The name. Tell me the name."

"Twenty-One Scars."

She heard the shot again as if it were inside her head. She felt him shudder against her back, and heard the moan that broke from his throat. "Sam," she whispered as the gray light deepened to an all-encompassing dark.

Rosa stood in the door. A lamp burned in the foyer behind her, casting her shadow across the boards of the porch. "It is getting late, señora." She shivered and rubbed her upper arms. "Chilly, too. Will you come in soon?"

Emma continued to rock, and as she rocked, she stared at the spot in the mountains where the sun had disappeared earlier. "Not just yet, Rosa," she said. "You go back in. I'll be along soon."

Emma looked pale and drawn. She was still wearing the gray skirt and white cotton blouse she had worn when Jay returned—alone. It was as if she hoped to stop time somehow by not changing clothes. As if, were she to put on a new outfit, she would be admitting the past and acknowledging the future. Emma kept her old clothes on, kept silent most of the time and kept gazing west.

Rosa sighed. "He is gone, señora. Señor Sam is dead."

Emma drew her lower lip between her teeth. She shook her head as if to ward off the words. "No," she said.

Stepping onto the porch, Rosa lowered herself awkwardly beside the rocker. "He is dead. They are both dead. Señor Jay buried them."

The tempo of her rocking increased. "Jay *said* he buried them."

Rosa gripped the arm of her chair, wresting it to a halt. "I saw their saddles, señora. On the horses your son brought back. They were covered with blood."

"You saw what my son wanted you to see," Emma said. She turned her eyes to the girl's worried face and spoke in a low, measured tone. "Have you forgotten what happened to Natividad?"

Eyes wide, Rosa struggled to her feet. "What are you saying, señora? I cannot believe...Señor Jay is sick with grief. He is a changed man. He has been so kind to me this past week."

Emma merely nodded. Not only had her younger son been kind, but he had also been calm and quiet. Like a crazed horse who'd just had a burr removed from beneath his saddle. Like a man who'd just rid himself of a powerful and hated enemy. Like Cain, perhaps, after he'd killed Abel.

She had no proof, of course. Only the word of the young Apache girl who'd knocked on the kitchen door a

few days ago. Sent by Sam to allay his mother's fears, the
girl said he had been shot in the back. The Apaches had
discovered them, both Sam and Anne, and had taken
them to their campsite in the foothills of the Sangre de
Cristos. Emma kept the girl's visit a secret as she turned
the ugly possibilities over and over in her heart.

It could have been any of the Indian-hating cowhands
in the territory who had done it. Lord knew there were
enough of them who could be roused to shoot a half-
breed in the back, especially seeing him with a pale creature like Anne McIntire. Emma hoped so. She prayed it
was true. But Jay's strange mood and his deliberate lie
about burying his brother kept haunting her.

Both Jay and Rosa thought she was grieving as she sat
for hours, rocking, looking west. The truth was that she
was contemplating her life, trying to figure out just what
it was she had done wrong. Had she loved one son too
much, the other not enough? Had her sympathies for her
Apache child's plight drained her of the ability to express love for her natural child? Had she made a mistake
when she took that dark, squalling baby into her arms?
Should she have kept silent about his father? She didn't
know. She didn't know.

Emma raised her red-rimmed, watery eyes to Rosa
now. Poor Rosa. Jay had the girl beguiled with his sudden warmth and concern. Emma thought somehow it was
all her own fault, that if she had been a different kind of
mother, she might have had two contented sons. She
reached out a hand to touch Rosa's.

"I expect you will marry one day and have children,
Rosa. When you do, be careful of your sons. Be oh, so
careful of your sons."

The circle of light over her head was the smoke hole.
The rough dome was the roof of the wickiup. Anne stared

up at the pale blue morning sky. Her head was fine now. The crashing headaches were gone. The gash at her temple had healed. It had even been artfully concealed by Chirrihuaca, her moon-faced, copper-colored nursemaid, who had singed off a few locks of hair above the wound, then gave Anne a mirror so she could see how well the short curls hid the scar.

Anne was shocked at the face that peered back at her from the mirror. In the three weeks since the shooting, she had lost weight, enough to hollow out her cheeks and sharpen her nose. Her complexion, pale to begin with, looked chalky, and her eyes were shadowed, almost bruised looking.

She was lucky to be alive. She knew that. Now that her headaches and dizziness were gone, now that she felt certain that her baby had not been harmed, she should have felt happier. But she didn't. Worries about Sam plagued her constantly, gnawing at her mind day and night.

The Apache women would not allow her to go near him, claiming it was bad medicine, not only for Sam but for the child. As soon as she had been well enough to argue, Anne had begun a vigorous campaign to see him. So far nothing had worked. The reply was always no; the reason, bad medicine. Be glad your man is alive, they kept telling her. Trust the spirits to make him better. In the meantime, they made sure she stayed away by keeping a constant watch on her. Chirrihuaca continued to sleep in the wickiup with her, no longer an attentive nurse but a vigilant watchdog.

As she lay gazing up through the smoke hole now, Anne tried to think of a new argument to use on Smart Woman. Chirrihuaca had told her that female shamans were rare, but very powerful. According to the copper-faced nurse, Smart Woman possessed strong magic. But what the wrinkled, bright-eyed woman possessed, Anne thought, was a keen intelligence and a stubborn streak as wide as the New Mexico sky. Anne was stubborn, too, though, and she was going to see Sam. Today.

Smart Woman was so tiny she barely had to bend at the waist to enter the hide-curtained door of the wickiup. This morning she was wearing five necklaces over the cotton blouse that topped her buckskin skirt. One of the necklaces, Anne noticed, was made of teeth. Animal, not human, she hoped.

"Big magic today," the wrinkled woman said as she folded her legs and lowered herself to the floor of the wickiup with the ease and grace of a young girl. One of her gnarled hands began to trace patterns on the buffalo hide that she now shared with Anne.

Now or never, Anne said to herself. She stiffened her shoulders and faced the shaman. "I do not believe in your magic, Smart Woman. My spirits—" Anne pointed up through the smoke hole "—have told me my man is dead. They say you are lying to me, that your magic failed."

Smart Woman's lips crooked into an impish grin. "These spirits of yours, did they tell you that your man said to keep you away from him?"

Anne couldn't hide her shock, couldn't keep her jaw from dropping perceptibly. "What? What are you saying?"

The shaman continued to trace intricate patterns on the brown buffalo robe. "Your man cannot move his legs. He is afraid. He is also ashamed."

There was a buzzing in Anne's head—of old words, words she had heard years ago. *We're sorry. The captain cannot move his legs.* She could barely find her own voice. "No, Smart Woman. It was Daniel who couldn't move. Daniel, not Sam."

For a second the old woman looked confused. Her forehead creased and a deep line furrowed between her eyes. Then she grimaced and spat, as if confusion were forbidden or, at the very least, unwelcome. She grasped Anne's chin between her thumb and index finger. "Sam," she said. "Twenty-One Scars. Sam is afraid. Sam is ashamed. He needs powerful magic."

"I don't understand," Anne said, her own face now distorted with bafflement.

"You will." Smart Woman rose to her feet. "Come."

Sam lay on his back, head and shoulders propped on rolled buffalo skins. A thin, soft doeskin covered his naked body from his waist to his knees. His forehead was beaded with sweat as he stared at his toes, trying desperately to get a fix on whatever muscles and nerves controlled them. He'd spent the better part of the morning remembering how as a child he had learned to wiggle his ears.

For hours, when he was eight or nine, he'd stood in front of his mother's pier glass, trying to wiggle his ears. With each random twitch, he would try to locate the source, the part of him that controlled the movement. It took a long time, but finally he narrowed it down to a muscle behind his ear. Using that, and a slight but imperceptible tensing of his jaw, he was successful.

It occurred to him that the same principle ought to apply to toes. Ears, after all, weren't supposed to move. Toes were. Goddammit, they were supposed to move!

"Move," he commanded, his head raised from the buffalo skin pillow, the cords in his neck strung tight and glistening with sweat. "Move, damn you!"

His feet—one with its heel planted solidly on the ground, the other canted sideways—did not respond. He was as helpless as a newborn babe. With a harsh curse, he let his head drop back. He'd rest, he thought, and then try again. And again.

He wanted to believe what the old woman had told him—that the bullet she'd fished out of his back had been lodged in muscle; that it hadn't damaged his spine, his "white chain of bone." Smart Woman had tapped a gnarled finger to his forehead. "Think walking," she had said.

Sam closed his eyes. Christ, he hadn't thought of anything else since his senses returned after the long days and nights of fever. All there was to do was think and stare at the thatched wall of the hut, or, when they finally turned him on his back, at the ceiling and the smoke hole.

At first he had been grateful for the ministrations of the Apache women, for their cool hands when his skin was on fire, for their warm eyes when his heart was chilled with hopelessness. Slowly, though, his gratitude had hardened to resentment as he continued to be dependent on the women. He avoided their eyes now as they washed him, replaced the soiled mats and hides beneath him, massaged his useless legs.

He despised being at their mercy, and at the mercy of his own jagged emotions. Hopeful and determined one moment, he would become listless and defeated the next. Sometimes rage would nearly lift him off the woven mat beneath him. More often despair beat him down.

And always there was Annie. He'd asked Smart Woman to keep her away at first, not wanting her to see him reduced to the same dependency as her late husband, believing then that it would only be a matter of days before feeling and movement returned to his legs.

But the days had stretched to weeks now, and he was no better. Sometimes, when he stopped feeling sorry for himself, it was Annie who was the focus of his sorrow. She hadn't come clear across the country to wind up where she'd begun, playing nursemaid to a cripple. Sam wasn't going to let that happen. Helpless as he was, there were still one or two things he could control.

Sometimes, when his mood turned bitter and black, he thought about Jay. Smart Woman had shown him the bullet she'd taken from his back. She had worked a hole through the brass-and-iron slug, then threaded it on a string of dried antelope gut. When he refused to wear it around his neck, the shaman put it around her own. "An amulet," she said, "to keep evil spirits away." Only one cartridge Sam knew of was made of brass and iron. And only one rifle in the territory—Jay's British Snider—used them.

His rage would swirl around his brother like a storm, then turn back upon himself. He should have known, Sam thought. He should have been more careful. In hindsight, the ambush was the obvious conclusion of Jay's plan. Sam had walked right into it.

His lips twisted in a mournful grin. Well, he wouldn't be walking into any more of them, that was for damn sure.

At the hide curtain over the door of Sam's wickiup, Anne's knees turned to liquid. She couldn't go in. "Not just yet," she said to Smart Woman as she took a faltering step backward and then breathed in a great draft of cool autumn air. Then she chided herself for her hesitancy. She longed to see Sam, to touch him and talk to him, to take care of him. She was going to be his wife. Her place was beside him—anywhere. And yet...

A wave of dizziness overcame her and Anne dropped to the ground. Smart Woman said nothing, but stood close, her hand touching Anne's head lightly, once again moving in strange repetitive patterns.

A nameless fear had been haunting Anne ever since Smart Woman told her Sam was paralyzed. That fear suddenly gripped her heart. And now it had a name: Daniel. Only this wasn't Daniel. It was Sam. Did she love him enough? she wondered. Was she strong enough to bear his pain and his sorrow and his anger? She hadn't been strong enough to bear Daniel's. But maybe that was because she hadn't loved him with her entire being, the way she loved Sam.

Anne crossed her arms over her stomach. She could feel the beginnings of a swelling there, despite the fact that she had lost weight. Oh, Sam, she thought, no matter what difficulties we face, it isn't just the two of us anymore.

Smart Woman crooked a finger under Anne's chin. "Come," she said. "It is time."

Anne touched the singed hair at her temple, suddenly aware of the scar from the bullet. Then she smoothed her trembling fingers across the front of the doeskin skirt that Chirrihuaca had made for her. Oh, Lord, she thought, she was too thin and too tired and far too different from the woman Sam had last seen several weeks ago. But then, Sam wasn't the same either, was he? As she rose to her feet, Anne nodded to the old wrinkled woman, indicating her readiness.

Pointing to her own deep brown eyes, Smart Woman then shook her finger. "No tears," she said.

Anne took in another deep breath and nodded toward the curtain that covered the door. Smart Woman reached

out a thin brown arm and pulled it back, allowing Anne
to step through into the dimness of the wickiup.

Sam blinked at the bright October light as it streamed
into the thatched hut. The woman who entered was little
more than a silhouette in fringed garments. It wasn't
Smart Woman, that was for sure. The aged shaman always strode right toward him, as if she were going to walk
over him. This woman paused in the doorway, as if she
were lost or afraid.

He'd been surly lately, he knew. Earlier that morning
he had even pushed Fourth Daughter halfway across the
hut when she fussed too long over the tangles in his hair.
He couldn't blame anybody for hesitating at the door.

"It's all right," he said to the tiny silhouette. "I won't
bite."

When he heard the delicate chime of her laughter,
Sam's hands curled into fists. "Annie," he said, squinting as he tried to bring her into focus. "Go away. I don't
want you here."

She didn't say a word. She just moved forward, picking her way toward him through the various clay pots and
woven baskets on the floor of the wickiup. The long
fringe on her skirt shimmied with each step.

Sam turned his head away, as if not looking would
make her disappear. He didn't think he could bear the
sight of her sweet oval face, her sky blue eyes, her moon-
colored hair. He knew he couldn't bear having her see
him this way. He wanted to think of something hard and
cruel to say to her to make her turn on her heels and flee.
But there were no words. Even if there had been, they
couldn't have made it past the lump in his throat.

She knelt beside him, and Sam could feel her warmth
altering the air around him. He kept his eyes closed as she
gently touched his arm, tracing her fingertips along the

bare skin from his shoulder to his elbow. Her hand covered his fist. Then he felt the light touch of her lips on his collarbone, the feathered drift of her hair, her warm cheek pressed against his chest.

A tear escaped from his eye, and he took in a great, ragged breath before he turned to nestle his rough chin against her soft, fragrant hair.

The instant he moved to touch her, Anne knew how foolish she had been to have harbored a single fear or doubt. This man was her love, completely and forever. There was nothing—no trial too difficult, no circumstance too grim—that could keep her from his side. This was where she belonged. She breathed his name in a sigh of sweet relief.

Sam smoothed his big hand over her hair. His thumb grazed back and forth across her cheek. His hard chest rose and fell as he struggled to control his emotions. "Annie. Oh, God, Annie," he murmured.

"I won't go away. I'm not leaving you, Sam. Not now. Not ever."

He blinked to clear his eyes. His hand stilled on her hair. "You've already been through this once. I don't want you to have to do it again."

"It's not the same," she protested.

"The hell it's not. I will not allow you to become my goddamn nursemaid. Is that clear?"

"Smart Woman says you'll walk again."

His tone roughened. "I know what she says. Believe me, Annie, I know." He tapped his finger against her head. "Think walking," he said in imitation of the shaman's high-pitched voice.

She lifted her head from his chest. "Think kissing," she said with a grin, as she brought her lips close to his.

Sam's mouth tightened and he turned his head away. "That's all over, too, Annie. Or didn't the old lady tell you that?"

"She told me you need encouragement," Anne said, refusing to be put off.

"Encouragement!" Sam spat. "What I need is some feeling below my belt."

"We'll work on it. Together. It will come, Sam."

"Will it, Annie?" He grabbed her hand, then pulled back enough of the doeskin covering him to expose his thigh. "I want to show you something." He held her hand over his leg so that the nail of her index finger pointed down, then he scraped it over his skin, hard and deep. As a red, ragged line of blood oozed to the surface, he never flinched.

Anne tried to pull away, but his grasp was harsh and tight. "Stop it, Sam," she cried. "You're bleeding."

"Am I?" he asked in a mocking tone. "I can't feel a thing." Sam jerked her hand roughly to the warmth of his manhood. "I can't feel that either," he rasped, "so don't think kissing anymore."

When he released her, Anne—her eyes stinging with tears she wouldn't let fall—grabbed his hand and brought it to her belly. "Can you feel that, Sam Hook?" she asked. "That's your child inside me. He's going to need a father to hold him and to love him. And I don't think he's going to give a damn whether that father is horizontal or vertical. I know I don't."

He stared at her, struck dumb by the news, his hand frozen on the soft curve of her belly.

"I'm not leaving you, Sam," she whispered as tears began to stream down her cheeks. "*We're* not leaving you."

Chapter Eighteen

Emma's wagon had barely rolled to a stop in front of the livery stable when Father José approached, his sandalled feet kicking up little clouds of dust that were dispersed by the folds of his long brown cassock.

"Señora Hook, I must speak with you."

She looked down at him from the wagon, surprised to find his brown eyes lusterless and his normally cheerful face overcast with worry now. "Of course, Father," she said immediately.

He tipped his head to indicate the two cowhands who had accompanied her on the trip from The Hook. "In private," he said as he raised an arm to help her down from the high seat. "Come. We can speak in the church."

It felt good to walk after so many hours in the wagon, and Emma continued to stand once they were inside the mission. She noticed the warm glow of a score of votive candles burning in crimson glasses. The air inside the little church was heavy with incense. Emma couldn't help but think she much preferred the crisp, clean air in the Presbyterian church she'd attended as a girl back East.

"What was it you wanted to discuss, Father?" she asked.

He fidgeted with the crucifix that hung around his neck. "One hears rumors, señora...."

"About Sam," she said quietly.

The priest nodded. *"Sí."*

"My son is dead." Inwardly, Emma prayed that she would be forgiven for her lie—to a man of God, uttered within the walls of a church. But much as she respected Father José, the man tended to be loose-lipped. Emma trusted no one with her secret. If word got back to Jay somehow, there was no telling what her younger son might do.

Father José lowered himself to a wooden bench, his crucifix now clutched in both hands. He murmured something in Spanish, then said to Emma, "I fear for little Benito. It was my hope that these rumors were false."

"Is the boy ill?" There was a note of alarm in her voice.

"No, no. He is strong as a little mule. But I fear we are going to lose him. My fears increase now with your sad news."

"I don't understand, Father."

"The boy's people want him back."

"His people? You mean the Apaches?"

The priest nodded. "It seems the woman who left him on our doorstep did it to spite her husband. He was unfaithful to her and she was punishing him by getting rid of what he wanted most—a son. The woman confessed to him as she was dying."

"I thought the boy was a half-breed," Emma said. "I assumed his mother was white." Her heart beat faster as she imagined how she might have felt if the Apaches had tried to take her Sam away from her.

"Because of his abandonment, so did we all." He shook his head in dismay. "I was so hoping that Sam could help. But now... Raging Owl has threatened to destroy all of San Miguel if I fail to give up the boy."

Emma's hand flew to her mouth. "Is there time to send for help?"

"I have already notified the army in Santa Fe. They said they have enough problems already. They said—" the priest's mouth slid into an uncharacteristic sneer "—they said 'Give the little bastard back to his own kind.'"

"Oh, my," gasped Emma. When Sam returned, whenever that happened, he would be devastated by the loss of little Benito. Her mind raced. There had to be something she could do. Perhaps there was a way to get word to Sam. But how? And how could she do anything without Jay finding out?

Anne sat outside her wickiup in the warm afternoon sun. She was using two flat stones to grind herbs, helping Smart Woman prepare a medicinal drink for Sam. Chirrihuaca sat with her, her short legs crossed and her coppery face deep in concentration as she wove strands of dried bear grass to mend a large hole in a strainer. Anne had been asking her nurse and constant companion about some of the other women, very few of whom spoke any English at all.

"Where's the tall woman with the odd nose?" Anne asked her now. "I haven't seen her for several weeks."

Chirrihuaca looked up from her weaving, first at Anne and then over her shoulder to see if anyone was within hearing distance. "She died," the woman whispered.

"Why are you whispering, Chirrihuaca?"

Again, the woman looked around her before speaking. "It is bad luck to speak of the dead. Her ghost might return. I would not want to meet Dancing Child's ugly ghost."

Anne scooped the crushed herbs into the palm of her hand, then put them in a small basket lined with antelope hide. "What happened to Dancing Child's nose? Did she have an accident?"

Chirrihuaca laughed coarsely. "No accident. Raging Owl cut off the tip of her nose because she let another man come into her."

Anne's eyes widened. "How awful!"

"Raging Owl was her husband. It was his right to do it." Now the round-faced woman leaned closer to Anne. "But he betrayed her first. She was very angry."

"I don't suppose she got to cut his nose off, did she?" Anne asked.

"Worse. Dancing Child left their male child at the sacred place with the bell in San Miguel. She confessed just before she died."

Anne's eyes grew even wider now. "How long ago did this happen?"

The woman began weaving again, moving her lips in silence for a moment. "Six, perhaps seven harvests ago. Raging Owl never knew he had a son. He is going to claim him from the long-robed shaman in San Miguel."

"Does Sam know anything about this?"

Chirrihuaca gave her a quizzical look. "No. Why do you ask such a question?"

"No reason. I was just curious." And suddenly scared out of her wits. The child had to be Benito; there was no other boy of the same age or heritage. This would hurt Sam deeply. Losing the boy he already considered his son would break his heart. And to lose him to the Apache who was terrorizing the countryside would shatter his soul.

Anne reached into another basket for a fresh supply of leaves and began grinding them with such force that tiny sparks flared between the two rocks. Perhaps it was a sign, she thought, then chastised herself for falling under the Apache shaman's spell and believing in signs and portents. Still, there was nothing she alone could do but hope that the powerful magic Smart Woman had promised was truly powerful enough.

The wrinkled old shaman joined Anne and her companion later in the afternoon. Smart Woman poked a finger in the basket of ground herbs, swirled them around and nodded in satisfaction.

"It is time for talking," she said, putting her hand on Anne's bent knee. "There is an evil man called Jay."

Anne looked at Smart Woman the way she might have looked at a carnival mind reader who had just rattled off the exact contents of her handbag without once looking inside.

Smart Woman chortled. Then she tapped her ear. "I listened when Twenty-One Scars was sick with heat. He spoke much."

"Jay is his brother, the natural son of the white woman who took Sam into her home and her heart. They are…" Anne looked at Chirrihuaca for help. "I want to tell Smart Woman they are rivals. That they have fought against each other since they were small boys."

The moon-faced woman said something to the shaman in Apache. Smart Woman nodded somberly as she fingered one of the amulets around her neck. She held the metal fragment out toward Anne. "From Jay's gun," she said. "Twenty-One Scars knows this."

"Are you telling me that Sam was shot by his brother?" She turned to Chirrihuaca again. "Is that what she's saying?"

Both Apache women nodded.

Then Smart Woman clamped her hand around Anne's calf. "It is not the bullet that keeps his legs still. It is the man."

Anne shook her head in bafflement. She had no idea what the woman was trying to tell her.

"Twenty-One Scars chooses not to kill his brother. He chooses with his legs."

"He has no feeling in his legs," Anne said, "or—" She felt her cheeks color as she lowered her gaze to her fidgeting hands. "He can't..."

Smart Woman patted her leg. "He will," she said. "Tonight."

Anne's eyes snapped up. The old shaman was grinning. Then, with Chirrihuaca's assistance, Smart Woman began to outline her plan in minute and vivid detail. By the time she was finished, Anne's cheeks were flaming.

"I don't know if I can do that, Smart Woman," she said.

"You must."

As soon as the sun went down, the women led Anne inside her wickiup, where they whisked off her doeskin tunic, sat her down and began a lengthy toilette. Chirrihuaca rubbed a fragrant oil into her skin. Fourth Daughter powdered her long, silver hair with ground yucca root, then spent half an hour combing her fingers through the fragrant tresses. Two other women sang softly.

When Anne asked her about the song, Chirrihuaca replied, "They sing of the seasons and how they change. How 'ghost face' turns to 'little eagles.'"

"Ghost face?"

The Indian woman continued to smooth the fragrant oil on Anne's feet. "What the whites call winter."

"Then 'little eagles' must be spring," Anne said.

Chirrihuaca nodded. "It is also a love song. They are cold because they miss their men. They want to be warm. They wish for their men to stop making war, to go back to the reservation and live in peace."

"Do you think that will ever happen, Chirrihuaca?"

The woman shrugged, as if it were far beyond her control. "We should not talk of sad things now. We must prepare you for Twenty-One Scars."

After the women left, Anne sat alone for what seemed an eternity. She fingered the fringe on the new tunic the women had given her. It was decorated with signs and symbols she didn't comprehend. What if Smart Woman's plan didn't work? she wondered. What if, in spite of all her amorous efforts, Sam was still unable to feel anything? What if the magic wasn't powerful enough?

She squeezed her eyes closed, trying to banish such thoughts. It would work. It would. She was going to do her damndest to turn "ghost face" to "little eagles," to turn cold winter to warm, burgeoning spring.

And if Smart Woman was right about Sam—that his wish to kill his brother was keeping him flat on his back, that his need for revenge was at war with his will—then maybe Anne would have to take matters into her own hands. If she failed tonight, maybe she would have to kill Jay herself in order to free him. She could do it. And she would do it if she had to.

But before she had to deal with that, there was still tonight. There was magic to be done. Her own white witchcraft.

Smart Woman came and led her by the hand outside into the October night. "Look," the shaman whispered as she pointed a bony arm toward the sky, where an enormous moon hung like a silver amulet on a chain of bright stars. Smart Woman touched Anne's hair.

"Same," she said. "The moon is strong magic. It is yours."

Perhaps, thought Anne as her fingers trembled. Perhaps.

Every once in a while, when the smoke from his fire dispersed, Sam could discern the stars in the dark circle of sky visible through the roof of the wickiup. He could tell time by the stars—the hour of the night, the month of the year—but he needed the whole sky to do it, not a scrap of firmament viewed through a smoke hole.

That was going to be the story of his life now that he was no longer whole, now that he was a useless shadow of a man. He'd been thinking all day and into the night about the child Anne was carrying. His head was reeling with the news, and his mood kept swinging wildly from joy to sorrow. He was going to be a father! But what kind? Horizontal, in Annie's words. What could a horizontal father teach a child? His own father hadn't taught him with words, but by showing him—how to ride, how to rope a steer, how to lift a hundred-pound bale of hay from a wagon bed so it didn't strain the muscles of his back, how to stand tall and proud.

Sam kept telling himself he should be glad he was alive, but there was no gladness in his heart.

And Annie. Stubborn, loyal Annie. How many years could she endure another prison of a marriage? How long before her passions would tire of the solitary confinement and she turned elsewhere for love? How long before she'd finally bring him a gun and leave it quietly on the table by his pitiful bed?

Sam closed his eyes to block out the stars, to hold back the flood of tears that could so easily come if he allowed it. He cursed his brother once more, and cursed himself for creating the monster Jay had become. "Kill the monster," a voice deep inside him urged.

His lips moved almost imperceptibly. "Thou shalt not... though shalt not..."

He thought he was dreaming when the hide covering the doorway was pulled back and women began drifting into the wickiup. One after another they came, their long dark hair flowing softly around their faces, their tunics shimmying with long fringe, their bare feet moving soundlessly over the woven mats. The stifling, fetid air inside the hut seemed to cool, and was suddenly replete with heady fragrances—pine and musk, rose and juniper.

Smart Woman's face was powdered. The old shaman looked like an apparition as she stood by the door, motioning impatiently with a gnarled hand to someone outside.

Annie. Annie stepped through the door. She was pale as the moon with her hair streaming over her shoulders. Her blue eyes shone like diamonds in the firelight. The soft fringe on her dress whispered as she walked, as she bent her slim bare legs and sat beside him, taking his hand in hers.

He wanted to flee from her beguiling beauty—beauty he would never again possess, loveliness he'd never bend again to kiss, bewitching warmth he'd never again penetrate. But he couldn't flee. He could only turn his head away.

Smart Woman began to chant, her withered arms held over her head toward the disk of dark, starry sky. The words of her haunting song came from deep in her throat and reverberated against the thatched walls of the wickiup.

She turned as she sang, to all four corners of the earth, and ended by facing Sam. From the hide pouch that hung at her beaded belt, Smart Woman took a handful of sacred pollen. She walked slowly around the hut then, pressing some of the golden dust into each of the women's upturned hands. The women began to chant and sway.

Sam stared up at the smoke hole. When Smart Woman threw pollen on the fire, smoke billowed up and blotted out the stars. He clenched his teeth and pulled his hand from Annie's, aware of what the women were trying to accomplish, moved by their efforts but angered by them all the same. What mournful songs would they sing when they failed? he wondered. What pitiful chants would they intone when all their magic and all their feminine beauty failed to arouse him?

One by one they placed their pollen-streaked hands on him. He could smell the pungent odor of the dust, could taste it as they touched it to his lips, could feel it mixing with the sweat on his chest. If they touched him elsewhere, he didn't know.

They moved slowly out of the wickiup in a single file, each woman turning back briefly and nodding to Smart Woman. Finally, just the old shaman and Annie were left. The light in the wickiup was golden, filled with pollen dust. The mixture of fragrances in the air was powerful.

Smart Woman took a necklace of feathers and carved bone from around her neck. She placed it over Anne's head. Then she sprinkled sacred pollen on Anne's hair before turning and disappearing silently through the door. The hide curtain dropped behind her with a soft and conclusive thud.

Annie began tracing her fingertips over his chest. Sam pushed her hands away.

"You don't really believe this hocus-pocus, do you?" His voice had a bitter edge. "A little song or two. Turning around four times and smearing yellow grit all over. What's supposed to happen now, Annie? Am I supposed to miraculously get up and walk?" He grabbed her shoulders and shook her roughly. "Because if that was supposed to be the end result of all this mumbo jumbo, take a good look. I'm still flat on my back. My damn legs are as dead as they ever were."

Sam let go of her and turned his head away once more.

She gazed at his chiselled profile, at the hard line of his jaw and the little muscle that twitched in his cheek. "That isn't what was supposed to happen next," she said softly as she rose to her knees and began to lift the buckskin tunic over her head.

"What the hell do you think you're doing?" Sam snarled. He had turned his head back at the faint rustling of the hide garment. Now he took a fistful of the tunic and pulled it down so it covered her once more. "Don't embarrass us both, Annie. I don't know what Smart Woman told you, but this isn't going to change anything."

Her blue eyes locked fiercely on his. "Smart Woman said if the middle leg rises, the other two are bound to follow. She said—"

Sam laughed harshly. "My middle leg, as that old crone so aptly described it, is as dead as the other two. Forget it, Annie."

She dropped her gaze to her trembling hands. It was tempting to obey him, to scramble out of there as quickly as her legs would carry her, to avoid doing what Smart Woman had told her she had to do. "I'm nervous, Sam," she confessed with a quavering voice. "I don't think I was ever cut out to be a temptress, especially now when I'm thin as a stick except for my little potbelly." Anne felt her face growing hot. "But if Smart Woman is right, if there's a ghost of a chance that this will help you... And it's been so long, Sam. I want you. I—I need you." Tears splashed on the backs of her hands.

When Sam reached out to her, his hands, too, were watered by her tears. "Ssh. Hush, love. I'm sorry I made you cry." He drew her to him, cradled her head against his chest. He'd been so mired in his own problems, he really hadn't given a thought to what Annie might be feeling, to what she might be needing.

"I don't know how to do this, Sam," she sniffed. "Just let me be close to you."

He sat her up and began to lift her dress. "Go ahead, Annie. I want to be close to you, too, love." Even if that was all he could do, Sam thought morosely. Well, hell, he still had hands, didn't he? He knew how to slake a woman's passion. He could give her that if he couldn't give her his body.

She drew the soft buckskin over her head. Her pollen-sprinkled flesh glowed in the firelight. She was like a flower, Sam thought, a delectable blossom waiting for the deft and passionate touch of the bee. But before he could reach for her lushness, Anne dipped her head and traced her tongue around his rough nipple. His throat thickened with desire and he drew in a sharp breath. Christ, how he wanted her! Would this sweet torture last his entire life? The hunger was still there, but not the means to satisfy it. "Annie," he moaned.

She stilled his lips with a kiss, soft then searing as her hot, honeyed tongue sought his. Gently, her fingers skimmed down to the soft doeskin that was draped over him. She pulled it away and tossed it well out of his reach. As their lips clung, she slid one leg over him, then shifted her weight until she straddled him.

Anne eased from his ravenous kiss then, and sat up. He could only stare at the alabaster perfection of her breasts, the sweet curve of her belly, the soft tangle of curls that hid her velvet depths.

Her eyes were brimming with need. "Touch me, Sam," she whispered, bringing his hesitant hand up to her mouth. "Please," she murmured, her eyes closed as he drew his thumb across her lips, then let his fingers drift down her ivory flesh to brush across a taut nipple. It wasn't enough for either one of them. Anne leaned forward as he lifted his head.

"Oh, yes," she breathed as his famished mouth drew succor and sustenance from her breast.

Her hips began to move over him, rocking from side to side, forward and back. Far back in his head, a voice cautioned Sam to stop her, to keep disappointment at bay. But her rhythmic movements and the sweet feast of her breast overwhelmed his thoughts, as they were overwhelming all of his senses.

Her pale hair streamed over his face, so he couldn't see as she reached beneath her and stroked him, but he felt a fire being stoked in his loins, a hot, rising fire. It was a fantasy, Sam thought. A phantom surge his mind was creating, like the rising heat of a mirage from desolate ground.

She sat back then. Her eyes were shuttered with passion as she moved over him and took him into her, sheathed him and rode him with a fierce, driving need while Sam lay still. Except for his hands, which gripped her insistent hips. Except for his eyes, which burned over her moist and stunning ivory flesh. Except for his mouth, which framed her name again and again. "Annie."

She shuddered exquisitely as she felt Sam's sweet release inside her, as he closed his eyes, arched his head so that the cords of his neck stood out in throbbing relief and called her name. She leaned forward, pressing her face into his solid neck, her heart pounding against his.

"Annie. Oh, God, Annie. What did you do, love?" he murmured. "What the hell did you do?"

She smiled softly, nuzzling more deeply into him. Sam began laughing, a slow laugh, low and warm, as his hands smoothed over her slick back. "Christ, woman, you curled my toes."

"I'm glad," she whispered.

"No, I mean it, Annie. You really did. Look."

"What?" She lifted her head and turned to look down the length of his bronzed legs. His toes indeed were curled down. She held her breath. "Can you uncurl them?"

"I don't know," he said. There was a note of disbelief in his voice, coupled with joy and wonderment.

"Try, Sam," she urged.

As she watched, his feet moved. His toes pointed once more toward the roof of the wickiup.

"Oh, yes," she sighed, nestling again into the warm crevice of his neck. "Oh, yes."

She fell into an exhausted sleep in his arms, while Sam stroked her hair softly and continued, determinedly, to wiggle his toes.

Chapter Nineteen

Two days later Sam was on his feet. He wasn't ready to walk any distance. In fact, at first he was capable of going only a few yards outside the wickiup, with Anne and Chirrihuaca under his shoulders like a pair of mismatched crutches. His legs were weak from lack of use and there was stiffness and pain in his back from the bullet wound. His mood, however, could only be described as sunny.

Because he was so cheerful, Anne decided not to tell Sam about Raging Owl's plan to claim Benito. Chirrihuaca had told her the braves had ridden north when they last left the campsite. The Apache woman didn't think the men were heading directly for San Miguel, but probably intended to raid several ranches north of there first.

"Raging Owl will probably wait for the dark moon so the ghost of Dancing Child cannot see him take the boy," Chirrihuaca said.

"How many days till then?" Anne asked her.

The woman held up four fingers.

"How long will it take me to return to San Miguel?"

Chirrihuaca's coppery forehead creased. "Does Smart Woman know your thoughts?"

Probably, Anne was thinking. The old shaman seemed to know everything. But she shook her head in reply to the question. "I have said nothing to Smart Woman."

Chirrihuaca shrugged, as if to say, "What difference does that make?" Then she said, "It takes nearly two suns to make the journey."

If she left immediately, Anne thought, she could get there before Raging Owl and she could warn Father José. Perhaps she could even take Benito away for a while, or, at the very least, hide him somewhere in town or at The Hook.

"Does Twenty-One Scars know your thoughts?" Chirrihuaca asked, smiling slyly.

"No. And don't you tell him, either," Anne said. "He isn't strong enough to travel yet. But he's stubborn enough to try to anyway."

"You cannot go alone," Chirrihuaca said.

Anne gazed at her former nursemaid, now her confidante and friend. Her eyes communicated her silent appeal.

The Apache woman was quiet as a stone, her expression unreadable for what seemed a very long time. Then she smiled. "I will go half the distance with you. One sun only. Do not ask more."

Anne let out a grateful sigh. "Thank you, Chirrihuaca. And you must promise me you won't tell Sam about this."

Chirrihuaca laughed. "And you must promise me you won't tell Smart Woman."

Anne joined in her laughter, and then the two women sat with their heads together—light against dark—planning their secret trek.

Anne approached the door with a steaming bowl of herb tea cupped in her hands. She would be leaving for

San Miguel soon and this would be her last moment alone with Sam, although she dared not let him know.

"That's a fetching sight," Sam said as she entered the wickiup backwards, her buckskin tunic hiked up to reveal a shapely, ivory length of thigh. When she turned, her pale beauty took his breath away again. Sometimes, he thought, it was hard to believe she was truly his. It was still difficult to believe her slim hips sheltered his child.

"Smart Woman says you're to drink every drop of this," she said as she folded her legs and lowered herself beside him on the soft buffalo skin.

He took a whiff of the pungent steam and wrinkled his nose. "Another of her foul-tasting magic potions?"

"Drink it, Sam," Anne warned.

Sam took the clay bowl from her hands and put it aside. "I'll let it cool off a little first," he said as he reached out and gathered her against his bare chest.

"You won't just dump it out and say you drank it, will you?" she asked, sliding her arms around his ribs. "Smart Woman's been right about everything so far, you know."

Anne could feel his arms stiffen around her. She sensed the tension snaking through him.

"Not everything," he said sharply.

"Something has to be done about Jay," she said, trying again to bring up a subject Sam kept avoiding. "Someone has to do something. Why don't we talk to the sheriff in San Miguel? Maybe there's—"

"That's enough, Annie." He set her away from him brusquely, then picked up the bowl and began sipping.

"You can't just keep ignoring it, Sam," she said, up on her knees now, hands planted on her hips. "The man shot you in the back. He—"

"Enough!" he bellowed, flinging the clay bowl against the thatched wall of the wickiup. Warm tea sprayed all over Anne, and the fire sizzled as the liquid touched the hot rocks and glowing coals. The bowl fell with a thud onto the grass-mat floor as Sam sat with his fists clenched and his lips drawn tight.

Anne scrambled to her feet, her tunic dripping. "You're the most obstinate man I've ever met, Sam Hook. You're like a damn mule," she shrieked. "Go ahead. Do what you want. Forget about Jay. But don't ask me to forget, because I won't. I can't. Ever." She spun on her heel and nearly tore the hide covering off the doorway as she left.

If there had been anything within his reach, Sam would have thrown that, too. Instead, he cursed mightily and slammed his fist into the palm of his hand.

She was right. He had to do something. If he were still alone, he might be able to keep his rage bottled up forever, might endure any torment Jay dreamed up. But he wasn't alone. There was Annie to think of. And there was his child. Knowing his brother as he did, Sam realized Jay's next angle of attack would be an oblique one. He didn't even have to hurt Sam anymore. All he had to do was harm Annie and the baby.

Sam had thought long and hard about leaving, perhaps going back East where they could live a normal life. But not only would that mean giving up his claim to the land he loved, it would also mean leaving his mother at Jay's mercy. And no matter where they went, no matter how far, he'd still be looking over his shoulder as long as his brother was alive.

There was only one choice, he thought as he flexed the slowly strengthening muscles of his calves and thighs.

One way or another he had to deal with Jay. He had to stop him.

An unbidden thought kept taunting him, sharp as a knife in his heart. *Only a savage kills his brother.*

Anne stood on the bank of the Canadian River, watching as Chirrihuaca rode away. "Goodbye, my good friend," she called one last time. Someday, Anne thought, she would return the favor the Apache woman had done her by bringing her so close to San Miguel. Someday. But today she had to walk as fast as her legs would carry her. If Chirrihuaca was right, Raging Owl was only a day or two away.

Turning east, Anne began her trek. She was once again wearing her "white woman's" clothes—her black velvet riding habit and the black leather shoes that pinched her feet now and made her long for the soft moccasins she had worn while she was with the Apaches. Her skirt hobbled her gait and her jacket chafed beneath her arms, despite the fact that she had lost weight. She gazed over her shoulder one last time, to catch a final glimpse of Chirrihuaca riding away in her comfortable buckskin tunic and moccasins.

Once this ordeal was over, Anne vowed to herself, she would dress for comfort rather than style. She didn't care what anybody said, and if it made her look like an Apache, so much the better. Then she and Sam would indeed be a matched pair.

She saw the smoke long before she reached the town. It rose high in the late-afternoon sky and hung in the windless air like a black plume.

"No," she cried out loud. She couldn't be too late. She couldn't. She had to get to San Miguel before Raging Owl took Benito away. The fact that the warrior was the boy's natural father made no difference to her. Chirrihuaca had told her that he planned to abuse the boy in order to taunt Dancing Child's ghost. If she couldn't reach him in time, the child was doomed.

She wondered now if she had made a mistake by not telling Sam. He seemed to be getting stronger by the hour. Lord knew, with his long legs, he could have made this trip twice as fast as she. If anything happened to Benito, Sam might not be able to forgive her for not giving him the chance to save the boy.

"It's this damn skirt holding me back," Anne muttered. She grabbed the hem, hunted for a seam and ripped it. The soft velvet fabric parted with a dull whisper, revealing the white cotton of her pantalets.

Freed somewhat from the constraints of her clothing, Anne quickened her pace toward San Miguel—toward the terrible, towering smoke.

Before long her lungs were burning and her lips were parched. She was covered with dust, for she had stumbled repeatedly in the waning light, over roots and rocks, in ruts and crevices. Her ankle, weakened from the wagon accident, throbbed as she finally hobbled into the little town. She stood a moment, leaning an arm against the side of the café, trying to catch her breath and still the pounding of her heart. That was all she could hear—her own ragged inhalations and the hammering of blood in her ears.

She limped to the street, looked east and west. It was Sally Mendoza's place that was burning. Flames thrust through the black smoke like bright orange fingers. The front wall had collapsed. On what was left of a side wall, Anne could see a big mirror. As she watched, it cracked and fell in huge shards into the flames.

Where was everyone? Why wasn't someone trying to put out the fire? What—

"Miz McIntire?"

Anne's heart jumped into her throat at the sound. She whirled to her right.

"I didn't mean to scare you, ma'am," Tom Atkinson drawled. The burly sheriff grasped her around the waist as she sagged against him. "We best get you inside."

"I have to warn Father José," she said, her breath still coming in gasps and her throat raspy with dust and smoke. She tried to say more, but her voice failed her.

The sheriff took a step, his arm still clutching her. "Well, you just come on along with me now, ma'am."

Anne pulled away. "I need to speak to Father José. It's a matter of life and death, Sheriff. Please."

Tom Atkinson tipped his hat back on his head. "Yes, ma'am. I know it is. You're worried about the boy."

Eyes big and round, Anne stammered. "Yes. How did you know that? How—?"

"Benito's doing fine. Sam's got him all stowed away inside the church."

"Sam?" She blinked now as if she had heard him wrong.

The sheriff's mouth twitched into a brief grin. "Yes, ma'am." He took her arm again. "Come on along. I'll let him do all the explaining."

Anne let him lead her along the edge of the street toward the church. When they were almost there, a flaming arrow streaked past them. Tom Atkinson shoved her behind his back. She heard him swear roughly, then watched as the roof of the livery stable went up in flames.

"Raging Owl is burning the town!" she whispered.

"He's sure trying," Tom Atkinson spat, gripping her arm again and propelling her the final few yards toward the church.

When he opened the heavily carved door and ushered her inside, Anne was shocked to see what looked like the entire population of the town gathered there. People were everywhere—sitting on pews, on the floor, on windowsills. The altar was lit with crimson candlelight, and other candles were scattered around the crowded room. There was barely enough light to make out faces, but there was enough to see that none of those faces was smiling. The sweet fragrance of incense blended with the sour smell of a multitude of frightened people.

"Well, lookee who's here," a loud female voice proclaimed. The bulk of Mrs. Thiel rose directly in front of Anne. "I'm surprised you're not wearing a stinking animal hide, Mrs. McIntire. But you look like an Indian-loving strumpet, anyway."

Anne followed the woman's harsh gaze. Her velvet riding habit was torn clear up the side of her hip and her pantalets hung in shreds.

"You've got your nerve bringing her in here, Tom," Mrs. Thiel said, turning her dark little raisin eyes to the sheriff. "Let the tart stay out there with the savages she loves so much."

"Do you want to get out of our way now, Mrs. Thiel?" the bearish sheriff growled through clenched teeth.

The big woman backed up. "I'll get out of your way, all right. I don't want to be anywhere near *her*."

"This way, Miz McIntire," Tom Atkinson said, placing his hand at the small of her back. "Don't pay anybody no mind. Folks're pretty upset tonight and they're all saying things they're gonna regret tomorrow."

"If we live to see tomorrow," somebody yelled.

There was a rough chorus of grumbling as Anne let the sheriff guide her toward the front of the church. As her eyes became more accustomed to the dim, flickering light, she could see the sheriff's deputy standing in front of the crowd, a shotgun levelled on the townspeople. Nearby, Father José stood with his curly head bowed and his hands clasped in prayer. And, as her eyes moved to the priest's right, she saw Sam's moccasined feet and long, buckskin-clad legs. He was sitting alone in the front pew. Her gaze travelled to the hard sculpture of his naked chest, where one of Smart Woman's necklaces of feathers and carved bone hung. So that was how he got here before her, Anne thought. Smart Woman must have told him.

Anne slid into the pew beside him. He looked bone-tired and he smelled more like a horse than a man. There was a hard glint in his obsidian eyes.

"You should have told me," he said with more weariness than anger in his voice. "What the hell did you think you could do alone?"

She didn't know anymore. She only knew he was here and that somehow Sam would make everything all right. "How do you feel?" she asked him, covering his hand with hers. "You look so tired, Sam."

His eyes warmed a little as they took in the cream-colored length of her exposed thigh. "You look a little worse for wear yourself, Annie." He slipped his big hand discreetly over her abdomen. "You have to take care of him, you know."

"Right now, I'm a lot more worried about you." She lifted her hand to touch the necklace. "I suppose Smart Woman told you about Raging Owl's plan, but I can't for the life of me understand why."

He nodded. "Simple," he said. "The women are tired of hiding in the hills. They want to go back to the reservation. The only one preventing that is Raging Owl. Smart Woman wants him defeated."

"She wants him killed?"

Sam shrugged. "Killed. Humiliated. Whatever it takes to make the men stop following him and return to the reservation."

Anne looked over her shoulder at the grumbling crowd. "No one's doing much to accomplish that." She sniffed. "What are they waiting for?"

"Me," he said somberly. "And I was just waiting for you." Sam took both her hands in his and his dark eyes sought hers. "Don't say anything, Annie. Just listen. I've challenged Raging Owl's manhood by claiming I'm the boy's natural father. It's a matter of honor now. He has no choice but to fight me, hand to hand, for Benito."

She opened her mouth to protest, but he tightened his grip on her hands and then further silenced her with a hard, almost brutal look.

"If I win, he'll leave in shame. His braves won't follow him long."

The blood rushed from her face, leaving her light-headed. "And if he wins?" she murmured. "If Raging Owl wins?"

"He won't," Sam said.

"Don't do this, Sam," she pleaded. "For God's sake, you've been flat on your back for weeks. Let somebody else be a hero."

"Annie," he sighed with strained patience, "there is nobody else."

"Well, can't the sheriff—"

He took her face in both his hands, his warm palms on her cheeks. "They want to hand over the boy," he said roughly, his dark eyes glistening.

Her eyelids fluttered. "Oh, my God. But surely they wouldn't . . ."

"They were just about to do it when I got here," Sam said, then he laughed bitterly. "The good people of San Miguel have agreed to let me fight for the boy. They talked it over and decided they'd win either way. If something happens to me, they can still hand over Benito."

Father José turned from the altar and walked toward them. His face was pale and drawn. His silver crucifix trembled in his hand as he spoke. "It is time, my friend."

Sam nodded. "Padre, will you take Annie into the orphanage with Benito?"

"*Sí.* We shall wait for you there."

"Go with him, love," Sam whispered. "I'll come back for you. I promise."

Anne couldn't even speak. Her lips were twisted with grief, salty with tears. He kissed each wet corner of her mouth, then held her against him a moment, and when he stood up to leave, his hard chest glistened with her tears.

The minute he saw her, Benito rushed across the central room of the orphanage and threw his arms around Anne's legs. She pressed her hand against his head while staring at her Aunt Emma, who was approaching her. Emma Hook's face had a gray, almost ghostly cast.

Anne slipped to her knees and hugged the little boy, burying her face in his sweet-smelling cotton shirt.

"Don't cry, *Viuda*. Please don't cry." Benito's little hand reached up to her head, hesitated a moment, then touched her hair. A surprised gasp issued from his lips.

Anne leaned back to look at him through a shimmer of tears. "What is it, *niño?*"

"Sam told me that your hair was soft as the silk of spiders. I thought he was lying to me. But it is so soft. Did the spiders spin your hair, *Viuda?*"

She laughed and hugged the boy to her. "No, Benito. It's just hair, sweetheart. And not nearly as nice and shiny as your beautiful black hair."

Emma put a hand on her shoulder. "I'm so glad you're all right, Anne. Sam told me...everything."

Anne stood up, keeping Benito's hand tightly in hers. She kissed her aunt on the cheek, then searched the woman's gaunt face. "Everything, Aunt Emma?"

Emma Hook nodded. "Jay. Yes. I already suspected. We'll have to get help for him once this—this..." Her voice broke.

A shiver of dread edged up Anne's spine. "Where is Jay? Is he here in San Miguel?"

"He brought me into town. He was concerned that Raging Owl might attack The Hook. I haven't seen him since yesterday." Worry creased her forehead. "What are you thinking, Anne?"

She tried to shrug off her fears about Jay. Right now there was a more pressing fear. "Sam's gone to meet Raging Owl," she whispered over Benito's head. "Oh, Aunt Emma, I love him so. I don't know if I can bear—" Her throat closed with a soft sob.

Emma placed an arm around her shoulders. "Come over here and sit. Father José, could someone fix Anne a cup of coffee? You look like you're all done in, dear."

Anne sat, Benito close by her side, on one of the long benches the children used at mealtimes. She fussed distractedly with the rip in her skirt a moment, then let her hands fall listlessly into her lap.

Her aunt sat nearby. "He'll be all right, Anne. I know it. Sam is a cautious man. He wouldn't challenge Raging Owl unless he knew he could win." Her eyes flicked to Benito. "He wouldn't take the risk."

"Did Sam tell you he was flat on his back for weeks?" Anne asked, wishing she were as certain and as hopeful as Aunt Emma. "He only started walking a few days ago. He isn't as strong as you may think." She pressed her lips together as she looked down at Benito's dark head.

"I didn't know," said Emma, her voice catching in her throat.

The two women sat in silence then. Father José placed a tray on the table. "Shall I get milk for your coffee, Mrs. McIntire?" he asked as he set a steaming mug before her.

Anne looked up at him as if she had just come out of a daze. "No, thank you, Father. But can you get me a rifle?"

He nearly dropped the mug he was passing to Emma. "A what, Mrs. McIntire?"

"A gun, Father José. A rifle, if you have one. If not, a pistol will do."

Emma's eyes rounded with surprise. "What in the world are you thinking, Anne?"

Just then they heard shouts and cries from the street.

Emma grew more pale. Her lips moved in silent prayer.

"It has begun," Father José said. He made the sign of the cross over his heart.

Anne stood up. "Get me a gun," she demanded. "Now."

"Sam said for you to remain here with the boy," Father José said. As he spoke, he looked around. "Where is Benito?"

The women looked at each other. No one had seen him slip away.

The priest called to an older boy on the other side of the room. "Carlos, where is Benito? Have you seen him?"

The child pointed to a door. "There, Padre."

"*¡Madre de Dios!*" exclaimed Father José. "We must bring him back."

"What is it, Father? Where does that door lead?" Anne asked.

"Up to the bell tower," the priest said. "He will have a perfect view of the street below. Of the fight."

Anne was already heading for the door. "I'll get him. And you get me that gun, Father. Please hurry."

Chapter Twenty

Anne scrambled up a narrow flight of stairs, pausing once as fatigue and nausea swept through her. Not now, she admonished herself. There would be plenty of time to be sick later. The rest of her life. Right now she had to get to the bell tower.

Access to the tower was through a heavy trap-door, which she heaved upward with one shoulder.

"Go away," Benito yelled.

She managed to lift the door a few more inches. "Benito, it's me. It's *La Viuda*. Help me with the door."

His small hands gripped the wooden edges and pulled the heavy planks until there was room for her to climb through.

Anne sat for a moment, trying to stop the spinning in her head and the pain that was beginning to slice through her abdomen. Benito touched her shoulder. He pointed over the adobe wall of the bell tower.

"Come look, *Viuda*," he said.

She rose unsteadily to her feet.

The crowd in the street below had formed a ragged circle. Anne looked down on bonnet tops and billowy skirts, on big Stetsons and plaid shoulders and pointed boot tips. The townspeople made up most of the circle.

Many of them held torches high overhead, and the flames swayed and cast wavering wedges of golden light. Soft gray shadows shifted on the dust of the street.

There were about two dozen Apache braves standing shoulder to shoulder on the far side of the circle. Their weapons were stacked in a pile—stone clubs, bows and arrows, long sharp lances, a scattering of rifles. Their painted faces were eerie in the shifting light.

In the center, in a bare dusty space already sprinkled with blood, were Sam and Raging Owl. As Anne looked, they faced one another, their legs spread wide, weapons in their upraised hands. Both men were stripped to the waist and their hard muscles surged and shimmered. Raging Owl wore only a breechcloth, and the long cords of his legs stood out like bound coils of strong rope. Sam's buckskin trousers were split over one powerful thigh.

In the wavering torchlight, their black hair shone with deep blue glints. Both their bodies glistened with sweat and smears of blood. Their naked chests heaved as they circled one another.

"Sam cut the Apache," Benito whispered. "But then he fell down."

"Hush," Anne snapped, shoving the boy down so he could no longer see over the wall. She looked again, in time to see Raging Owl lunge forward, a knife in one hand, a stone club in the other. As Sam grasped and twisted the wrist that held the knife, the blunt end of the club thudded into his back.

Anne sucked in her breath as if the blow had struck her own flesh. As she watched, blood began to trickle from the partially healed bullet wound just above Sam's waist. The trickle increased to a flow, already reddening the buckskin at his waist. But he had Raging Owl on the ground now, one knee planted on the Indian's massive forearm, one hand gripping his throat. Raging Owl clubbed him again, spattering blood in a wide arc on the dusty street. He rolled away and broke Sam's hold.

She averted her eyes. Where was Father José with the gun? She wondered if there was time for her to climb back down and hunt for one herself. Just then the trap-door near her feet began to rise.

Benito stomped down on it with a bare foot, but the door rose further, pushing him aside. Tom Atkinson's gray hair and rugged face appeared. As he emerged fully through the trap-door, Anne saw that he was carrying a rifle.

"Thank God, Sheriff," she said.

He glanced over the wall, then returned his gaze to Anne. "It won't work, Miz McIntire. Not with all those people down there. Those redskins would slaughter them all in the blink of an eye."

Anne pressed Benito's head into her leg, covering his ears. "I am not going to let Raging Owl kill Sam and take this child away."

Tom Atkinson peered over the wall again. "Sam's holding his own. He's three inches taller and a good twenty pounds heavier than the Indian. Plus he's a born fighter. I'd say if there's going to be anybody killed, it's going to be Raging Owl."

Anne forced herself to look again just as the Indian's bare foot lashed out and gave Sam's arm a stunning blow that sent his knife flying from his hand. The crowd shrank back as the bloody knife landed among them. Everyone just stood there, staring down at it.

Her jaw hardened with tension. "Don't just stand there," she hissed. "Somebody pick it up and give it back to him. Pick it up, dammit!"

A woman rushed forward and clutched the knife. Anne knew from her dark hair and white blouse that it was Sally Mendoza. She pitched the knife, hilt first, so it landed near Sam's feet.

"Thank you," Anne breathed as she watched Sam slowly bend his knees and gather up the weapon with his fingertips.

Tom Atkinson was looking at Anne now rather than at the bloody struggle below. "How about if I take you and the boy back down now, Miz McIntire? He shouldn't watch, and you're looking a bit peaked."

When he reached out to grasp her elbow, she batted his hand away. "Take Benito," she said. "But leave the rifle, Sheriff."

"No, ma'am," he said in a firm voice. "I can't do that."

They stood silently then while the battle raged on below. Sam's superior size and strength were negated by the wounds he had suffered, leaving the men evenly matched. It began to look as if no one would win, or they would kill each other slowly with knife slashes and kicks and clubbings. The circle of spectators kept changing shape—moving outward when Raging Owl fell backward, moving in when the two men grappled on the ground.

Tom Atkinson's eyes scanned the rooftops on both sides of the street. He nudged Anne's arm with his elbow and angled his head toward the roof of the mercantile. "Looks like you're not the only one who wanted to get up high with a rifle," he said. "Jay's got the same idea."

Anne looked with horror in the direction of his gaze. Jay was hunkered down on the flat roof, his gun sighted on the center of the circle below. "Oh, my God," she whispered. "Shoot him, Sheriff."

Tom Atkinson stared down at her. "That's Jay Hook, ma'am."

"I know who it is," she snapped. "And I know what he's waiting for."

"Same thing you are, I expect."

"Not quite, Sheriff. I'm waiting to shoot if Sam loses. Jay's waiting to shoot if Sam wins."

He pushed his hat back. "You're being a little unfair, aren't you?" he asked. "Jay's a mean customer, and he hasn't got a lot of use for his brother, but—"

His words were cut off by a loud cheer from the street below. They both turned to look. Raging Own was down. Blood streamed the length of one arm as he tried to reach for his fallen club, but his fingers appeared limp, unable to curl around the weapon's wooden handle. As the Apache warrior reached helplessly, Sam planted a solid kick in his ribs, then held him to the ground with his knee.

For a long moment, Sam's head was bent over the fallen Apache. Anne could see him labor to catch his breath, could see him shift the broad muscles of his back as if to ease the pain from his wound. Then, in the flash of a hand, he grabbed one of Raging Owl's black braids and yanked the Indian's head back to expose his neck. Even from the bell tower Anne could see the glint of fear in Raging Owl's dark eyes as Sam held the blade of his knife poised against his throat.

"Kill him, Sam," someone in the crowd yelled. "Kill the red bastard."

An ugly chant of "Kill him! Kill him!" began then, and moved around the circle. The torches swayed in rhythm with the chant. As she listened, Anne looked toward the roof of the mercantile. Jay had his gun trained on Sam's back.

"Look," she told Sam Atkinson, pointing across the rooftops. "Take a good look, Sheriff."

The big lawman chewed on his lower lip, blinking once or twice as if he couldn't quite comprehend what he was seeing. Then he cursed softly and raised his rifle to his shoulder.

Anne shifted her gaze back to the street. The knife glinted near Raging Owl's straining neck just before Sam whisked it back and instead cut through one of the man's thick braids. Raging Owl dropped in the dust in defeat. Slowly, with great effort, Sam stood up. His head was bowed over his erstwhile foe. The Indian's black braid dangled loosely from his hand.

The shot rang out high over the street. Dozens of faces turned up in time to see Jay Hook stumble to the edge of the mercantile roof, stand for a moment as if he meant to fly and then pitch headfirst to the dusty street below, his rifle still clutched in his hand.

By the time she reached the bottom of the narrow stairs, Anne's head was swimming. With one hand on Benito's dark head and her elbow nestled in Tom Atkinson's sure grip, she walked into the central room of the orphanage just as Sam came through the door from the street, his brother's limp body in his arms. He paused, his eyes roaming from his mother's stricken face to Anne's. Slowly, with tenderness and great care, he placed Jay's body on one of the long benches, then knelt beside him as he folded Jay's arms over his chest.

When Sam stood, Anne was able to see the extent of his injuries. The open wound at the small of his back was pouring forth dark blood, which had completely soaked the back of one pant leg. His chest was sliced laterally just beneath the hard curve of his breast. His rib cage was already dark with bruises. He lifted his head to meet her eyes, a smile just touching his puffy lips.

Benito clung to Anne's legs, peeking from the folds of her skirt. She could feel his little body trembling as she bent down to him.

"It's all over, *niño,*" she said softly. "You're safe now. Sam is going to be fine. He's going to be just fine."

"But there's so much blood," the little boy whimpered. "I am afraid."

Anne nudged his shoulder gently. "Go to him, Benito. Tell Sam that you love him. He needs you now."

The boy released his hold on her legs, then took a faltering step toward Sam. He stood still then, his dark eyes big and frightened.

Sam eased down on one knee, did his best to wipe his bloody hand on his pant leg, then held it out in the boy's direction. "Come here, squirt," he said.

Benito let out a tiny squeal and raced into Sam's arms.

"You best sit down, Miz McIntire," Tom Atkinson said as he stood by her side.

His voice seemed to come from some distance away. "Yes. All right," she said wearily, letting him guide her to a chair. She felt a sticky warmth between her thighs, and the room suddenly reeled before her eyes. There was a roaring in her ears. Bright lights skittered across her vision just as a hard arm clamped around her waist and another swept beneath her knees.

She was safe…yes…in Sam's arms. She felt his warm lips on her forehead and then she heard him say, "I think we both could use the doc, Tom."

"Sam, if you don't sit quietly, I will be sewing your arm to your chest. *Por favor.*" Dr. Lopez held the threaded needle still until Sam turned his gaze back from the bed where Anne was lying, so small beneath the quilt, so still.

"She's going to lose the baby, isn't she, Doc?"

The stocky little Mexican glared at him. "We will talk when I have finished with you, *amigo*. You have lost much blood, Sam. It is difficult to believe you can even sit up or speak."

Sam dismissed his concerns with a scowl and a brusque wave of his hand, then sucked in his breath as the vet poked the needle through his skin and began taking small stitches to close the gaping slash on his chest. He had already applied a dressing to the wound on Sam's back and had wrapped it tightly.

"So," the doctor murmured as he sewed, "they tell me the Apaches will probably go back to the reservation now. Is that true?"

"I guess," Sam sighed. He looked down at the man's skilled, steady fingers. "Can't you hurry that up?" he asked through clenched teeth.

The doctor ignored him as he continued to weave the needle and the dark thread back and forth. "How many months along is Mrs. McIntire, Sam? Do you know?" He glanced up. "I am assuming you are the father, no?"

Even though Lopez was a veterinarian, it never occurred to Sam not to trust the man's skills. He had delivered—along with colts and calves—innumerable Mexican and half-breed babies, all of them hale and hearty.

"Four months, four and a half," Sam said. "The little fool probably ran five miles yesterday, after riding thirty the day before that."

Lopez nodded soberly. "She has suffered from a good deal of worry, too," he added. "Put the two together— the physical activity and the worries... I don't know what to tell you, Sam. There is not much I can do other than to keep her quiet. She, too, has lost much blood. I just don't know.''

Sam's head snapped up. "You're not saying Annie's life is in danger, are you?''

"No, that is not what I said. But *your* life could be in jeopardy if you do not hold still, *mi amigo*.''

Reassured at least that Annie wouldn't die, Sam sat quietly and submitted to the needle. Dr. Lopez finally tied a small knot and cut the thread.

"There. What you need now is a good night's rest, Sam. You may sleep on my sofa if you like, in order to be near your lady.''

Sam glanced again at Annie, pallid and blanketed to her chin on the narrow bed. "I'll stay right here, Doc. Thanks.''

"I don't think you understand how seriously you are hurt,'' Lopez said.

Sam's dark eyes skewered him. "I don't think *you* understand, Doc. I'm not leaving her.''

The stocky Mexican shrugged. "As you wish. Do me a favor though, will you?''

"What's that?''

The doctor grinned. "When you pass out from loss of blood and lack of sleep, please do it by the door so I will not have far to drag you.''

The fat candle that Dr. Lopez left burning in a saucer was now just a pool of tallow around a flickering wick. Sam could barely keep his eyes open, but he fought the sleep that would carry him far away from Annie. When she stirred, he took her hand. Her eyes fluttered open and he managed a smile, despite his puffy lips.

"Everything's going to be fine, love,'' he said. He reached for a glass of water, then slipped his arm beneath her head. "Drink a little of this. The doc says you need it."

Anne sipped, but most of the liquid dripped down her chin. Sam lifted a corner of the quilt to dab at the moisture.

Her eyes were glossy in the dim light. "I love you, Sam Hook," she whispered. "Are you all right?"

"Don't worry about me," he said, using gruffness to mask the catch in his voice.

"I'll always worry about you," she said. "Oh, Sam, I'm trying so hard to hang on to this baby for you."

He lifted her hand to his mouth and pressed his lips to her cool fingers, because he knew he would cry if he tried to speak. For a long while he kept watch as Anne slipped back into a restless sleep. Then Sam's head sagged upon his chest as sleep, at last, claimed him.

Emma Hook walked from the church, where she had spent the night, to Dr. Lopez's house at the far end of town. She could hear the ring of Tula's hammer as he worked behind the burned-out livery stable, crafting her son's coffin. Odd, she thought, that the rhythm of the carpenter's hammer was almost cheerful. *TAP-tap-tap*. *TAP-tap-tap*. Odd, too, that what she was feeling right now was relief rather than sadness. One son was dead, but one was alive. She would have years to grieve for Jay. Today she was concerned with the living.

Mrs. Thiel was sweeping ashes and chunks of burnt wood away from her front door. The fat woman leaned her broom against the door, brushed her hands together and patted her steel-gray hair, preparing a greeting. But Emma passed by without so much as a glance in her direction, and when the big woman huffed in displeasure, Emma pretended not to hear. By the time she had reached

Lopez's door, Emma had ignored half the citizens of San Miguel.

She raised her hand and knocked in time with the carpenter. *TAP-tap-tap.*

The doctor opened the door. The little vet had obviously slept in his clothes. His hair was uncombed, his cheeks darkened with stubble. "Señora Hook," he said. "Please come in."

Emma's stern demeanor cracked for the first time that morning. "I've come to see Sam." She had to steady herself on the door frame as she crossed the threshold into the small house.

Dr. Lopez escorted her into his cramped but tidy parlor where he gestured to a chair. "Please have a seat, señora. May I bring you a cup of coffee? I have just made it."

Emma seemed not to hear him. "How is my son, Dr. Lopez? And Anne? Is the child—"

"I'm fine, Mama." Sam stood in the door that led down a short hallway. He was wearing a pair of denim pants that Dr. Lopez had borrowed for him. His open shirt revealed a fresh white bandage on his chest.

Her hands trembled as she held her arms out to him. When he came to her, she hugged him fiercely.

"Mama, I'm sorry about Jay," he whispered. "I'm so sorry."

Emma stiffened. She pulled a lace handkerchief from her sleeve and dabbed at her eyes. "We'll take Jay home and bury him next to your father. After that, I never want to hear his name again. I mean that, Sam."

Sam's silence was his assent.

"Now," Emma said, poking her hankie back into her sleeve, "let me look at you." She reached up to push a stray lock of hair off his bruised cheek.

"Annie's four months pregnant, Mama. She might lose the baby."

She pressed her palm to his cheek now. "I'm so sorry, Sam." Emma's eyes welled with tears. "You did a very brave thing last night. Your little Benito is strutting around this morning like a bandy rooster, crowing about you."

"They all would have handed him over like a worthless scrap of paper," Sam gritted, his face darkening with suppressed rage.

"I think there are a lot of folks in San Miguel who aren't terribly proud of themselves this morning."

They heard a wagon roll to a stop in front of the house.

"That'll be Tom Atkinson," Emma said. "He's offered to drive me back to The Hook. I'd like to look in on Anne before I go."

He pointed down the short hallway. "Maybe you can do a better job of cheering her up than I did." Sam stared at the floor. "This is some mess I've gotten her into."

Emma clucked her tongue and let herself smile for the first time that morning. "As I recall, it takes two to get in this particular mess." She patted his shoulder as she passed. "Tell Tom I'll be out directly."

The bearlike sheriff leaned against the wagon. He shifted upright when Sam came outside, whipped his hat off his head and smoothed back his graying hair.

"I'm real sorry about last night, Sam," he said, his gray eyes locking on Sam's face. "There wasn't no other way, as far as I could see."

As he extended his hand to the sheriff, Sam's eyes were drawn to the rear of the wagon where the pine casket was roped in place. He could smell the fresh-cut wood and see the gouges where Tula's hammer had missed the nails.

For a moment he couldn't breathe and his head felt light and airy as a tumbleweed.

"Sam? You all right?"

"I'm all right," Sam insisted, firmly clasping the sheriff's proffered hand. "You did what you had to do, Tom. Nobody bears you any grudge, least of all me. Thanks." The knowledge that it would have been Sam in the coffin if it weren't for Tom Atkinson's perfect aim from the bell tower went unspoken.

The sheriff sucked in his lower lip and stared at his boot tips. "I'll see that your mother gets back to The Hook safely. You have any problems here, you let my deputy know."

Emma emerged from the door. "I'm ready to go home now," she said, then she patted Sam's arm. "Anne's bound and determined to be back on her feet in a few days. I'll be watching for you, son."

Sam kissed the top of her head, then helped her into the wagon. Tom shook the reins over the horses' backs and the wagon rolled forward. The casket creaked against the ropes that held it in place.

So long, little brother, Sam thought as he watched the wagon stir up low clouds of dust. Maybe you're at peace now.

Then, as tears stung his eyes, Sam's mouth twisted into a mournful grin. Jay had finally bested him at something. His brother had found peace in death, while Sam, the survivor, faced a lifetime of battles.

Chapter Twenty-One

"This must be what it's like to travel in a private railroad coach," Anne said, hoping Dr. Lopez could hear her over the creaks and rattles of the ramshackle wagon he had borrowed to bring her back to The Hook. She was lying on a mattress in back, quilts tucked around her and two soft pillows under her head.

"I would not know about that, señora," he called back. "I have only ridden one time on a train and that was in a stinking, crowded boxcar."

Anne watched a hawk soar and dip in the bright blue sky above her. The bird's wings barely moved as it sailed on a current of wind. She remembered how she had wanted to find her own wings. To fly. To be free. She smiled, recalling that her freedom had lasted a scant two weeks—from the time she left Syracuse to the moment she stepped off the stagecoach in San Miguel.

"Some wings," she muttered to herself as her body rocked with the rhythm of the wagon.

Lopez eased back on the reins. "Too rough?" he called over his shoulder.

"No, it's fine. I was just talking to myself. You've been so kind to me, Dr. Lopez. I don't know how I can ever thank you." Kind was putting it mildly, she thought. The Mexican veterinarian had made his home hers for the past two weeks. He had checked on her at all hours of the day and night, forced her to eat, forced her to consume vast quantities of liquids, reassured her with words and smiles and, finally, with an unspotted linen cloth he removed from between her legs and waved like a flag of victory. Then he had made her stay in bed another week just to be sure.

"You need not thank me, señora. It is I who thank you, both you and Sam, for what you did for San Miguel. That is the debt that can never be repaid."

"Sam did it for the boy," she replied a bit testily, "not for the town."

"The result was the same, señora. Our town is free of the Apache threat once and for all. We are all grateful. It has brought the people together."

Maybe it had, she thought, but their togetherness was still a tight, white circle. Maybe they were grateful, but hardly anyone had bothered to express it. Certainly not to Sam. He'd gone back to The Hook a week ago without so much as a pat on his poor back. He pretended it didn't bother him, but Anne knew otherwise. She knew, too, that Sam was still eaten up with worry about their future.

"I see the ranch up ahead," the doctor called.

A moment later she heard a shout and fast hoofbeats hitting the hard ground. She raised her head and craned her neck, then her heart warmed as if it had been touched by pure sunshine. Sam was coming like the wind, his black hair streaming out behind him, his lithe body leaning forward as if he wanted to arrive ahead of his barrelling gray horse. And he nearly did, for when the horse drew even with the wagon, in one fluid motion Sam swung from his saddle into the wagon bed to gather Anne, blankets and all, into his arms.

"You're all right? The baby's all right? Oh, God, Annie!" He crushed her to him, then drew back. A dark cloud moved over his bronze features. "Everything is all right, isn't it, Doc?" Sam looked to Lopez for reassurance.

"*Sí.* Everything is fine. Everything has been fine for one entire week. I believe it will continue to be fine."

Sam bit his lower lip as his eyes roved over Anne's wet, tear-stained face. He appealed to the doctor once more. "She's crying, Doc."

Lopez turned and grinned down at his bewildered new passenger. "I expect they are tears of joy, Sam."

Anne finally managed to extract her arms from the tangle of blankets. She threw them around his neck. "Oh, Sam. It's so good to be home."

When they arrived at the house, Sam lifted her gently down from the wagon bed, carried her to the front door and pushed it open with his foot. "Mama! Rosa! Annie's home," he called.

She was home, she thought. But then home was wherever Sam was—out on the high plains by a campfire or in a dim, smoky wickiup. She hugged his neck more tightly.

After hugs and happy tears from Emma and Rosa, Sam carried her upstairs. Dr. Lopez had been adamant about that as he joined them inside the house. "No stairs," he had cautioned them, "and no hot baths."

Sam had winked at him. "Sounds like I'm going to be spending all my time lugging around a filthy fat lady."

"That isn't funny, Sam," Anne snapped, though secretly she was thrilled that his sense of humor seemed to have returned.

Upstairs, Sam carried Anne into the room that had been her aunt's. He set her gently down on the huge carved walnut bed. When she commented on it, he said,

"Mother's moved into my old room. She said this bed was way too big for her now."

"That was sweet of her," Anne said as Sam placed a pillow under her head.

"No, that was crafty of her. That way she'll be right next door to the nursery and she'll get to sneak in and see her grandbaby at night." Sam eased down beside her on the high bed, crooking his arm to prop up his head. "I just want to look at you, Annie. God, you're beautiful."

She pushed out her lower lip in a fair imitation of a pout. "I thought you said I was fat and filthy."

His thumb grazed her cheek. "Not yet. You're all soft and sweet-smelling and hardly bigger than a child yourself." His hand drifted to caress the delicate skin of her throat, and then he began to undo the tiny buttons on the bodice of her dress.

A warm current of wanting flowed through her. "Damn," she murmured.

Sam's dark eyes widened, but his nimble fingers continued to loosen button after button. "What?" he asked softly.

"I'm not just going to be fat and filthy," she said, "I'm also going to be frustrated. Dr. Lopez said no more making love before the baby comes, just to be on the safe side."

Sam parted the halves of her bodice and drew down the thin cotton camisole to expose one full rose-tipped breast. He bent his head and circled the taut nipple with his tongue. "Did he say I couldn't do this?"

Her eyes fluttered toward the ceiling. "I didn't ask."

He drew her more fully into his warm mouth, moaning softly as he took his fill of her soft flesh. Then he raised his head. His dark eyes were warm. His white teeth flashed in an irresistible grin. "What else did he say we couldn't do!" As he spoke he brought her hand to the lacings of his buckskin trousers.

A warm flush spread over her face as her fingers began to work at the soft leather thongs. "I don't believe he mentioned this."

When her small hand found him, he sighed contentedly at her touch. And when she slid slowly down to taste him and please him as he had so often pleased her, a low groan welled up from the depths of his being and his big hands twisted in her pale, soft hair.

She nestled against him later and pressed her hand over his surging heart, feeling it slowly settle back to a normal rhythm. "I love you, Sam Hook," she said. "Are you sure you want to marry a fat, filthy, frustrated female?"

"No." His voice was somber.

Anne sat up and stared at him. He was wearing his Indian look again—a hard bronze mask. Then the mask split into a broad grin.

"I want to marry *you*. I want to marry the beautiful *Viuda de la Luna*." He spread his hand over her belly. "And the sooner the better, don't you think?"

After one of Rosa's huge breakfasts of beef steak and eggs, Dr. Lopez pushed his plate away with a sigh.

"I hate to leave your wonderful hospitality, Señora Hook, but I must be getting back to town. I really should have returned last night."

"We're very grateful, Doctor, for all that you've done."

The Mexican looked across the table at Anne. "I will be seeing you in a few months, no?"

She nodded.

"Send for me in plenty of time," he continued. "Or, if you like, when your time approaches, come stay in my house."

At the head of the table, Sam's coffee cup clattered back in its saucer. "You're not anticipating any problems, are you, Doc?" His dark brows drew together in a worried frown.

"On the contrary," Lopez said. He shifted his gaze to Anne. "No problems at all, as long as you follow my instructions—*all* of my instructions."

Anne fumbled with the napkin in her lap as her cheeks colored. She wasn't surprised the doctor suspected they had made love last night, not after the way she had clung to Sam when he carried her downstairs this morning and from the looks and little smiles they had been exchanging over their steak and eggs.

Sam leaned back in his chair now, his frown replaced by a grin that played over his wide mouth and crinkled the corners of his eyes. "I'll see that she behaves," he said.

"I hope you will invite me to your wedding," Lopez said.

"You'd better stay then," Anne said quietly.

All eyes turned in her direction as she raised her head and flashed Sam a smile.

"I didn't know if Father José would consent to marry us, so when I found out a circuit judge from Santa Fe was due on last night's stage, I asked Tom Atkinson if he would bring him out to The Hook. He promised me he'd bring him out today."

Sam's jaw dropped. He shifted forward in his chair. "Why the hell didn't you tell me?"

"Cold feet, Sam?" taunted Anne playfully.

"No, I..." He looked down the table at Emma, his hands turned up helplessly before him.

Emma Hook smiled. "There goes your surprise," she said to her son.

Anne raised her eyebrows. "What surprise?"

"Well, hell," growled Sam.

"I was remaking my wedding dress for you, Anne," her aunt said, "but I'm afraid it's not quite ready."

Anne breathed a tiny sigh of relief. Although her comment about Sam's cold feet had been made in jest, there was still the nagging remembrance that he had refused to marry her before, even going so far as to dump her back in Syracuse. "I have plenty of dresses," she said.

"Widow's weeds," sniffed Emma. "We're going to have to put together a whole new wardrobe for you, dear. Of course, we'll wait until after the baby comes. But then—"

She was interrupted by a sharp knock on the front door and the urgent shout of one of the cowhands. "Riders coming from the west, Sam. A lot of 'em!"

Sam was up out of his chair before anyone else had a chance to react to the news. Anne watched in horror as he grabbed the Spencer from the gun rack and strode out onto the porch.

By the time the rest of them rose from the table and followed him out, there was a thick cloud of dust to the west.

"Mother, get the spyglass, will you, please?" Sam asked not taking his eyes off the menacing cloud.

Anne felt her mouth going dry. She saw her own fears reflected in Dr. Lopez's eyes.

"It could not be Apaches, could it, Sam?" the doctor asked.

"I don't know, Doc, but we're going to get ready for them just in case." Sam called to the gathering cowhands then and ordered them to collect every gun in the bunkhouse and bring them to the main house. The men sprinted into action.

Emma returned with the spyglass. "Here, son." She handed it to Sam, her fingers trembling.

Sam lifted the instrument to his eye and trained it on the horizon.

"Who is it, Sam?" Anne moved closer to him, lifting her hand to shade her eyes and squinting in the same direction.

"All that damn dust," Sam muttered. "Wait a minute...."

"What is it?" Anne's voice was a dry croak as she watched Sam's lips tauten over his teeth.

"It looks like half the townspeople of San Miguel," he said.

Dr. Lopez sagged back against the front wall of the house. *"Gracias a Dios,"* he breathed. "We are safe."

"Not necessarily." Sam gritted his teeth as he brought the spyglass down and turned his eyes to Anne. There was a welter of emotion in them—fear, rage, sorrow, desperation. "Get in the house, Annie. Stay in there with Mother and Rosa." He turned to Emma. "Keep her inside, Mama, no matter what."

Emma, her face ashen now, reached to take Anne's arm, but Anne shrugged out of her grasp and tore the spyglass from Sam's hand. She raised it to her eye and looked west.

Through the dust, she could barely make out shapes, much less faces. She concentrated harder, straining her eyes. There was a wagon. And there was a big bay horse with a burly figure in the saddle.

"It's Tom Atkinson!" she cried, swinging the spyglass a little to the right. She pressed her lips together, as if that would help her focus through the veil of dust. "There! That must be the circuit judge. He's a funny little man wearing a bowler hat.'' She let the glass fall to her side and turned to Sam with shining yes. ''Oh, Sam. It's our wedding day!''

Or a good day for a hanging, Sam thought.

''For heaven's sake, Anne! You must hold still.'' Aunt Emma yanked so hard on the hem of the dress that she nearly pulled Anne off her feet. ''Just a few more stitches and I'll be done.''

Anne bit her lip, trying to hold still, when all she wanted to do was race downstairs, grab Sam's arm and haul him in front of the judge.

She craned her neck toward the window, trying to see his towering figure in the crowd in the yard below. ''Isn't he dressed yet?'' she muttered.

Emma laughed around the pins in her mouth. ''Rosa said his hands shook the whole time she was helping him into his suit. She said he nearly strangled himself doing up his cravat.''

Anne laughed. ''At least he put that dratted gun down. I thought he never would.''

''Well, dear, I guess suspicion comes naturally after all these years,'' the older woman mused. ''Most people treated him worse than a dog. Like that horrible Doris Thiel.''

''I didn't see her in the crowd,'' Anne said. Nor, she thought, had she seen the vicious Sims and his dim-witted sidekick.

''Good,'' scoffed her aunt. ''You wouldn't want that fat old biddy at your wedding, anyway. There.'' Emma took a step back to admire her handiwork. ''Well, it could do with a few more flounces, but it's not so bad if I do say so myself. Considering it's forty years old.''

Anne smiled at her aunt, soon to be her mother-in-law. Her smile was touched with sadness for the woman who had so recently lost a son. "Aunt Emma, I wish—"

But the sturdy woman waved her hand, dismissing Anne's imminent tears. "Uh-uh. None of that. I won't have you feeling sorry for me on your wedding day. It's bad luck, and you and Sam need all the good luck you can get. You wait here," Emma continued. "I'm going to hunt up the groom, so he can carry the bride downstairs. I just hope his knees aren't knocking so badly that he trips and falls."

As Anne waited by the window, she caught a glimpse of Benito, chasing one of the barn cats. The poor tabby was running for all of its nine lives. She wondered where Father José had come up with the little suit for the boy. Earlier, when she had asked the priest if he would leave Benito here at The Hook with them, he had said he would consider it, but that perhaps she and Sam deserved a quiet time together, unburdened by children.

Her reply had been swift and immediate: Benito was no burden; he was their son.

She cast a sidelong glance in the mirror on the walnut dresser, scanning the yards of muslin in Aunt Emma's beautiful gown and smoothing the folds over the swelling that was probably obvious only to her.

Benito would be a loving big brother, she thought. The love she and Sam intended to shower on him would make him feel warm and whole. If a little brother came along, she intended to see that Benito never felt he had to compete for love or strive to be accepted. She would teach him to be proud of his Apache blood, would maybe even take him to visit Chirrihuaca and Smart Woman at the reservation.

There was a soft tap on the door. It opened as she turned, and Anne felt her heart quicken at the sight of

Sam's wide shoulders filling the door frame. For a moment he appeared shy, almost sheepish, as he stood there in a dark suit that molded his muscular form. His hair was tied back with a dark silk cord, but as always, one errant black strand had escaped its bond. His dark eyes drank in every inch of her and gleamed with silent praise.

"Are you ready, love?" he asked, taking her into the circle of his arms.

He smelled of sunshine and citrus as she buried her face into his soft, white shirt. Her cheek encountered something hard beneath the fabric. She explored the object with her fingers.

"What's this, Sam?" she asked as she undid two buttons to look closer. "Why, it's Smart Woman's necklace. What a good idea. It's bound to bring us luck, just like my wearing your mother's dress. Here. Why not wear it outside your shirt?"

As she began lifting the bone-and-feather necklace, Sam raised a hand to stop her. "Wait, Annie. There's something I should probably tell you."

The tone of his voice disturbed her and she raised her eyes to his face, somber now. "Sam, what is it?"

He adjusted the necklace so it was no longer visible and did the buttons back up. "I don't want my mother to see this."

"Whyever not?"

Sam took her by the hand and led her to the big walnut bed, where he sat, pulling her down beside him. "Smart Woman is my natural mother, Annie. She told me the day I left their camp. That's when she gave me the necklace."

Anne's mouth had fallen open. "But I thought . . ."

"You thought my mother was a white woman captured by the Apaches. That's what my mother thinks, too, and I want her to go on thinking it. I'm afraid the truth would devastate her, even after all these years.''

"The truth?'' Anne had no idea what he was talking about. ''If Smart Woman is your mother, then who...?''

His dark eyes locked on hers. ''My father. John Hook.''

Anne took in a deep breath. ''Good Lord!''

"Seems he went to Smart woman hoping to get some kind of charm or amulet that would help my mother conceive. I don't know for sure. The old gal was pretty vague about what happened. She gave birth to me in the mountains, away from the tribe, then handed me over to my father. They never saw each other again.''

A spark of anger flashed in Anne and her fingers splayed protectively over her belly. ''How could she give you away?''

"She loved him, I guess. She told me I was her gift to Whispering Eyes—that's what she called him. I pressed her for details but she wouldn't tell me anymore.''

Anne's expression gentled. She took his big, warm hand in both of hers. ''I wish you had known that when your father was alive,'' she said softly. ''I wish you could have shared his secret.''

"The important thing is that my mother doesn't find out about it. She adored my father. It would hurt her to know the truth.''

"I think you're underestimating her, Sam,'' Anne said.

"You may be right, but I don't want to take the chance. Not a word, all right?'' His somber visage cracked with a grin. ''Your husband has spoken, Wife.''

She slipped her arms around his middle and leaned her head on his shoulder. ''Well, that explains it,'' she mused.

"Explains what?''

Anne sighed dramatically. "The magic you make me feel. Now that I know you're half shaman, I understand."

He stood, drawing her into his arms. "Let's go get married," he said, "so all these people will leave and I can bring you back up here."

Anne reached toward the nightstand for the lace hankie Emma had given her, tucking it into the long sleeve of her white muslin dress until just a corner of it peeked out, like a little white wing. One wing was plenty, she thought; with it she would circle happily around Sam for the rest of her life.

She nestled in his strong arms as he carried her down the stairs and outside, where their arrival sent a momentary hush through the gathering. As he set her gently on her feet, the hush was rent by the yowling of a tomcat. The cat streaked past Anne's white skirt, followed by Benito, who was covered with dust from head to foot.

Sam caught him by the collar. "Hold it, squirt," he said, picking straw from his thick black hair. "There's going to be a wedding, Benito. Then you're going to come live with us."

The boy eyed the voluminous white muslin skirt directly in front of him, then buried his head in Sam's pant leg, sobbing uncontrollably. Sam had to untangle the child's arms from his leg in order to kneel down.

"Benito, what's wrong?"

With tears and dust intermingling to make muddy streaks on his cheeks, the little boy whispered, "I wanted you to marry *La Viuda*, Sam. Not—" a grimy finger pointed to the white skirt "—not this one."

As he gazed from one to the other—from his dark child to his fair-haired bride—he suddenly felt complete. Wild dark Benito and Annie with her moonlit hair had brought Sam's warring halves together. His Apache son and his white wife combined to make him whole. A sense of peace settled in his soul as he hugged the sobbing little boy.

"I've got news for you, squirt," he said. He gathered the little boy up in his arms and straightened his knees to stand beside Anne. "She's not *La Viuda* anymore. She's *La Esposa*."

Benito gaped at Anne's glowing face, then he reached out to feel a lock of her pale hair. He tipped his face up to Sam's. *"La Esposa de la Luna,"* he said.

Sam grinned. "'Fraid not, kid. *La esposa de Sam.*"

Benito opened his mouth as if he were about to correct him, then thought better of it. Instead he turned to Anne and said, "I think I will just call you Mama."

Her eyes glistened with joyous tears.

"Well, come on," Sam said with mock gruffness. "Let's get this over with."

"Just a minute," Anne said. She whisked the winged hankie from her sleeve, and began to apply it with motherly precision to Benito's muddy face, while Sam smiled at the two of them.

Who needs wings at all? she thought.

* * * * *

Harlequin® Historical

WESTERN SKIES

This September, celebrate the coming of fall with four exciting Westerns from Harlequin Historicals!

BLESSING by Debbi Bedford—A rollicking tale set in the madcap mining town of Tin Cup, Colorado.

WINTER FIRE by Pat Tracy—The steamy story of a marshal determined to reclaim his father's land.

FLY AWAY HOME by Mary McBride—A half-Apache rancher rescues an Eastern woman fleeing from her past.

WAIT FOR THE SUNRISE by Cassandra Austin—Blinded by an accident, a cowboy learns the meaning of courage—and love.

Four terrific romances full of the excitement and promise of America's last frontier.

Look for them, wherever Harlequin Historicals are sold.

Harlequin® Historical

HARLEQUIN HISTORICALS ARE GETTING BIGGER!

This fall, Harlequin Historicals will bring you bigger books. Along with our traditional high-quality historicals, we will be including selected reissues of favorite titles, as well as longer originals.

Reissues from popular authors like Elizabeth Lowell, Veronica Sattler and Marianne Willman.

Originals like ACROSS TIME—an historical time-travel by Nina Beaumont, UNICORN BRIDE—a medieval tale by Claire Delacroix, and SUSPICION—a title by Judith McWilliams set during Regency times.

Leave it to Harlequin Historicals to deliver enduring love stories, larger-than-life characters, and history as you've never before experienced it.

And now, leave it to Harlequin Historicals, to deliver even more!

Look for *The Bargain* by Veronica Sattler in October, *Pieces of Sky* by Marianne Willman in November, and *Reckless Love* by Elizabeth Lowell in December.

Harlequin® Historical

Nora O'Shea had fled to Arizona seeking freedom,
but could she ever find love as a mail-order bride?

MARIANNE WILLMAN

From the author of THE CYGNET and ROSE RED,
ROSE WHITE comes a haunting love story full of
passion and power, set against the backdrop of the
new frontier.

Coming in November 1993 from Harlequin

Don't miss it! Wherever Harlequin books are sold.